ABOUT THE AUTHOR

JULIET MARILLIER was born and brought up in Dunedin, New Zealand, and now lives in Western Australia. Her historical fantasy novels for adults and young adults have been translated into many languages and have won a number of awards including the Aurealis (three times), the American Library Association's Alex Award, the Sir Julius Vogel Award and the Prix Imaginales. Her lifelong love of folklore, fairy tales and mythology is a major influence on her writing, as is her membership of a druid order, OBOD (The Order of Bards, Ovates and Druids). Juliet's novels include the Sevenwaters series, the Bridei Chronicles and the Shadowfell series. She is currently working on a new project for adult readers.

Juliet is passionate about animal rescue and shares her home with a small pack of rescued canines. She blogs monthly on http://www.writerunboxed.com and her website is at http://www.julietmarillier.com

prickle moon

Also by JULIET MARILLIER

prickle moon

juliet marillier

T℘ Ticonderoga
p℘ publications

For my granddaughter Calypso

Prickle Moon by Juliet Marillier

Published by Ticonderoga Publications

Introduction copyright © 2013 Sophie Masson

Afterword copyright © 2013 Juliet Marillier

Cover artwork by Pia Ravenari

Designed and edited by Russell B. Farr
Typeset in Sabon and Baskerville Old Face

A Cataloging-in-Publications entry for this title is available from The National Library of Australia.

ISBN 978-1-921857-37-9 (limited hardcover)
     978-1-921857-38-6 (trade paperback)
     978-1-921857-39-3 (trade hardcover)
     978-1-921857-40-9 (ebook)

Ticonderoga Publications
PO Box 29 Greenwood
Western Australia 6924

www.ticonderogapublications.com

10 9 8 7 6 5 4 3 2 1

Thanks to Pia Ravenari for her meticulous and beautiful cover art, which so sensitively interprets the title story; and to the inimitable Sophie Masson, whose wisdom I greatly esteem. Her introduction really enhances the collection.

A big thank-you to my four adult children for always being ready to brainstorm and for giving honest feedback. Over the years of writing development represented by this collection, they've helped me more than they realise. Thanks to Satima Flavell and Fiona Leonard for their perceptive editorial advice. Last but not least, my gratitude to Russell B. Farr at Ticonderoga for providing me with this wonderful opportunity.

contents

introduction

sophie masson

I remember precisely the first time I ever read Juliet Marillier's work. It was 1999, I was about to start a long train journey from my home in rural Northern New South Wales to Sydney, and I had a brand new book to read and review: *Daughter of the Forest*. Around me were noisy students and crying babies and a quarrelling couple who didn't seem to mind washing their dirty linen in public, and the train rattled and clattered and stopped much too often; but from the moment that I plunged into the enthralling story of Sevenwaters, it all ceased to matter. I was completely spellbound, taken into a world that I both recognised instinctively because it chimed with my own deep inclinations: a traditional world where fairytale, myth and history mixed effortlessly, and yet also a world that was utterly original, magically reinventing tradition, with vivid characters and prose that flowed as fresh and beautiful as a spring. The effect was as though I'd been on one of those journeys to the Otherworld where time passes differently, so that those seven hours vanished as though they'd never been and I emerged blinking to find that we were arriving at Central Station.

What was exciting too was the fact that though the novel had such a satisfactory ending, it was also promised to be the first in a series. I could hardly wait. I was an adult, an author myself who'd already published many books, including *Knight by the Pool,* the first volume of my *Lay Lines* adult fantasy trilogy(later published as the omnibus volume *Forest of Dreams*). As well, I'd been reviewing books for quite a while. I was pretty much a professional reader. Not jaded, just rather detached, seeing the machinery of construction all too clearly and rarely tumbling into books with the headlong enthusiasm of youth. But *Daughter of the Forest* was different. It filled me with just the same sense of heady enchantment as when I was a child reader. It did not hurt of course that it was based on one of my favourite fairytales, the Six Swans, which is so full of longing, tragedy and romance, or that it was rooted deep in the Celtic traditions I was absorbed by. But those echoes weren't the only reason that I was so completely involved in the world depicted so vividly by its creator, or I believed in it so utterly that even now the delight that made me forget seven hours of tedium in a train is still with me. This was pure storytelling magic, the kind that never forgets the deep human truths underlying the fantasy, which feels utterly real and yet headily other. And even when I looked at it as a professional reader, as it were, my admiration for the author's achievement did not lessen. Though it was her first published novel, it was remarkably accomplished, showing a lightness of touch, a beauty of writing, and a sureness of pitch and construction that showed a consummate writer was at work.

Well, I was of course not the only reader who fell in love with the world of Sevenwaters, and the work of Juliet Marillier. Readers all over the world fell for it in a big way, and since that first book, it's not only the Sevenwaters series that have captured the attention of a large international readership, but also Juliet's other books: from the series such as the *Saga of the Light Isles* and *The Bridei Chronicles,* to the stand-alone *Heart's Blood* (another particular favourite of mine) and two novels for young adults, *Wildwood Dancing* and *Cybele's Secret.*

As well as the wonderful novels, however, Juliet has also written many short stories, which have appeared individually over the years in publications ranging from magazines to anthologies. I was lucky enough to commission her to write one for the anthology I edited, *The Road to Camelot* (Random House Australia 2002, reprinted 2010), which was themed around the childhood and youth of Arthurian characters. And I'm delighted that this story,

"In Coed Celyddon", centred on Arthur himself, appears in this new collection, amongst many others.

Amazingly, this is Juliet Marillier's first short-story collection, and it really showcases the wide range and the depth of her talent. Though many of these stories have been published before, several were written specially for this book, including the title story, "Prickle Moon", with its touching, richly-layered depiction of the terrible dilemma of an old Scottish wise woman, whose love for wild woodland creatures must be balanced against the demands of a grief-stricken powerful lord. "Angel of Death", another new story, which is set in a neglected dog farm, also offers a glimpse into the relationship of humans and animals, both good and bad, while "Poppy Seeds", which is also new, is a lively, wry re-imagining of the youngest-son trope of fairytale. "Wraith Level One", meantime, which is also published for the first time, is a jaunty re-imagining of the ghost story, complete with eccentric version of heaven.

Fairy tale has always been an important inspiration in Juliet's work and that element is very strong in the brand-new story "By Bone-Light", a chilling, powerful updating of another of my own favourite fairy tales, the Russian story of Vassilissa the Fair and the witch Baba Yaga, while the previously-published "Let Down Your Hair" dips deep into the storytelling cauldron of Rapunzel, and "Juggling Silver" is a bright excursion into the world of the sea-folktale. The griefs of life, and death, are movingly depicted in such stories as "Jack's Day" and "Back and Beyond". But humour is as much a part of this collection as fantasy, romance, tragedy and drama, and the funny twist on writers' workshop groups offered in "Tough Love 3001", where participants are aliens, will have many readers chuckling, while "Letters to Robert" is an entertaining, tart little take on the nineteenth-century romance.

Though most of the stories are stand-alone, a couple also offer intriguing extra glimpses into the worlds of some of her longer works: the haunting "'Twixt Firelight and Water", which is the longest in the collection and set in the world of Sevenwaters, and the tough, Nordic-flavoured "Otherling" (which has echoes of the uncompromising Viking world of *Wolfskin*).

Whatever your narrative inclination, and whether you'll devour this book cover to cover like me or dip into it at your leisure, there's something in this wonderful, rich collection for everyone. Ticonderoga Publications, known for its long contribution to the speculative fiction publishing scene in Australia, and role in bringing it to an international audience, is to be warmly congratulated on bringing Juliet Marillier's short fiction together in such an attractive package, for the enjoyment of her many readers all over the world.

SOPHIE MASSON
FEBRUARY 2013

☽

prickle moon

"Come up Littlefoot, Primrose, Sandy
Twinkletoes, Snufflenose, Bright Eyes and Dandy
Snugglepig, Fuzzywig, Rattlecap, Spiny
Squeaker, Peeker, Scufflepaws, Tiny.
Whiskers, Snaggletooth, Trencherman, Pearlie
Three-toes, Parsnip, Conker and Girlie."

She sang them in, verse by verse, name by sweet name, till the whole rattling, prickling assemblage of them was at her doorstep, or as near as made no difference. A few hung back, shy ones, old ones, too fearful or too canny to venture beyond the straggle of bushes that marked the end of her garden and the start of the wildwood. They waited there, bright eyes in the shadows, as the rhyme came to an end and she trod quiet and careful to set down the wee bowls. Dusk hung over the garden; from the window of her little house, warm light spilled out, laying a golden cloth on grass already dew-damp. Her guests would eat like lords and ladies.

'Twas the best time of the day, tender and true: bidding the sun farewell, waiting for the moonrise, touching the edge of strangeness as the tribe crept out to accept her offerings. A time of trust. No need for the defensive shields of daytime, when dogs and wheels and booted feet would be abroad. There were foxes in the wood, owls, weasels. But 'twas rare for them to tackle a prickler, even a young one. The spring before last, a farmer's terrier had done for

Pearlie's young, all of them gone in one wild frenzy of digging. The wee ones, their spikes still soft, no match for the grip of a dog's sharp teeth. Nothing Pearlie could do but roll up and wait for it to be over. Imagine that; imagine the listening. But that was the only time she could remember.

Sometimes they sickened. The lives of pricklers were short, and they had their share of ailments and injuries. Every evening, when they came in to drink, she gave them a look-over to see if any needed her help. Parsnip was old now, white hairs around her muzzle, her feet slow on the grass and her eyes dimming. Snaggletooth had taken a ferret bite on the foreleg last autumn. From one full moon to the next she'd had him in a box of straw by the fireside, mending with the help of parsley salves and warm rest. He was there with the others, healed now, but not quite as he'd been before. As the little one lapped up the last drops from the bowl, 'twas plain to see something was gone from him.

They stayed awhile after the milk was finished, foraging in the garden for bits and pieces, the bold ones coming right up to her feet where she sat on the step watching them in the deepening dark. Pearlie was always first; 'twas as if her terrible loss had made her braver, or maybe she knew a friend when she saw one, even if that friend was in human form. Pearlie had bred a healthy new litter; her young were there among the rest, grown and able to fend for themselves. And now, as Pearlie accepted a rub under the chin, a stroke down the soft belly, here was Conker nosing forward for a share of the attention, and after him Rattlecap with his broken spines, and here—unusually bold—was one of the wee ones, not yet named.

She'd wondered, sometimes, if they had their own names, spoken in a language of squeaks and grumbles, or passed on by subtle glints of the eye and slight movements of the body. The rhyme was hers, not theirs—something given because she loved them, quaint and delicate and mysterious as they were. When a new litter grew strong enough to come abroad with their mother, the names helped her tell one from another. 'Twas funny how, when she sang her rhyme, each came out in turn to its name, as if they had some understanding of the pattern she'd made. 'Twas all patterns in the wood. The patterns of hunting and flight. The daily songs of thrush and robin, the nightly calls of owls. The high dance of the lark, the gliding, ominous flight of the hawk. The furtive ways of the weasel, the clever weaving path of the fox. The industrious work of spiders; the brief lives of pond skimmers and dragonflies. This wee pattern of her own, maybe it marked her out as one of them, the wild ones, the ones that did not belong on Pringle's field or along the pathways of Gimmerburn settlement, but up here in the tangled shadows.

No. However much her heart wanted to believe that, it was wrong. She was as human as Pringle with his shouted orders and his felling of trees if they happened to stand in his way. She was as human as the laird with his grand house and his fast-shut doors. She was a woman like the village wives and half-grown girls who made their way up here when they needed her help. She was a sister; a mother; a widow. She'd had her losses and her sorrows, same as the rest of them. The folk down there in the settlement, they both feared and pitied her, imagining her lonely. She lived alone, true enough, but solitude suited her. She liked quiet. Besides, with this wee tribe at her feet, accepting her offerings, letting her sing to them, tend to them, love them for their short lives, she was hardly on her own.

She kept her thoughts away from the old times, mostly. Sometimes, when night had fallen, she'd lie in bed and let waking dreams come whispering to her ears. Her fingers would trace the seams of the heart quilt. No need of lamp or candle to show her the pieces; her touch knew them all. Here was cloth cut from the coat of a feckless man, a fellow she lay with on a long-ago, wild midsummer's night. Here the last of a flower-patterned kerchief that had been her sister's. Here was a fragment from a wee gown, yellowed now, a scrap of lacy stuff. Her baby boy had worn it, half a lifetime since. Sweet Rose, withered on the stem at three days old, had never had her turn.

She'd wept her tears for the lassie long ago. Rosie was tucked safe and sound in a corner of her mind, a warm, safe place where she could never come to harm. In the dark, before sleep, 'twas another loss that haunted her. She'd lie there with her fingers on the quilt, humming a snatch of lullaby, cradling her fine laddie in her mind. *Oh, hie and baw birdie, ma bonnie wee man.* Gone now, her firstborn, gone to the long tides and the deep. The pain of that would be in her bones until the day she died.

But this, now, when the sun was gone and the moon was yet to rise, and her wee ones came to her call; this, when they crept forward to lap from their bowls, and lingered afterwards to greet her in their shy and silent way, this eased her heart and soothed her mind. It brought her day to a fine, right ending.

When 'twas almost dark, they made their rustling, creaking way back into the wood. She went inside, bolted her door and sat by firelight to take a bit of supper. Soon it would be bed, and the quilt, and the old memories. *Lie safe, my son. Waves, cradle his bones kindly.*

Some nights, sleep was slow to come. Sometimes she'd wake from a tangle of dreams, a net dragging her down into past hurts and future regrets. But with the coming of light the sadness always faded. She loved the early mornings, when the sun slanted low between the leaves and the birds sang out their first greetings to the new day. A single pure note of question: *Time?* A rising fanfare of response: *See, the dawn!* A jubilant shout: *Rise up!* A body could not hold on to sorrow, hearing that.

If tomorrow was fair, as it promised to be, she'd maybe go up the top of Pringle's field when her morning's work was done. She'd sit awhile and watch the long-haired sheep as they made their meandering ways, and the quick small meadow birds. The sun's warmth would seep into her body, easing the aches and pains. Odd, it was, how she found a remedy for each one who came to her door, weary wife, lovesick lad, injured farmer or troubled girl, and yet her own ailments stayed with her, familiar as a set of long-worn clothing. Some kind of price that needed to be paid, perhaps.

The pain was not yet so great that she could not do her work. She considered her hands each morning as she gathered, chopped, shredded, mixed and brewed, and judged that she had still a few years left before they would no longer obey her will. Some time to go before her legs would not carry her out into the woods in search of roots and leaves and fungi; some time before her back seized up and her strength gave out. Until then, there was work to be done. Good work.

Trust had been slow-learned in this place. When she'd first come here the hut had been an old ruin, deserted and sagging, and there'd been no wise woman in Gimmerburn. And she'd been young; well, younger. She'd made a home of the wrecked cottage, mended the thatch, patched the walls, dug and hoed and planted a garden. Exchanged brews and salves and possets for eggs and bread and a bit of help with the heavy work, though even then she'd been happiest in her own company.

She'd learned, slow as slow, to know the pricklers in all their little differences. At first they'd been no more than a rustle in the undergrowth, a stirring in the leaves. In those days there'd been a cat, Malkin. The big old tom had come out of the woods the day the thatching was finished and moved calmly in. Thinking, plainly, that she'd made the place comfortable for his benefit. She remembered him stalking along the bean rows as if there might be fat mice or errant chickens to be found. When the days grew cooler he'd come quick enough to her call, eating what she gave him, settling in his warm spot by the hearth fire.

Nobody had told her the pricklers were in the wood, not when she first came to Gimmerburn. But she knew; not much slipped by her sharp eyes. So, at dusk, with Malkin safely shut in, she'd taken to wrapping her shawl around her against the chill, and carrying out the pail of milk, the scraps of food, the bowls, the bits and pieces she might need if one was sick or hurt or out of sorts. Nobody else would tend to them. Folk were happy enough to come to the cottage of a morning, when the sun was up and people were about their work on Pringle's fields or in the settlement down below, a straggle of houses along the burn. Farmers and their wives, lads and lasses would visit her by day, one or two at a time. They looked over their shoulders if they were coming for a love potion or a cure for an awkward ailment. The village was small; secrets were hard to keep. At night folk kept away from the wood, and away from her. The prickle tribe was hers alone, a delicate, precious thing she'd held close to her heart for generation on generation now, since they were short-lived creatures. There were many, many lines to her rhyme, name after name, though she sang only for the ones still living. Once they were gone, let them lie quiet. Let those who lived out their small lives and died in their sleep never know the terrible thing that might have been.

Once she heard it, once she found out what lay in the past here, she thought it no wonder this place had been without a wise woman for so long. No matter how kind the folk might be, no matter how comfortable the cottage or how generous the farmers, who'd want to live under such a shadow of wrongness? Only a body with nowhere else to go.

She'd wondered, when one of the village crones told her the story, if it was all lies, for it was passing strange. She'd thought of moving on, so she did not have to consider the possibility that it might be true. The pricklers had held her; by the time she'd learned the tale, she'd found she couldna leave them.

So she'd stayed on, doing her work, making her brews, easing the bodies and minds of Gimmerburn's folk, glad, in a way, that this was where she'd come at last, for the simple pattern of this life went some way to salve the hurt she'd borne since the day they carried her boy out of the sea, his face snow and ashes, his fine strong body limp as a rabbit taken from the snare, and the woollen jersey she'd made him with her own hands still wrapping him, its cables and knots and twists drawing him home too late, oh, too late for anything but tears. Dougal, the wee bairn she'd cradled in her arms. Dougal, the fine big son she'd waved off from shore time after time. Never to father a lad of his own; never again to sit by her and put his hand on her knee and tell her his hopes and his dreams. When the first grief had passed, a restlessness had grown in her, a river deep in the spirit that would not stop flowing, and she'd let it bear her away, and away again, until she'd fetched up here, with a cottage to mend and work to be done. There was a pattern in that, too, if a body looked deep enough. Comfort in that, if a body could make herself see it.

Malkin was long gone, and no other cat had come to take his place. 'Twas just herself and the pricklers, and in between a string of visitors, none of them talkative. And wee Ishbel, the lassie who might, one day, take her own place here. Ishbel was up to the cottage most mornings, learning the herbs and their uses, preparing salves and possets, and making herself useful in other ways: a bit of sweeping here, a bit of wood-chopping there. The girl was capable. And quiet; she'd tell what was going on down the hill, but only if she was asked. 'Twas Ishbel who had tended to Snaggletooth by day, when the wee one was recovering by the fire. She'd helped bathe Squeaker's eyes, the time ill humours swelled the flesh around them and seemed like to blind the creature. The lassie had gentle hands and a strong heart. She knew the old tale, and still she kept coming.

◯

Morning, and Ishbel's three little taps on the door.

"Missus Janet? I'm here."

"Come you in, lassie. Dinna forget to shut the door after you; the wind's whipping hard." If it kept up, there'd be no sitting idle above Pringle's field today. Maybe she should ask the lass to cut more wood. They'd be needing the fire.

"Missus Janet?"

Ishbel was standing close, right beside her as she worked on a salve for old Jennie MacGregor's nettle rash. There was something in the lassie's face, the set of the lips, the shadow in the clear hazel eyes, that stilled her hands.

"What is it, Ishbel?" And then, "Sit you down, lassie."

Ishbel sank to the bench. She hadna so much as taken off her shawl.

Janet went to the bucket, rinsed her hands, took the steaming kettle off the fire and made a brew, peppermint for mind's ease, chamomile for calm. The sweet, healing smell spread out through the cottage. The fire crackled; outside, the wind clawed at the shutters and whistled over the thatch. All the while, the lassie spoke not a word.

"A bittie tea for you. Wrap your hands around the cup, let it warm you, and tell me what's made you so sad and quiet. You ken what folk say about bad news: better out than in." *And some news, a body wishes she'd never heard spoken.*

"Missus Janet, it's . . . I've . . . "

"Out with it, lassie." Something was creeping into her bones, colder than midwinter.

"I saw . . . " Ishbel took a sip of the tea, drew a deep breath, pulled herself together. "I saw Willie Scott up by the edge of the wood, digging. I asked my brother what Willie was doing, and he told me the laird's boy, wee Iain, has fallen sick."

"They didna call me to tend to the laddie." The cold thing had its fingers around her heart. Oh, let this not be what her bones told her it must be. Let the laird, the ill-begotten Hamish Buchanan, not be putting his trust in wicked superstition, not after so many years of turning his back on the good magic of hearth and herb patch. She might have saved the wee ones that died, three sons, two daughters all lost before they reached their third year. She might, if the laird had let her near his grand establishment to tend to them.

Their mother wouldna have been so proud. But in that household Hamish was laird, king and emperor all rolled in together, and if a town doctor was the only one he'd have, dead children or no, then that was who'd be attending his son's sickbed. "What ails the wee laddie?"

"'Tis the same thing 'twas with the others, a fever and a cough, so I've heard. Missus Janet," Ishbel's voice had fallen to a whisper, "do you think Willie's making a prickle house?"

She took her time, breathing before she spoke, keeping her voice calm. 'Twasna Ishbel's fault that she was the bearer of such tidings. "Take me to the place," she said. "We'll ask the lad ourselves."

Willie had been working hard. Where yesterday had been a patch of level sward sheltered by young oaks, now a pattern of neatly dug trenches and holes marked out the foundations of a wee house. She watched as Willie took out the last of the pegs and strings that had guided keen eye and sharp spade. He bent to pick up his discarded shirt and wipe the sweat from his brow, and saw the two of them standing there.

"Missus Janet." Willie straightened. "Ishbel."

"What's that you're building, Willie? 'Tis awful close to the wood. Not a spot where a body would be wanting to bide, I'd have thought."

Willie gazed at her. His face said: *I am too brave to turn my eyes away; I am not brave enough to tell you the truth.*

"*Tell me.*" She could almost taste the iron in her mouth. "Yon housie, 'tis awful small. You building a palace for trowies, maybe?"

Willie cleared his throat. "He didna tell you?"

"He didna. Seems that task falls to yourself, Willie. Spit it out, bad news doesna improve with keeping." Her words came like stones hurled in bitterness, but the lad spoke quiet-like.

"'Tis a prickle house, Missus Janet. The laird give me the order last night. His wee lad's poorly. 'Tis the only way to save him." The young man's cheeks reddened. "That's what the laird said. And he . . . he'll be wanting you to gather what's needed, later, he told me. Seeing as you have the knowing of the pricklers and all."

Very still, she stood; still enough to let the rage burn through her without bursting from her lips in a scream. Only her hands moved, squeezing up into furious fists.

"Shame on you, Willie Scott!" Into her silence came the shout of Ishbel, the shy wee lassie who never opened her mouth in anger. Her cheeks were red with fury, her tongue a whip. "Could you not have told him you wouldna?"

"I'm sorry. I'm sorry, Missus Janet. The laird pays my wages. I've my family to support, you ken."

'Twas not possible to stay silent after that. "You're sorry. Is this the showing of your sorrow, that you come up here and dig a neat wee foundation for the laird's monstrosity? You ken 'tis nonsense. You ken 'tis no more than superstitious rubbish. Acting on a foolish old tale willna help Hamish Buchanan's wee lad. If the man wasna so torn up by grief, he'd see that the same as the rest of us do. Maybe I could help the bairn. Maybe I could have helped the others that slipped away. Since he wouldna let me near them, we'll never know. And now the man expects me to—he wants me to . . . " She could not put it in words.

"It could be true, that old tale." Willie's face had flushed as red as Ishbel's. "Maybe a prickle house can make a man's dearest wish come true. Life to the dying. Hope to the grieving. You never know, Missus Janet."

"Life to the dying? Hope to the grieving? Whoever told you the story must have left out the part about death to the innocent." Oh, she was cold; so cold. "You seem done with the digging, Willie Scott. So you can take yourself back down the hill and tell Hamish Buchanan I willna do it. I willna tolerate the thing in this wood, and I willna gather what I know he's wanting. I canna."

Silence, then, save for the ordinary sounds of the place: birds in the trees, sheep in the field, someone chopping wood down in the settlement, the creak and splash of the mill wheel. Willie did not move, and nor did Ishbel. Both watched her in silence, as if waiting. Nobody needed to say a word.

The cold truth was, there'd be no refusing. She could say the words, of course, words of pride and defiance. The laird owned the wood and her garden and her cottage. He could turn her out any time he wanted to. She'd been lucky it hadna happened before, lucky that Hamish Buchanan had taken so long, endured so many losses before he grew desperate enough to try this. But you couldna call the deaths of children lucky.

There'd be no following her heart, no telling the laird it was all foolishness, no saying that he should have asked her to tend to his ailing babes, and that she simply wouldna do what he wanted, even at the price of her home and hearth. What was better, kind hands taking the pricklers from the wood, gentleness and trust until the very end—almost the end—or Pringle with his men and his dogs tramping up here to dig them out, balled up with fear? *Oh, my wee ones, my bonny wee ones . . .*

"There's other pricklers in the wood," Ishbel offered in a whisper. "On the far side. They dinna come here, but there's a whole other clan."

A moment's temptation, no more. "Would you send raiders to the next village to murder and maim there, so you could keep your own bairnies safe?" She heard the rasp of grief and fury in her own voice. "Could you listen to the sound of screaming, and watch the cottages burning, knowing the price you paid?"

It was quiet for a few breaths, then Willie said, "You want me to tell the laird you said no, Missus Janet?"

Ishbel had taken Scribbet from her apron pocket and was holding it against her breast as if she might find some comfort in it. Janet had made the wee thing for the lassie years ago, when Ishbel was five or six and coming up to the cottage for girdle scones and stories. Scribbet's body was a pine cone, the spines an assortment of old knitting pins, the eyes dark bone buttons, the mouth a seed pod. 'Twas a wonder the wee creature hadna fallen apart long ago; 'twas remarkable that Ishbel, halfway between child and woman now, still loved Scribbet and carried it about with her. And now Ishbel raised her eyes and turned a steady look on her teacher and friend. 'Twas the look of a far older woman.

"Missus Janet?" Somewhere in that look, Willie Scott had got lost. But he still stood there, blue eyes troubled, fair skin flushed from the unexpected hurt of Ishbel's earlier words. He and she were not courting, exactly; 'twas more of a silent understanding. "What would you have me tell the laird?"

"Only that you told me about the prickle house. No more. Ishbel, go you down to the village and ask Granny Cameron to give you the old tale again, and make sure she doesna leave out a single word. Willie, how long?"

"Full moon, he told me. It's to be finished by full moon. All but the . . . the wee places, you know."

Ach, my own dearies. Fear set claws in her belly and fastened sharp teeth on her mind. She ordered it away. "Three days, then. Only three. You'll be busy with the building."

"There's other fellows coming up to help. 'Twill be done in time. I'll take your message. But I'll be back up here after, working till sunset."

"Best be off, then."

When he was a short way down the hill, out of earshot, she said, "Ishbel."

"Missus Janet?"

"Bide a bit. Come back home with me. I'll give you something to take down to Cameron's. Doesna their lassie help about the house, up at the laird's?"

"Aye." Ishbel's eyes had grown big as saucers.

"'Tisna poison I have in mind, lassie. The lady bears no blame for this wretched thing, nor her bairn neither. 'Tis healing I'm thinking of."

"Annie Cameron might be dusting the lady's bedchamber or cleaning out the coals," Ishbel said as they walked back to the cottage together. "She wouldna be talking to the lady, nor making her supper."

"Who looks after the sick bairn?"

"A nurse. A woman from outside Gimmerburn. Willie knows her, a bit."

"Ah. Then we must make more use of Willie."

"I dinna want to see his face again, after this. I dinna want to hear his voice. Not a word." Ishbel's lip was trembling.

"'Tis bad and sad, no doubt of that. I canna rightly see a way out of it. But this isna Willie's doing."

The lassie folded her arms, saying nothing.

"Get you down to Cameron's, then. The potion can wait. We canna make an enemy of Willie, lass, for following the laird's orders. If I canna summon the strength to say no, 'tis not fair to expect it of the laddie, with so many folk depending on the few coppers he brings home. Off with you, and bring me back every wee bit of that tale, every last scrap, mind."

☾

She made the potion. Whatever came of this, for good or ill, there was an anxious mother down the hill, and a sickly child. If she could help them, she would. Enough of this nonsense, town doctors who didna ken up from down. Sorrow had robbed the laird of his good judgement. Willie must help her get the cure into the Big Man's house and into the hands of the lady; after that, it would surely be a matter of common sense.

When the brew was perfect, she decanted it into a wee bottle and put in the stopper. There was more work to be done, but her hands couldna seem to set about it. By the hearth, the straw-filled box where Snaggletooth had sheltered as his leg healed waited for a time when it would be needed again. On the shelf under the window were the salves and lotions she used for the prickle tribe: soothing balms for bites and scrapes; a healing wash for cuts gone sour. 'Twas her way to be ready for what might come. But some things a body could never be ready for. The death of a child. And this, today. A prickle house. She should have looked closer at those diggings, asked Willie Scott how many . . . *Wee places*, he'd called them. 'Twas a sizeable foundation. Four-and-thirty, that was the tribe now, with the new litters from Pearlie and Primrose and Spiny.

What was keeping Ishbel? Shouldna the lassie be back up the hill by now? Perhaps she couldna find Granny Cameron. But where would the old woman be but in her cottage down there, bent over her work with her eyes narrowed and her wrinkled hands firm and sure on the bobbins? There was a fine lace square on the chest over there, given by Granny in exchange for a brew. 'Twas a lovely thing, too good to wear. A picture came to her mind, a prickler lying dead and cold, and the lacework around it like a shroud.

Come on, Ishbel, dinna dawdle. Where was the lassie? Much longer, and she'd have to go down the hill herself and see what was keeping her. *The tale. Bring me the tale*, she willed Ishbel. *Quick, now!* All the time wondering if 'twas only foolishness to imagine there might be something in the old story, something she'd missed when she first heard it, a trick or secret that would give her a way out. Something that would save the prickle tribe. In truth, she didna see how that could be. Hamish Buchanan was the laird. In his eyes she was nobody, just a wild old woman. He didna trust her cures; his dead bairns proved that. At full moon he'd be watching her like a hawk, waiting for her to set a foot wrong. You couldna trick a man like that. Maybe she should put a bag on her back and walk away, so she didna have to see it, hear it, smell the blood and the taint of it all over the wood.

The lassie's tap at the door. "Missus Janet?"

She made a brew again, sat Ishbel down at the table, listened as the tale came out in all its oddity. Listened with ears tuned sharp as a hunting owl's for any scrap of hope there might be in it. When 'twas over, she looked at Ishbel and the lassie looked back at her.

"I dinna see much in that to help us. What put the notion in that fellow's head in the first place, that such a cruel and strange thing could pull his woman back from the brink of death?"

"I dinna know, Missus Janet. But that's how Granny Cameron told the tale."

"Did she say anything more?"

"Nothing much. But . . . " Ishbel's cheeks flushed pink. "She bid me be kinder to Willie Scott. Told me to remember Willie was the tallest man in Gimmerburn. 'Twas an odd thing to say. If a man's done ill, 'tis surely no matter if he's a great lummock or a wee shrimp."

A thinking kind of silence, then. Willie Scott was indeed tall; head and shoulders above the biggest of the other lads. His dad had been known as the Giant, back in the days before Jamie Scott fell foul of a drunken carter and got his head smashed in for speaking common sense.

Ishbel took Scribbet out of her pocket again, and held the wee thing against her breast. "'Tis getting late," she said. "Will you be singing them in tonight?"

Three days. There'd be no training them out of their evening ritual, not so quick. They would come, some at least, with or without the call.

"Aye, I will." She wouldna let herself think of it as a farewell. There must be an answer. If she'd been a different kind of woman, she'd have been praying. Any kind of god or goddess would do, as long as they'd ears to hear an old woman's plea. "And I'll be wishing there was a prickle goddess in this wood, a gnarly old thing she'd be, ready to stretch her hands out over the wee tribe, so they'd be safe from fools of lairds that dinna know right from wrong." She glanced at the girl, whose capable hands were curled around the well-loved form of Scribbet. The wee face with its pointed nose and seed-pod eyes poked out between her fingers. In the soft lantern light, Scribbet could have been a real prickler, a sister to Pearlie or Conker or Snaggletooth.

'Twas then the notion came to her. "Ishbel?"

"Aye?"

"The ritual, the thing . . . 'tis done at night, under the full moon, aye?"

"In the tale it says, *When the full moon touches the roof of the prickle house.* That's when they have to . . . when someone has to . . . " Ishbel faltered, unable to get the words out.

"Would they bring lanterns? Candles?"

"They'd be needing those to see their way up the hill. But in the tale it says, *by moonlight.* So maybe they douse the lanterns, before 'tis done."

"Who does it? Must the one who wants his dream-come-true perform the task with his own hands?"

The lass turned those big eyes on her, and there was a new knowing in them. "That wasna the way Granny Cameron said it. 'Twas more like: *The laird bid his man set the living pricklers into the wee house by moonlight, one by one, till all the empty corners were filled up. Before the moonlight left the thatch, he spoke what was in his heart: that this was a gift to the powers of the wood, to restore health to the wife dearer to him than all riches and all honour. And the man closed up the wee holes, so the prickle house was tight against storm and flood, fire and pestilence.* That was how she told the tale."

There was a wee silence, like a slow breath.

"Cruel. Bitter cruel. And the sick wife, she came good after 'twas done, aye?"

"The next morning she was on the mend. *She woke with eyes bright as stars and a smile on her lips,* was the way it went. *And the laird was forever grateful and respectful to the powers of the wood, that had granted him his heart's desire.*"

"Grateful and respectful, was it?" The words were sour in her mouth. "That laird of long ago, maybe, the one in the tale. Not Hamish Buchanan. 'Twould take more than a miracle to put respect in that man."

"His wee son's sick to death, Missus Janet. That's what they're saying."

"You canna be telling me you believe in this." Was the whole of Gimmerburn turning mad?

"I dinna. Only . . . a sorrow like that, it can make a body lose sight of common sense. The laird . . . he willna be thinking straight. Didna you yourself—"

"Dinna say it. Dinna speak my son's name."

"I willna. I ken how it grieves you, even now." There was a strength in the lassie's voice, a strength to match that look she'd had in her eye earlier, as if she'd suddenly grown up.

"If 'twere your bairn, Ishbel, lying there struggling for his next breath, and you believed this might help him, would you do it? Would you hold back, respecting the small lives of the wood? Or would you think the life of a human babe must be first, always?"

"'Twould take a god or goddess to weigh such a heavy thing, Missus Janet. I only know, if 'twere my babe, my heart would be breaking over it. The laird's a man like any other."

Since she had no answer to that, she gave none. A plan was forming in her mind, a plan that depended on the moonlight and the old tale and the cooperation of Willie Scott. And one more thing: that the prickle house was only superstitious nonsense. That the woman in the tale didna need the ritual to recover. For if she was wrong about that, she might be robbing a wee lad of his chance to live, and while she didna think much of Hamish Buchanan, his child was as blameless as any bairn, human or otherwise. "Let me be right about this," she muttered.

"What was that?"

"Nothing, lassie. We've work to do. If you'll help. The first thing is finding Willie Scott. I need a word with him."

She could almost see the words on Ishbel's lips, *I willna*, but the lass shut her mouth and went out without saying anything. Not long after, she was back. It seemed work on the prickle house was over for the day. Ishbel came in; Willie stood on the doorstep, twisting his hat in his big hands.

"Come you inside and shut the door, Willie Scott. You're letting in the chill." It was nearly time to call in the prickle tribe; how could she bear it? "I've a plan. Without the two of you, I canna make it work. Will you help?"

◑

Two days until full moon, and the sky veiled with drifting clouds. Rain fell, gentle and slow. The lads kept on working; 'twasna long to get a house finished, even a wee one. Willie's notion that the special nooks and crannies—four-and-twenty of them, as the laird had ordered—should be set up so high was a bit daft, but the laird had put Willie in charge, so they made the house the way he bid them.

When the day's work was over the wee place stood tall, with only the thatching to be done and some whitewash to be put on the walls. A sweet thing 'twas, like a fairy dwelling from an old tale of magic. Fergus, who was handy with a chisel, had carved rows of acorns on the shutters. They had laid a path of pale stones in a circle all around the house, as Willie bid them. Tomorrow, Angus and Sandy would lay the thatch, and the others would paint, and 'twould be ready. All ready for full moon. Nobody asked what would happen if the clouds didna lift.

The lads talked about it in whispers and murmurs. They were proud of the making, the fine thing they'd done together; but the strangeness of it, those wee chambers, the idea of it . . . That took the brightness off the thing. None of them would come up to watch, when 'twas time. Not one of them.

This was what Willie said when he came to her house late in the day, after the others had gone home to their families. They were at the table, she and Ishbel, not eating but making, the space between them a litter of cones and seed pods, beads and thread and scraps of this and that. Four-and-twenty; 'twas a lot. They were less than halfway to it. And 'twas time to sing the pricklers in.

She left Willie with Ishbel, bidding him set the kettle on the fire and make them all a brew. Then she went out. 'Twas the last time she would call them before the thing was over and done with, one way or another. If her trick didna work, and if the laird's son died, she'd be away from Gimmerburn before the prickle house saw another full moon. If it did work, and the laddie lived—whether from the pricklers or from the draught that had gone, with Willie, over the river to the laird's house, where Annie Cameron had passed it to another lass to give to the lady herself—she vowed she would leave anyway. If it could happen once, it could come around again. Even now her heart was all cracks, like a worn old pot.

'Twouldna take much to shatter it in pieces.

> *"Come up, Foxglove, Peppercorn, Sneaker,*
> *Parsley, Gentlefoot, Silvertips, Squeaker,*
> *Come in safe from the wind and the weather,*
> *Come in wee ones, come all together."*

Safe. 'Twas a lie. There was no safe place, not for prickler or fox or badger, not for man or woman or child taken before his time. She watched them come, one by one, as innocent as that wee laddie in the big house, maybe breathing his last this very night, maybe holding on thanks to the draught she'd made for him. She set down the bowls, then sat on the steps, the way she always did, to see them take their supper. If there was a goddess in the wood, now would be the time to ask her a favour. She couldna find the words for that, and besides, such things were nobbut folk's foolishness. "You might help a bit, when the time comes," she muttered. "Make Hamish Buchanan see what he needs to see, and only that. You might bid the wee ones go to ground, just this once. You might . . . " She stopped herself. If there'd been such a thing as a goddess, Dougal would have come safe home from the sea, to wed and father bairns and be happy. The laird and his lady wouldna have lost so many babes, and there'd be no need for a prickle house.

" . . . *Whiskers, Snaggletooth, Trencherman, Pearlie*
Three-toes, Parsnip, Conker and Girlie."

Pearlie wasna herself. Oft-times first to come forward, ready for a touch, a stroke, a kind word, tonight she was at the back, in the shadows. She hadna eaten a morsel nor drunk a drop. 'Twas Conker who came up to the steps, snuffling about, looking up at her with his shining dark eyes. Behind him Peppercorn, a bold young fellow. Give it a season or two, and he'd be fathering a new tribe of wee ones. If the laird didna get to him first.

"What's amiss with Pearlie?" Ishbel's soft voice came from behind her, along with a band of warm light from the part-open door. Willie was moving about inside, clinking dishes.

"I dinna ken. We'd best take a look. Tread quiet."

Just what ailed the wee one, there was no quick telling. She couldna get warm, even when Ishbel carried her inside and sat with her by the fire. She wouldna take milk or water, even with a drop of honey in it. Something was gripping her body tight, hurting her sore. Her eyes had a glaze on them, as if she were seeing through a cloud. They examined her, legs and feet, belly and back, mouth, ears, nose, looking for bites and stings, cuts and hurts, but there was nothing to be found.

"A night's rest, maybe that's all she needs," Janet said when the wee one was bedded down in the box by the hearth, and the three of them sat at the table to eat the meal Willie had made from the bread and cheese and fresh greens folk had brought up to the house during the day as payment for the remedies she gave them. Three times she and Ishbel had heard the knock at the door and had scooped their makings off the table quick, hiding them from curious eyes. Better that than draw attention by keeping the place locked up. When folk had spoken of the prickle house, she'd turned the talk to other things. The laird's son was still alive. That much they knew.

Willie wasna saying much. She saw him looking over at the shelf where their makings were set out, some needing the glue to dry, some still wanting bits and pieces added to make them more lifelike. He hadna said if he thought they would do. She couldna tell what he was thinking, and that was unusual, for mostly—when he looked at Ishbel, for instance—the lad's face was an open book.

She'd made six so far, Ishbel five. Some were like Scribbet, with a big pine cone for the body and seed pod eyes. One she'd fashioned from an old brush, the bristles sticking up, the flat part under, and stumpy legs made from cut-down corks. That wee thing stared back from the shelf, its button eyes sharp as sharp. 'Twas fancy, of course, but she could have sworn there was some kind of life in it.

Ishbel had fetched the rag bag out, and fleece waiting to be spun. The fruits of her day's work were on the shelf next to Janet's: three made from cloth patches in brown and grey and green, the hues of the woodland, stuffed with wool, with strips of birchbark scraped up in tufts and wrapped around, the better to look like prickles. One from the inside of an old shoe; one from a long-dried-out skin with the spines still on it and a pair of black stones stuck in the empty eye holes. That creature was like the ghaestie of a prickler; looking at it set her insides curdling.

"If clouds come over the moon," said Willie, "the laird willna be able to do it. Isna that right, Ishbel? The moonlight has to touch the roof, and then they go in."

"Aye," Ishbel said.

Janet knew what was coming. Let him say it; the help he'd be giving them might cost him dear indeed.

"If there are no clouds, Missus Janet, the laird would have to be blind to think those wee creatures were real pricklers. I like them well," Willie hastened to add. "I see you've done your best. But . . . "

"Shut your big mouth, Willie Scott," muttered Ishbel.

"I dinna mean—"

"I willna sing them in tomorrow." Janet spoke loud and firm, stopping the two of them. "I willna do it. We'll make the rest, and we'll go out to the prickle house, and the moon will shine or it won't, and we'll do what we agreed. Unless you have a better plan."

Pearlie rustled about in the straw. She'd been startled, maybe, by Janet's raised voice.

Willie went to look. He wasna often in the house, and never before when she'd had a prickler here to tend to. She saw him bend down; kneel down. Saw his young face soften. Caught there a fleeting memory of her Dougal, long ago, looking at a babe in a cradle.

"Who's this?" The lad's voice was all gentleness.

"Pearlie. She that lost her young to the dogs last spring. She's poorly."

He reached in to touch the wee one's spiny back; to lay a big, gentle finger on her neat small head. "How fine they're made," Willie breathed. "Every bit just so."

"Aye," she said after a moment. "'Tis almost enough to make a body believe in good gods."

Morning saw Willie Scott and the other lads hard at work on the prickle house. 'Twas a fine day. The sun shone. The watery clouds vanished away. Folk came up to the cottage for bits and pieces, and in between, she and Ishbel took turns going into the wood for supplies, for four-and-twenty pricklers took a deal of making. All day she wondered if Hamish Buchanan would come up the hill and demand to be shown the creatures alive and ready for his bit of foolish spell-casting, and all day he didna come, save to the prickle house itself, where he watched on as the lads did the finishing touches. Ishbel saw him there as she passed the edge of the wood, gathering bits and pieces.

By dusk they were ready. The four-and-twenty wee ones were packed into two baskets and covered with cloths. Ishbel had set mead and oatcakes on the table, but they stayed untouched. The fire burned low. In her straw-lined box, Pearlie lay quiet, her breathing a faint rasp in the stillness. Her eyes were dimming. 'Twas a small grief, but it felt awful hard. She didna want the wee one to die alone in the box there, while the rest of them were out at the prickle house wasting their time with foolishness. But she couldna put Pearlie outside. 'Twould be bitter cold once the sun went down.

They waited. Beyond the door, out the back, the pricklers would be in the garden, by the steps, waiting too. She wouldna go out. She wouldna think what it might mean for that wee lad down the hill if she was wrong and the laird was right.

The light faded, the shadows crept out, and the wood was in darkness. They'd have gone away now, the tribe, knowing 'twas too late for the food and the kind words. She sat at the table with Ishbel, and the sounds of night time came to their ears. An owl calling, hollow and mournful. The wind moaning in the trees. The shiver of the shutters. And then, loud enough to make them both jump, the tramp of booted feet up to the door, and a hard knocking.

"Janet MacTavish! Are you there?"

'Twas the laird himself. Moving quick as an eel, Ishbel snatched up the baskets and set them in a dark corner. Janet reached into the box and lifted up Pearlie. The wee one was deathly cold. She glanced around as the rapping got louder, and the voice ruder.

"Missus MacTavish! Open up!"

"What does the fool think I am, his slave?" She grabbed the lacy cloth from the shelf; 'twas the nearest thing to a blanket within reach. She wrapped the cloth around Pearlie, tucked the wee one into a fold of her shawl, then went to open the door. Her heart was jittering about like a creature beset by stinging wasps. When he saw what they'd done, likely he'd make her go out and fetch the four-and-twenty right now. And if she wouldna, he'd send his men to dig them out.

Her eyes met Ishbel's, just for a moment. The lassie had her chin up and her back straight. She said not a word, but Janet took heart. *Brave it out. Stand your ground. This fellow kens nothing of pricklers, nothing at all. He hardly kens the folk he rules over.*

She opened the door and the laird came striding in. There were men behind him, five or six, it looked like, but they kept outside. Cold air rushed into the cottage. Against her breast, Pearlie trembled.

"Have you done as I asked?" Hamish Buchanan glared around the place.

Ask was not the word; this man didna ken how to ask, only to give orders. "I have," she said, keeping it courteous.

"Where are they?"

"They . . . "

"We have them in these baskets, Mister Buchanan." 'Twas Ishbel who spoke up, and as she spoke she gave the laird her best smile. Who would have thought a shy lassie like her could smile like that? 'Twas just as well Willie Scott had kept outside with the rest of the laird's men.

"Show me!"

Ach, here it was. She opened her mouth, not knowing what would come out, but again 'twas Ishbel who spoke first.

"They're in these two baskets, Mister Buchanan. Canna you hear them squeaking and rustling about?" Ishbel put her head to one side as if listening. There was indeed a faint sound, perhaps the fire crackling and settling under the cold draught, perhaps rats in the thatch or twigs brushing the walls outside.

"Take off the cover. Show me." The laird's voice was quieter. He didna step toward Ishbel nor make to pick up the baskets.

"Oh, didna you ken, Mister Buchanan? You canna disturb them now. They feel it, you see. They sense what's coming. It affrights them. We dinna want the poison to rise into the quills, not before they're set in the wee house." Ishbel's eyes were wide, lovely, guileless in her bonny face.

"Poison?" The laird took a step back.

"Aye," Janet said, getting in quick. "'Tis a thing that happens when the wee creatures are distressed. Once it comes up into the quills, you canna handle them safely. One drop, and your skin burns and bubbles and festers. A man could lose his hand. I hope your fellow's got a good pair of gloves for later."

The laird glowered at her. She didna often wish to be young and sweet-faced like Ishbel, but now was one of the times when a bit of beauty wouldna have gone astray. "'Tis the truth, Hamish Buchanan. See these hands?" She waved one hand in his face, quick, so he hadna time to see it clearly. "Ruined, they are, from handling the creatures. Ishbel here, she always puts her gloves on."

"I hope you're not spinning tales to me, Janet MacTavish. You ken I own this cottage and all the land about it, aye?"

"Would a body lie when she stood to lose home and livelihood for it? If you dinna believe we did what you wanted, then look here."

She fished Pearlie out of the shawl, still wrapped in the fine lace, and stepped up to Hamish Buchanan. She lifted the wee one as high as she could. Pearlie's nose was right by the laird's face.

The Big Man shrank back. He'd gone the colour of soft cheese. Pearlie hadna rolled in a ball, the way a prickler does when it senses danger. She'd only the strength to move her wee paws a bit, and give a faint sigh.

"Hold her if you want," Janet said. "If you wrap your cloak around your hands, 'twill be safe enough."

"Willie!" the laird shouted.

Willie Scott came in. Didna look either woman in the eye. Stood with gaze down, hands clasped before him, picture of a laird's obedient servant.

"Do you have gloves with you?"

"Aye, Mister Buchanan."

"Put them on, take this creature, and you two—" looking at Janet and Ishbel, "—bring the rest of them. Make sure they don't escape the baskets. I don't want anyone hurt."

She hadna thought, when she fetched Pearlie out of the straw-lined box, that she'd see her wee one taken out into the woods to die alone and frightened. It didna matter that this was only one prickler; that Pearlie was near death already; that her passing might help save the rest. 'Twas wrong; cruelly wrong. Too late now. Pearlie rode along the pathway cupped in Willie's big hands, and the moon rose up into the night sky, bright and lovely, setting a glitter on the leaves, wakening a green glow on the mossy trunks. 'Twas a fine sight, no doubt of that. Another time, such beauty might have eased her heart.

She'd thought—hoped—that nobody would come but the laird and his men, and her and the lassie. But there on the new white path, in a shawl-huddled row, were the old women of Gimmerburn, Granny Cameron and her cronies. And there was Farmer Pringle, who thought himself the next thing to the laird, and Pringle's wife Lizzie who had been up the hill this very morning seeking a physic for the womb. Behind them stood one or two of the fellows who worked Pringle's fields, and on the other side a scattering of folk from the settlement, though none of the lads who'd built the prickle house had come, save for Willie.

They came up to the place. Hamish Buchanan bid his men quench their lanterns, and Pringle's folk put theirs out as well. By moonlight the prickle house was a marvel, tall and slender as the tower of a princess, though, in truth, it didna stand so very high. A big man like Willie Scott could reach the eaves with his hands stretched up. A shorter man—the laird, say, or Pringle—would need a box to stand on, or a ladder.

Now all was quiet. The creatures in the wood hushed their voices as white moonlight touched the corner of the wee house.

"Put them in." The laird didna rap out an order now, just spoke the words. Ishbel went forward, basket on her arm. Willie was standing by the wall of the prickle house, waiting. As Ishbel came between him and Hamish Buchanan, Janet saw the lad slip Pearlie into his workman's pouch, lace wrapping and all.

"Here," said Ishbel, dipping into her basket and handing up the first prickler.

Willie held the creature as carefully as if 'twas alive; for a lad with such a guileless face, he was good at dissembling. Every eye was fixed on him, as if the folk of Gimmerburn were only waiting for disaster to come. Or maybe they were expecting something wondrous, sparkling lights or fey music or an appearance by the goddess of the woods in person, with shining wings and a long gossamer gown.

She waited for it. One of the sharp-eyed crones saying, *That's no prickler, that's nobbut a pine cone with wee stones for eyes.*

Or the laird's voice, thundering, *Would you trick me, Willie Scott?* and telling the lad to forget the cottage that housed his family and the work that paid for their daily bread. She waited for Granny Cameron to cackle with mirth, or for someone, anyone, to ask for a closer look at the four-and-twenty pricklers, to make sure the spell was just so. But 'twas silent. In they went, the wee ones made of cloth and bark, the brush-and-cork creature, the ones that were copies of Ishbel's beloved Scribbet.

Twelve of the wee spots had their own pricklers, and Ishbel's basket was empty. Willie had set the little ones up under the eaves. After each was put in, he had covered its resting place with a flat stone, shaped to fit snug. The occupants would stay dry as they died of slow starvation. Or would have, if she hadna cheated. *Let the laird not see this. Let us be done here, quick, quick . . .*

Ishbel set her basket down and stepped back. Janet came forward, twitched the cloth off her own basket, handed the pricklers up to Willie one by one. A cold sweat on her like the breath of a dead thing. Her heart drumming fit to smash itself on her ribs. Another, and another. Here was the wee one Ishbel had made from the skin, with its baleful pebble eyes. A murmuring came at the sight of that; someone was affrighted. Who wouldna be, to see the look on its face?

Three more to go; two more . . . Now the last one. She handed it up. The moonlight still touched the roof of the prickle house, but 'twould soon be gone. She drew breath, feeling her heart slow at last.

Willie Scott was moving a step along the house; he was reaching out to her again.

"Last one, Missus Janet," he whispered.

Ach! They had counted their makings over and over. Twelve in each basket, sure as sure. Had she dropped one in the woods, stumbling on a tree root? Had Ishbel left one behind in the cottage?

Willie Scott looked right at her. The moonlight gleamed in his eyes. Not a word from him, or from Ishbel.

"Make haste," came the laird's voice. He didna need to shout; she knew what he meant. *Finish the job quick before the moonlight's off the thatch. Or a wee lad will die, and 'twill be on your head.*

Maybe she gave a nod. Maybe she only looked at Willie. He put a hand in his pouch and brought out Pearlie. There was no time to bid the wee one farewell. A moment, only, to lay her hand on the lacy cloth and feel the sharp prick of the spines through the softness of it. She clenched her jaw tight and held her head high. Later, when her door was shut fast behind her, there'd be time for weeping.

The lad lifted Pearlie up high and set her in the last of the wee secret places. As the prickler left Willie's hands, a great cry came from the woods, a sorry shrieking that turned every face chalk white. That sound didna come from man or woman. 'Twasna the cry of a hawk stooping on its prey, nor the scream of a rabbit in the owl's grip. 'Twas the voice of the wood itself.

Then Willie Scott took up the last of his four-and-twenty flat stones, and laid it on top of Pearlie's wee tomb, so careful it made no sound at all. The moonlight moved off the roof thatch. All was silent now, but the scream stayed in her head; 'twould be with her always.

"'Tis done," said Willie Scott, tall and quiet. He came to stand between them, her and the lass. He looked toward the laird, and his gaze was steady.

"Aye," said Hamish Buchanan. "Aye." He walked up to the prickle house and set his hands against the wall, and he bowed his head. Praying, maybe, or thinking of his wee boy.

He was a man like any other. A bullying, proud kind of man, no doubt of that, but a man all the same. A father, and full of hurt. Through the lake of tears behind her eyes, through the lump of grief in her throat, she saw that plain as plain.

"We'll be away home," Ishbel said, and took her arm. Willie gathered up the two baskets. Like ghosts folk drifted away, heading for home and the warmth of hearth fires, turning their backs on the strangeness of the wood.

"The wee one was already gone," Willie said as they walked back to the cottage, just the three of them. "Gone before I laid her in the prickle house. Died in my hands as I lifted her up. 'Tis the truth, Missus Janet."

She wouldna ask if those big, kind hands had hastened the moment of death, or whether the woodland goddess, the one she didna believe in, had breathed in Pearlie's ear that it was time to go. She wouldna say that cry they'd heard and trembled at was the voice of all wee creatures screaming out against cruelty and injustice and suffering. They were little lives, aye. So easy broken, so soon gone.

"My thanks to you, Willie Scott. And you, Ishbel. Quick-witted, you are. Off home now, the two of you. I dinna want company the night."

'Twas early when the lady came to her door, the sun not long risen, the dew still heavy on the grass. Janet was sorting out her supplies, fitting jars and packets into her travelling bag. The hearth was cold; she'd had no heart for breakfast, and she hadna expected visitors.

"Missus MacTavish?" The lady was a wee thing, a wisp of a woman, her hair caught up in a cloth, a warm shawl around her shoulders. Dressed fine, for all that; there was no doubting who she was, though Janet hadna met her before. Down the hill a bit, looking as if she'd sooner not be there, was Annie Cameron. Keeping watch, it looked like. Maybe Hamish Buchanan didna care to let his wife out.

"Aye." She didna ask the lady in. The place was cold as the grave; there wasna even a brew to offer.

"I came to thank you. For the remedy you sent. Iain—my wee lad—he's well this morning. The cough eased as soon as we started giving him the drops, and last night he slept so peacefully—I kept getting up to check was he still breathing. I cannot thank you enough, Missus MacTavish." A glance over her shoulder, as if something might be stalking her. "Do you think . . . " Her voice lowered, her manner awkward now. "My husband . . . My husband is sure it was the prickle house that did it, effected a cure, I mean, but . . . It was your remedy, wasn't it? Your potion that made Iain well again? And that means if we'd come to you before . . . What do you think? What do you believe?"

The lady's eyes were big and sad in a face worn down by grief. Today's good news wasna enough to banish that.'Twould take a powerful joy to wipe away the loss of all those bairns.

"I canna tell you, my lady."

"But you must have an idea, a notion . . . "

"I dinna ken."

A silence. The lady looked past her, through the open doorway, to the cold room and the half-packed bag standing ready. "I hope you are not going away for long. I have asked my husband to dismiss the town doctor; I have no trust in the man. We will need you in Gimmerburn."

"Aye, well. I'm glad the wee fellow is recovering." *Your son will grow up and wed and father sons of his own. For all your losses, you are a lucky woman.* "Best be off home to your breakfast, my lady. 'Tis early to be abroad."

"I'm sorry," the lady said. "About the pricklers. That must have been hard for you."

"Aye."

She watched the two of them go, down the hill and back toward the village. She didna seem to have the heart for the packing now, so she went to sit out the back on the steps, though 'twas bitter cold. With Pearlie gone, another would have to be the heart of the tribe, one of the younger females, Primrose or Spiny. What had ailed Pearlie, to take her so quick? Let it not be a sickness that would spread fast from one to another, or she'd be thinking the prickle house a milder death.

Her thoughts turned in circles. The careful counting of the four-and twenty, the packing of the twelve and twelve, the walk to the prickle house . . . She couldna have dropped one, could she? The baskets had been covered with cloths. How could the count have been wrong? 'Twasna possible, couldna be, that Pearlie had . . . had somehow sickened of her own will, had made an offering of her own life to save the tribe? 'Twas as foolish as believing in the magic of the wee house and the moonlight. Besides, Willie had told her Pearlie was dead before. That meant they hadna done the magic, not the way 'twas in the tale. They had cheated twice over. But Pearlie . . . and that screaming . . . Could it be that one was enough? A life for a life?

She folded her arms on her knees; laid her head down. 'Twas the time and place for her tears, and she let them fall. Maybe, for a bit, she slept, for when she lifted her head the sun was higher, and someone was in the cottage clanking pots about.

"Ishbel?"

"Aye, I'm here."

Inside, the fire was crackling, the place was warming up, and on the table was a platter of fresh bread and a crock of clover honey. From out the front came the sound of someone chopping wood.

"There's no need . . . " she began, but the fact was, the warmth was good. It eased her aching joints, and Ishbel's quick smile soothed her heart. 'Twould be foolish to leave with her stomach empty and her spirits low. She wouldna get far that way.

"Sit you down, Missus Janet," the lassie said.

The house had been tidied from top to toe. The wood basket was full to the brim and the hearth swept clean. The place shone with good care.

"You didna unpack my bag, I hope."

Ishbel stood there, hands on hips. The wee meek lassie of old times was gone; here was a new woman. "I didna, but not for lack of wishing to. Willie and me, we wouldna tell you, *you canna leave*. But you might wait till tomorrow. Sing the tribe in one last time, speak to them about Pearlie, give them some comfort."

She wrapped her hands around the cup Ishbel set before her. The scent of good herbs wreathed her: chamomile, spearmint, a bittie lavender. Healing herbs. "Some sadness, there's no easing," she said. And then, "They're pricklers, lassie. They dinna understand what I say to them."

"Not the words, maybe. They ken the meaning right enough. They need your kindness, Missus Janet. To make sense of what's happened."

How could losing your child ever make sense? How could foolish superstition and the death of the innocent be anything but cruel chance? She went out at dusk, bidding Ishbel and Willie leave her be for a while. The bond between the two young ones was plain now, no longer veiled by shyness and uncertainty. They'd seen the strength in each other, and she was glad of that. There was hope and promise on their path ahead. Let there be no sudden obstacles on that way, no losses and griefs beyond bearing.

'Twas time. Dusk settled over her garden like a soft blanket, grey and violet and deepest blue. It spread itself into every corner; it wrapped the bushes in shadow and darkened the sward, until Ishbel lit the lamp in the window, and the gold light shone forth as if to say, *Now you are home. Now you are safe at last.*

She found, all of a sudden, that she hadna a voice to sing them in. The rhyme was fled; her lips wouldna shape the words. But the pricklers were there. All about the garden, by the flowering lavender, under the tall comfrey, creeping out onto the sward, they gathered in, and the lamplight made a wee bright spark in their eyes.

She reached down and took up Parsnip, elder of the tribe. *Wee one. Dear one.* Now others came close, moving in their slow way, gathering around her feet as if they were wanting something beyond sippets of bread and milk. All of them here; all but Pearlie. All of them close up, even the shy and fearful ones. Rattlecap with his broken prickles; Snaggletooth, limping in; bold Conker and sweet-faced Gentlefoot. Primrose, who might take Pearlie's place in the tribe. The old ones. The young ones. The wee ones who hadna their names yet. All of them.

She found her voice. "Pearlie's gone. She was a good one, a fine one. Had more than her share of sadness. Didna let that stop her. She was mother to many of you, friend to all, and you'll be feeling her loss hard. What she did at the end, 'twas rare and brave. If we could all be as brave as her, our lives would be fine things, long or short."

She set Parsnip down slow, gathered up wee Silvertips, Pearlie's youngest son, gentle as she could so he wouldna curl up in fright. "You've set me thinking, wee ones," she said. "Seems to me there's a basket of good things: new babes, first love, folk getting wed. Courage and kindness. And to balance it, there's a basket of sad things: the breaking of a family, the death of a bairn. Anger and fear. 'Tis life, no more and no less. When it gets hard, there's a choice. Turn your back and walk away, or go forward as brave as Pearlie did."

Whether the pricklers understood her, there was no telling. They lingered by her feet, and she held each in turn, stroking soft and murmuring low. Then Ishbel came to the door, pushing it open wider, and Conker gave a wee squeak as if to remind them it was supper time.

"You'll be wanting the bowls now, aye?" said Ishbel.

They set them out together, her and the lassie, and the pricklers gathered around to take their supper. Willie came to the doorway with wonder in his eyes, and she didna stop him from looking on. When the bowls were licked clean, the tribe crept away into the shadows, and it was night.

Inside, Willie built up the fire for her, as if she were an old woman incapable of fending for herself, and she sat by and watched him do it. Then Ishbel headed off for home, and Willie went with her, for he didna want her going over Pringle's fields on her own at night.

Janet bolted her door behind the two of them. The lantern glowed; the fire burned bright; beyond the shutters, the wood was alive with the small sounds of the creatures about their business. With careful hands she took the jars and packets from her travelling bag and set them on the shelves, each in its right place.

☾

otherling

It was a harsh winter, a season of slicing winds and ice-fettered waterways, of hunger and endurance. The days were always short in the shadow season, but this year dark seemed hungry to devour light. Bellies yearned for fresh meat; hearts ached for the sun's blessing. The Songs told of the coming of seals, and sanctioned the killing of three: sufficient for a good feast for every man, woman and child of the Folk. Bard's Singing set out how the hunting must be done. The men went masked, their leader garbed in the hunt cloak, soft and grey, shining and supple as if he himself were a seal. The spearing was prefaced by apologies and words of gratitude. Afterwards there was feasting, and oil for lamps, and the Folk took new heart. Now they might endure until the days began to lengthen again, and the first cautious leaf-swellings appeared on the wind-battered trees.

But Bard felt the rasping in his chest, his cough like a stick drawn over wattles, and he knew he had seen his last spring. He watched his student. She had been apt to learn: she could draw forth the pipe's piercing keen and conjure the subtle rhythm of the bones. By candlelight she summoned the voice of the small harp strung with the gut of winter hares. Its melody hung bittersweet in air: call and echo, substance and shadow. The girl had endured the days of fasting, the sleepless nights, the necessary trials by water and fire and deep earth. She had heard the Songs; had held within her the voices of the ancestors, a burden precious as an unborn child. All this she had learned. But she was young: perhaps too young.

"Tonight's lesson is grave indeed." Bard spoke quietly as the harpsong ended. "You know already that Bard is born only from a twinning; that in the way of things there will be one such birth amongst the Folk in each generation. This allows time for one Bard to pass on the mysteries to the next, as I have done to you. If the cycle were broken, and Bard died before his student was ready, the Singing would be lost, and without it the Folk would perish. The Songs reveal the great pattern that must be followed. They are our true map and pathway: our balance and our lodestar."

The girl nodded, saying nothing.

"Our calling cannot be denied. It is a sacred trust. But . . . " He faltered. How could her mind encompass the desolation of a life spent without human touch? She was but half grown: barely a woman. "There is a darker side. The Songs must be taken unsullied from their source, and passed on pure and strong to the Folk. Bard must devote every scrap of will, every fibre of spirit, every last corner of mind to that. It will be long; you will bear the burden until your student is ready to take your place. There is no room for other things. So we remain alone; apart. But it is not enough. Bard must be stronger than an ordinary man or woman; strong enough to endure the power of the Singing and not splinter into madness; true enough to form unbreakable link and pure conduit from spirit to man." His sigh scraped like a blade on ice. "That is why Bard must be twinborn. That is why we have the Choosing."

"What is the Choosing?" The girl's small features were frost-white in the dimness of the stone hut, and her eyes had darkened to shadows. Outside, the wind roared across the thatch; the rope-hung weights knocked against the walls.

"If you had lived amongst the Folk, you would know a little of this already," the old man said wearily. "I have kept it from you; it is a mystery darker than any you have yet learned. Now you must know it, and begin to harden your will towards it. You may be lucky; for you the Choosing may come late, when you are practised in the disciplines of the mind. Have you asked yourself what becomes of the twin who is not Bard? How this choice is made?"

She pondered a moment. "I suppose one seems more apt. Perhaps the other is sent away. I have seen no likeness of myself amongst the Folk."

"Indeed not. Your brother died long ago, when you were no more than babes; mine met the same fate in a time before my memory. We hold their strength as well as our own, and are ourselves doubly strong: two in one. Without this, no man or woman has the endurance, the fortitude, the clear head and unsullied spirit a Bard must possess. You could not hear the Songs, you could not draw the voice of power from the harp, or sway the minds of the Folk, without your Otherling."

"My Otherling?" she breathed.

"Your twin; the one who was sacrificed so that you could become Bard."

Her eyes were mirrors of darkness. "They killed him?" she whispered.

The old man nodded, his features calm. He was still Bard; if he felt compassion, he did not let it show. "Soon after birth. It is always thus. A choice is made. The stronger, the more suitable, is preserved. The Otherling dies before he sees a second dawn, and his spirit flows into the brother or sister. That way, bard becomes strong enough for the Singing. It is necessary, child."

"Bard?" Her voice was very faint in the half-dark, and not quite steady. "Who makes the choice? Who performs the—the sacrifice?"

The old man looked at the girl, and she looked back at him. He needed no words to answer her; she read the truth in his eyes.

It was as well he told her when he did. Next morning when she arose, shivering, to make up the fire and heat some gruel for the old man's breakfast, she found him calm-faced and cold on his bed. She laid white shells on his eyelids and touched his shaven head with her fingertips. When a boy passed by, trudging to the outer field with a bucket of oats, she called her message from behind closed shutters. Before nightfall the elders came with a board and took the old man away. Now she was Bard. Later, she stood dry-eyed by the pyre as he burned hot and pungent in the freezing air of the solstice.

At her first Singing, she told the old man's life and his passing, and she told a good season to come, for all the harsh winter. Seed could be planted early; mackerel would be plentiful. The sea would take no men this spring, as long as they were careful. When she was done the people made their reverences and departed. Some lived close by in the settlement of Storna, but others had far to travel, across the island to Grimskaill, Settersby or distant Frostrim. They boarded their sledges and whipped on wiry dog or sturdy pony; they strapped bone skates to their boots and made their way by frozen stream and lake path. They would return for the great Singings Bard must give at each season's turning. At these times new Songs would be given: new wisdom from ancient voices. The Singings had names: Waking, Ripening, Reaping, Sleeping. But she had her own names for them, which she did not tell. Longing, Knowing, Sacrifice, Silence.

They said she was a good Bard in those days. She kept aloof, as she should. She'd greet them when she must, then withdraw inside her hut like a ghost-woman. Days and nights she waited at the stones, silent in their long shadows, listening. They said if you dared to speak to her at such a time, she would not hear you, though her eyes were open. All that she could hear was the silence of the Song.

One long winter a man brought a load of wood and stayed to chop it for her. She watched him from behind the shutters, marvelling at the strength and speed of it. When he was done, he did not simply go away as he should, but used his fist to play a firm little dance-beat on her door. She opened it the merest crack, looked out with her shadowy eyes, her face pale with knowledge.

"All finished," said the young man, his grin dimpled and generous, his hair standing on end, fair as ripe barley. "Stacked in the corner to keep dry for you. Cold up here."

"Thank you," she whispered, looking into his eyes: merry, kind eyes the colour of rock pools under a summer sky. "Thank you." The door began slowly to creak shut.

"Lonely life," said the young man.

Bard nodded, and looked again, and closed the door.

After that he would come up from time to time, not often, but perhaps more often than the natural pattern of things would allow. He would mend leaking thatch, or unblock a drain; she would watch him from behind the door, or through the chinks of a shutter, and thank him. There was never more than a word or two in it, but after a while she found she was looking for him in the crowd whenever she ventured into Storna. She found she was peering from her window when folk passed on the road, in case she might see him go by, and turn his head towards her shutters, and smile just for her. She learned his name: Ekka, a warrior's name, though a man with such a smile was surely no fighter, for all his strong arms that hewed the iron-hard logs as if cleaving through rounds of fresh cheese.

She found her attention wandering, and brought it sharply back. Under the stones, sitting cross-legged in silent pose of readiness, she waited for the Songs, and they did not come. Instead of their powerful voices, their ancient, binding truths, all she could hear was a faint fragment of melody, a little tinkling thing like the tunes played by the band of travelling folk who went about the island in summer, entertaining the crowds with tricks and dancing. It was the first time the Songs had ever eluded her, and when she came down to her hut, empty of the wisdom whose telling was her life's only purpose, she knew the old man's teaching had been sound. She must shut down those parts of herself that belonged to the spring season: the Longing. Bard must move forward quite alone.

From that time on her door was closed to him. Once or twice he called through fastened shutters, knowing she was there, and she set her jaw and held her silence. She went out hooded and kept her eyes on the ground. He could not be totally avoided, for he was a leader in the settlement, with a part to play in the gatherings. Bard taught herself to greet him and feel nothing. She taught herself to look at him as she looked at all the others: as if the space between them were as wide and as unbridgeable as the great bowl of the star-studded sky. She watched him withdraw, the blue eyes darkened, the smile quite gone. Later, she watched him fall in love and marry, and she kept her thoughts in perfect order. Sleep was another matter. Even Bard's training cannot teach the mastery of dreams.

Time passed. Ekka's young wife had a tiny daughter. There were bountiful seasons and harsh ones. In times of trouble, the Songs cannot of themselves make things good. They cannot calm stormy seas, or cure sheep of the murrain, or bring sunshine in place of endless drenching rain. But they do bring wisdom. A warning of bad times enables preparation: the mending of thatch, the strengthening of walls, the shepherding of stock into barns and the conservation of supplies. Such a warning makes it possible to get through the hard times. The Folk kept a careful balance, each decision governed by the pattern she gave them, an ancient pattern in which wind and tide, fire and earth, man and beast were all part of the one great dance. One year the Ripening Song told of raiders in high ships, vessels with names like Dragonflight and Sea Queen and Whalesway. The Folk moved north to Frostrim, driving their stock before them. The raiders came and passed the island by; a shed or two was burned, a boat taken. At Reaping the Folk returned, and Bard sang their safety and a mild winter. Another year the Songs told of death. That season an ague took Storna and twelve good folk perished, man, woman and babe. Ekka's wife was gravely ill, and Bard performed a Telling by the bedside. In a Telling one did not exactly ask the ancestors a favour. One simply set out a possible course of events, then hoped. Bard told how Sifri would bear more children: fine, bonny girls like her little daughter there, strong sons, blue-eyed and merry. She told the laughter of these children through the narrow ways of Storna and out across the fields, as they chased one another under the sun of an endless summer day. She finished, pulled the hood up over her shaven head, and left. The next morning Sifri was sitting up and drinking barley broth. By springtime her belly was swollen with child again, her small, sweet features flushed and mysterious with inner life.

At Reaping that year, Bard stood beneath the watchstone and heard the Song, and felt her heart grow cold, for all the discipline she laid on herself. One did not ask the ancestors, *Are you sure?* Before the first frost Sifri gave birth to twins, a pair of boys each the image of the other. They were named, though neither would keep his name for long: Halli and Gelli. It was time for the Choosing.

She came down the hill, each step a thudding heartbeat. The Folk watched silent and solemn-eyed as if she herself were the sacrifice. Outside the Choosing place, the elders waited. Sifri and Ekka stood hand in hand, faces ash-white with grief and pride. They would lose both sons today, though one they might keep for a little while. The small girl stood at Sifri's skirts, thumb in mouth. Bard nodded gravely, acknowledging their courage; and then she went in.

The noise was deafening. Her own hut was always quiet. No hearthside cat or watchful dog disturbed her days, no servant muttered greetings, no child yelled fit to split her head apart as these two did. But wait. Only one babe screamed thus, one lusty child turned his face red with wailing and beat his tiny fists helplessly in air, seeking the comfort of touch, the return to warmth and love. This babe struggled; the other was quiet, so quiet one might have thought him already dead. She moved closer. The crying set her teeth on edge; it made her own eyes water. The children were in rush baskets, the lids set each to the side. Between them a stool had been set, and on it lay a dagger, its hilt an ornate masterpiece of gilded wire and small red gems, its blade sturdy, sharp, purpose-made. The children were naked, washed clean of the residue of birth. Perhaps they were cold. Perhaps that was why one screamed so. Soon one would be warm again, and the other colder still. It would only take a moment. Grasp, thrust, turn the eyes away. It would be over quickly, so quickly. There was no doubt which must be chosen: the stronger, the more fit. The fighter.

She moved forward again. The screams went on. This lad would have a powerful voice for the Singing. As for the other . . . she looked down. There in the woven basket, still as some small woodland creature discovered by a sudden predator, he lay gazing up at her. His round eyes were the colour of rock pools under a summer sky. His hair was a fuzz of pure gold. He smiled, and a dimple showed in his infant cheek. He was the image of his father. She turned to the other, her heart lurching, her hands shaking so violently she could surely scarcely lift the knife, let alone use it. As if in recognition of the moment, the first twin fell suddenly quiet, though his small chest still heaved from the effort of his outcry. His face was blotched with crying. His hands clutched the air, eager for life.

Now that the sobbing was hushed, sounds filtered in from outside: the creak of cart wheels, children's voices, the lilt of a whistle. Her mind showed her the travelling folk passing by, motley in their ragged cavalcade, their faces painted in bizarre patterns of red and black and white, their hair knotted and plaited, feathered and ribboned. Even their children looked like a flock of exotic birds. The whistle played a small arch of melody, then ceased abruptly. Someone had told them this was no time for music. And her decision was made. With steady hand, now, Bard reached down and grasped the knife.

There was a form of ritual to be observed, a pattern for the right doing of things. She came out of the small hut, basket in arms. The rush lid now covered the still form that lay within. Atop this lay the knife, its iron blade gaudy with fresh blood. The mother, the father, they did not ask to look or touch. This was not the way of it. The Otherling was gone to shadow; become a part of the great Song which would one day sound from his brother's lips.

"Go to your child," Bard told them softly. "Comfort him well. In three years bring him to me, and I will teach him."

"Thank you," said Ekka, blue eyes deep and solemn.

"Thank you," said Sifri, her voice a very thread of grief, and the two of them went into the hut. Their son's voice called them; now that it was over, he had set to yelling again with double vigour.

Bard bore the little basket up to her own hut, where it lay quiet, encircled by candles, until dusk fell. Her hand was bleeding. She tore a strip of linen from an old shift and bound it around palm and fingers, using her teeth to pull the knot tight. Later, the elders came for the basket and put it on the pyre, and they burned the Otherling with due ceremony. It did not take long, for he was quite small.

It seemed she had chosen well. Halli was apt. He grew sturdy and strong, broad shouldered and fair haired like his father, and with a fierce determination to master all he must know. By day she might show a new pattern on the bones, a more challenging mode of harpsong. At night she would lie awake to the endless repetitions, the long struggle for perfection. She need not use discipline; her student's own discipline was more rigorous than any she might devise.

For him patience was a far harder lesson, and without patience there can be no listening. At twelve he underwent the trials and showed himself strong enough. That did not surprise her; it was what came after that made her belly tighten with unease, her mind cloud with misgiving.

They stood beneath the watchstone in summer dawn, Bard and student.

"You know what must be done," she said.

There was a shallow depression below the great monolith, a hollow grave-like in its proportions, lined with soft grasses as if to encourage sleep. At summer solstice this place of listening caught the sun, and was a vessel of gold light on the green hill. At midwinter the shadow of the watchstone stretched out across the circle, shrouding the small hollow in profound, mysterious darkness.

Today there were clouds. Halli sat cross-legged, silent. Even so had she waited once, while the old Bard stood by the stones as still and patient as if he were himself one of these guardians of ancient truth; as if the lichens, pyre-red, sun-gold, corn-yellow, might in time grow up across his grey-cloaked form and make a gentle cap for his close-shaven skull. Even so had she waited, and emptied her mind of thought, and willed her breathing slow and slower. Then the Song had come to her, pure and certain, welling in the heart, sounding in the spirit, flooding the receptive mind with truth. It was the voice of the ancestors, ringing forth from the stones themselves, from the deep earth where they stood rooted firm, from the wind and the light and the unfathomable depth of the sky. She still held it within her somewhere: that first transcendent moment of joy.

Time passed. It could be long, a day and a night, maybe more. She knew the boy's strength. He would sit there immobile as long as he must, to hear it. And yet, as the sky darkened to rose and violet and pigeon grey, she wondered. He was apt, anyone could see that. Clever, quick, dedicated. Why was it so long? Inside her, memory stirred and shivered.

At dawn she spoke softly, breaking into his trance, bidding him cease. Another time, she told him. Next time. Halli was angry: with her, with the ancestors, with himself.

"You must learn patience," Bard said.

He clamoured to try again. Tomorrow. Tomorrow. Not yet, she said. If the ancestors would not speak, it was not time. His eyes narrowed with resentment, his mouth twisted with frustration.

"You must learn calm," Bard said.

He played the bones like a dance of death. He sounded the pipe in a piercing wail of need. His fingers dragged notes of aching emptiness from the small harp. She made him wait.

The season passed. At Reaping the travelling folk came through Storna with juggling and dances, with coloured streamers and performing dogs. A whistle tune floated up the hill, clean and innocent on the easterly breeze: a tune wrought untutored and free, yet exquisite in its form and feeling. The melody made its way in at her window and tugged at Bard's memory. Behind a closed door Halli played his own pipe, his music intricate, tangled on itself. She heard the two tunes meet and mingle, and she put her hands over her ears and used a technique long practised to shut out unwelcome thoughts. When she emerged from her trance, all was quiet. At last her student slept, his sturdy form relaxed as a child's, his strong features wan with exhaustion. The pipe had slipped from his fingers to the earthen floor. She laid the blanket over him.

Three Ripenings passed before he began to hear the Songs, and before she let him sing one he was already a man. Halli chafed against her restrictions. Why did she hold him back thus? He could do it, he knew he could. Didn't she trust him?

"You must learn humility," Bard said. "We are vessels, no more." His anger troubled her. Dreams came, and left her weary.

In his eighteenth summer Halli gave the Folk his first Singing. Bard listened as he told of early frost and the coming of whales; of a far shore where green fields and fruitful vines might be discovered; of the building of boats. His Singing was like the call of a war horn, deep and resonant. By the end of it, the young men's eyes were alight with excitement: here was a challenge beyond any yet imagined. Did not the ancestors bid them set forth on a great adventure? In the crowd Sifri stood quiet, her three fair daughters by her. There had been no more sons.

Before the turning of the season they made a fine ship of wattles and skins, tarred for seaworthiness, with oars of larch wood. On the prow they set the great skull of a whale. They called the vessel *Seaskimmer,* and in her the young men of the island journeyed forth one sparkling dawn in search of the fruitful land to the west, a land where one day they might all live and prosper under a smiling sun. They did not return at Reaping. The women, the old people, the children cut the barley and stacked the straw. They did not return as the year moved on and the days began to shorten. It was in the shadow time that they came back to the island, those bold venturers of the Folk. A boy and his dog wandered the cold beach of Grimskaill, gathering driftwood. Shrouded in weed, cloaked in ribbons of sea wrack, the young men of Storna and

Settersby, Grimskaill and far Frostrim lay quiet under the winter sky. For seven long days the Folk stood there by the water as the ocean delivered up their sons, each at his own time, each riding his own last wave. Then there was a burning such as the island had not seen in many a long year. The people looked at Bard with doubt in their eyes.

"This was wrong," she told him afterwards.

Halli lifted his fair brows. "How can the Singing be wrong? I told only the Song the ancestors gave me."

"It was wrong. The Songs help us avoid such acts of foolish waste, such harvests of anguish. It could not be meant thus."

"Why not?" her student said. "Who can say what the ancestors intend?"

"Surely not the wiping out of a full generation of young men. Who will father sons here? Who will fish and hunt? How will the Folk survive this?"

He smiled: his father's sunny, dimpled smile. "Perhaps the ancestors see a short future for us. Perhaps raiders will come and beget children. Who knows? I cannot answer your questions. You said yourself, we are no more than vessels."

That winter grandmothers and grandfathers swept floors and tended infants and stirred pots of thin gruel, while women cleared snow from thatch and broke ice from fishing holes. The few men of middle years slaughtered stock and hauled up the boats. It was a harsh season, but wisdom was remembered from times past, and they survived. At Waking, when the air held a deceptive whisper of new season's warmth, she would not let him listen for the Song.

"I am Bard," she told him, "and I will do it. You are not yet ready. You must learn something more."

"What?" Halli demanded fiercely. "What?"

But Bard gave no answer, for she had none.

The Song was an anthem to the lost ones, and a warning. The Folk must keep the balance or perish. Their children had survived the savage winter. Now all must be watchful. Bard thought the ancestors' message was not without hope. But she was tired, so tired that she stumbled as she went to stand before the Folk in the ritual place; so weak that she could scarcely summon the breath for the Singing. Afterwards her mind felt drained, her thoughts scattered. She could hardly remember what she had told them.

The weariness continued. Maybe she was sick. Maybe she should get a potion from the travelling folk, ever renowned for their elixirs. There was wisdom amongst that colourful, elusive band of wanderers: they had sent no sons voyaging across the ocean to return in a tumble of bleached and broken bone. But she was too tired to seek them out.

Halli was solicitous. He brought her warm infusions. He ensured the fire was made up and the floor swept clean. It was he who performed the Singing at midsummer, telling of fine shoals of fish south of Storna Bay, and favourable winds. Before the season's end deer might be taken and the meat smoked for winter.

The few men left on the island were not over-keen to put to sea, but the Singing removed any choice. They came to her afterwards with questions. How many deer? How many days may we fish in safety? With our young men gone, who will lead the hunt? She could not answer them. She had not heard this Song, for the stones were far, a weary distance up the hill. It was Halli who answered.

"Since the Singing did not tell of this, take what you will," he said.

There were some men of middle years, too old to sail for new horizons, still young enough for work. They found mackerel in great numbers and, thinking of winter, brought in netful after shining netful. The salting huts were crammed to bursting, and still there were more, a bountiful harvest. They went for deer, and found them in wooded valleys beyond Settersby. They were gone seven days; they returned bearing two great antlered carcasses and the body of a fine, fair haired man. Ekka was dead, slipped from an outcrop as he readied his spear to take the stag cleanly. Bard could hear the sound of Sifri's grieving all the way up the hill and through the shutters. She looked into her student's clear blue eyes, reading the iron there, and something shivered deep inside her. This was her doing. This was her Choosing. The boy had killed his own father. A Telling came to her mind as she lay shivering under her thick blankets, a Telling of times to come: of a spring with no mackerel, a spring where the young of puffin and albatross starved on the cliffs for lack of nourishment. In the season after, their numbers were less, and less again next Waking. Then weasel and fox, wolf and bear grew bolder, and neither chicken nor goose, young lamb nor younger babe in cradle was safe. The men grew old and feeble, the women gaunt and weary. Children were few. The Telling turned Bard's bones to ice. In such a time, all it would take was one hard winter to finish the Folk.

"You look tired," Halli observed. "You must rest. Leave everything to me." And indeed, there seemed a great urge in her to sleep; to melt into darkness, and let it all slip away. After all, what could she do? She had made her choice long years ago. All stemmed from that, and there was no changing it.

On the edge of slumber she heard again the sweet voice of a whistle, played somewhere out in the night, as deep and subtle, for all its simplicity, as the voices of the ancestors themselves. Bard slid out of bed, careful to make no sound. From Halli's chamber the small harp rang out. Still he drilled his fingers, the patterns ever more complex, as if he would never be satisfied. The sound of it frightened her. He frightened her. Unchecked, he would be the end of them all. But she felt so weak. The Folk no longer trusted her. Ekka was dead. She was alone, all alone . . .

A long time she knelt there on the earthen floor, shivering in her worn nightrobe. The old learning seemed almost forgotten: how to empty the mind and slow the breath, how to calm the body and control the will, how to listen. Somehow it had almost slipped away from her. She had forgotten she was Bard.

Of course you are alone, she thought fiercely. *Bard is always alone. Have you let even that most basic lesson escape you?*

"Not quite. But you have misremembered."

Her head jerked upwards. For a moment she thought—but no, the harp still sounded from the far chamber, servant of his will. The figure which stood before her was another entirely, and yet as familiar as the image she saw when she bent over the water trough to cup hands and drink. This wraith with hollow eyes and pallid cheeks, with shaven head, with ragged cloak and long hands apt for the making of music, this phantom was . . . herself. And yet . . . and yet . . .

"You know me," said her visitor, moving closer. She reached out a hand to touch, scarcely believing what she saw, and her fingers moved though him, cloak, flesh, bone all nebulous as shadow.

"You are my brother," she whispered, her eyes sliding fearful towards the inner door.

"He will not hear us."

"Why have you come? Why journey from—from death to seek me out?"

"You are afraid. You see no answers. Yet you hold the key to this yourself, Bard." His voice was grave and quiet. "The pattern is gone awry; that is your doing. It is for you to weave it straight and even once more."

"Why didn't you come before?" she asked him urgently. "I needed help. Why not come before good folk died, before he did what he did? Where were you?"

"You have carried me within you all this time, sister. If not for your error, you could have heard my voice, stronger as the years passed. Bard is never truly alone; always she has her Otherling. But you disobeyed the ancestors. Your choice was flawed. Now its influence spreads dark over you."

Bard stared at him, aware once more of her leaden limbs, her burdened heart. "The Folk will perish. Maybe not this year, maybe not next, but in time all will be lost. I've seen it."

The Otherling gazed back. His eyes seemed empty sockets, yet full of light. He was both old and young: an infant in a rush basket, a strong man in his prime, an ancient wise in spirit. "You made it so," he said quietly. "Now unmake it. Do what you could not do, long years ago. One does not lightly disregard the wisdom of the ancestors. Since the day you did so the Folk have walked under a shadow, a darkness that will in time engulf them. You hold their very future at the point of your knife."

"But—"

"The Otherling must die, Bard. There is no avoiding it. He cannot live in the light; he cannot be left to walk the land and whisper his stories in the ear of farmer and fisherwoman, merchant and seamstress. And Bard cannot do her work without him. The two must be one, for they are reality and reflection, light and dark, substance and shadow."

Bard shivered. "You mean the Otherling is—evil? That if he lives he must inevitably work destruction?"

"Ah, no. It is not so simple. The two are halves of the one whole: complement and completion of each other. Can day exist without night, light without shade, waking without sleeping? Can the Folk survive without the death of the mackerel in the net, the spear in the seal's heart, the hen's surrender of her unborn children? The Otherling must stand behind, in darkness, to make the balance. Only then can Bard sing truth. Now go, do what you must do before it is too late."

"I'm so tired."

"I will help you." He moved to embrace her; his encircling arms were as insubstantial as vapour. She felt a shudder like a cool breath through her, and he was gone.

The travellers were encamped by the seafront, children gathering shells under a blood-red dawn, the smoke of campfires rising sluggishly. There was a rumble of approaching storm, its deep music a counterpoint to the whistle's plangent tone. The young man sat watching the sky, as if his tune might coax the sun to show himself between the rain-heavy clouds. As Bard approached him the melody faltered and ceased.

She had not known how she would speak to him. How can you say, *Come with me, I will tell you whose brother you are, and then you will die?* Ah, those eyes, those fine, merry eyes she had seen gazing up at her once, open and guileless. He had been so quiet. He had been so good. Never a sound from him, as she had borne him forth, basket closed tight, all the way up the hill to her hut. Never a peep out of him, as she bribed the little girls to take him, the little girls with plaited crests to their hair, and faces all painted in spirals and dots of red and white. What was one more infant amongst so many? Who would know, when every one of them wore a guise of rainbow colours, a cloak of dazzling anonymity? She had paid handsomely; the women would feed him and care for him. They were a generous kind, and made their own rules. The rush basket, weighted with the carcase of a fat goose, had burned to nothing. Nobody had known. Nobody but Bard, whose heart shivered every time the travellers came by, whose eyes filled with tears to hear the voice of the whistle, so sad, so pure. What had she done to him? What had she done to them both?

"Come with me. I want to show you something."

He had no questions as they walked together under dark skies, up the hill to the place of the stones. She asked his name; he said, Sam.

"Were you at the last Singing?" she asked him.

He nodded and said nothing. At the old water trough they halted.

"Wash your face," Bard told him. Washed clean, the two of them, naked and clean.

The young man, Sam, looked at her a moment, eyes wide. His features were daubed with spiral and link, dot and line. His hair stood in rows of hedgehog prickles, waxed honey-dark. He bent to the water and splashed his face, washing the markings away. The water clouded.

"Wait," Bard said.

The water cleared. The sun pierced the cloud for one bright moment.

"Now look," she said.

The image was murky; specks of coloured clay floated across his mirrored features. But it was plain enough. He glanced up at her.

"I did wrong," Bard said. "He is your brother. I saved you, because—because—no matter. Now all is awry because of what I did not do." In its way, it was an apology.

There were no desperate denials, no protests.

"Can I see him?" Sam asked. "I'd like to see him first." It was as if he knew. Clouds rolled across, heavy with rain. The sky growled like a wild beast.

"Come, then," said Bard.

Halli was by the watchstone, hands outstretched, eyes shut in pose of meditation. Often before a storm she had found him thus; the soughing of the wind, the uneasy movement of trees, the air's strange pungent smell excited him. At such times of danger, he said, who knew what powerful voices might speak from the stones?

They stood by the hollow's rim, Bard and the young man Sam. Under the dark folds of her long cloak, her fingers touched cold iron.

"He is your brother," she said again, and Halli's blue eyes snapped open. No need for explanations. The two stood frozen, one in astonished wonderment, the other in sudden furious realisation. There was a moment of silence. Then Halli drew ragged breath.

"You saved him!" he whispered, accusatory, furious. "No wonder I was never good enough, no wonder I could not hear them! You saved the Otherling! Why? Why?"

Because of love, Bard answered, but not aloud. *I did wrong, and now he must die.*

"Brother, well met indeed!" Sam's dimpled smile was generous. Below the bizarre spiked hair his blue eyes spoke a bright welcome. He took a step forward, hand outstretched in friendship. Now she was behind him. Halli's agonised eyes met hers over his twin's shoulder, their message starkly clear. *Do it now. Do what you could not do before. Make it right again.* Perhaps it was her own Otherling who spoke these words: the shadow within. She drew out the knife. She saw the dimple appear in Halli's cheek, the curve of his mouth as he watched her. Sam went very still. He did not turn. Bard raised her hand.

A great blade speared down from above; there was a thunderous crack like the very ending of the world, and a sudden rending. It was not her own small weapon that set the earth shuddering, and came like a wave through the damp air, hurtling her head over heels to land sprawling, gasping, face down in wet grass with her two hands clutching for purchase and her ears ringing, deafened by the immense voice that had spoken. Her heart thudded; her head swam. Slowly she got to her knees. The knife lay on the ground at her feet, its blade clean as a new-washed babe. She looked up. The watchstone was split asunder, its monumental form chiselled in two pieces by the force of the blast. One part still stood tall, reaching its lichen-crusted head to touch the storm-tossed sky. The other part lay prone now, like shadow given substance: dark testament to the sky's ferocity. This slab would never be lifted, not should all the Folk of the island come with ropes and oxen. It was grave and cradle; ending and beginning. After all, she had not had to choose. The ancestors had spoken, and the choice was made.

"You're weeping," she said. "Bard does not weep."

"How can I not weep?" he asked her. "He was my brother."

"Come, Halli," said Bard gently. "There is no more to be done here. And it's starting to rain." She unfastened her cloak and reached to put it around his shoulders.

He stared at her, face ashen with the shock of finding, and losing, and finding again. "I have so much to learn," he whispered, and she saw that he had recognised her meaning. "So much."

Bard nodded. "I am not so old yet that I cannot teach you what you must know. Already you are rich in understanding. Already you hear the Songs and tell them, unaware. He will help you. His fingers know the harp, his lips the pipe. The heart that beats new wisdom into the Songs belongs now to the two of you."

He bowed his head, looking towards the gentle hollow, now hidden beneath the huge slab of stone. Rain fell like tears on the fresh-hewn surface, making a pattern of spiral and curve, dot and line.

"Best put your hood up," she said, "until I attend to that hair of yours. No student of mine goes unshaven. Now come. There's work to be done."

☽

let down your hair

The price of my future was a bunch of lettuce. That's what my mother agreed to in a moment of weakness, when the cravings of pregnancy sent her stealing in a forbidden garden. The witch let her keep me until I was three years old, and then she took me to the tower.

The tower was tall and slender, its base in a ring of birches, its tip in the clouds. It had a door at the bottom and a door at the top, both of them locked. The witch kept the key in her pocket; for me, there was no getting out.

She didn't take me from sheer wickedness. She needed me to do a job. There was a pot to watch, an iron cauldron hanging from a three-legged stand with a hook and chain. Soup bubbled inside, but we never ate it. The witch went out foraging for our meals: a scrawny bird, a dried-up lizard. And she grew things in her special garden: golden carrots, ruby-red beets. Lettuces.

The witch never gave me a name, and I forgot my old one. As I grew bigger, I made up names for myself. Confined to the chamber at the top of the tower, I only had the images I could see, and the words the witch gave me when I asked, "What's that called? And that?" So I named myself Willow one day, and Stream the next, and at night I was Moon or Owl.

As she stirred her bubbling brew, the witch muttered stories. Thus I learned new words and new ideas. I did not know if the world where folk fell in love and wed and had children, fought battles, slew dragons and ruled kingdoms was a real place beyond my tower or only existed in the witch's head. The people in the tales had wonderful names, names to conjure by. I called myself Emilia, and Adelbert, and Chrysoprase. I imagined a cat for myself, a little dog, a dragon. I imagined a friend to whom I could whisper secrets.

But there were no secrets in the tower, not for all the years of my growing up. There were the locked doors, the privy in its little alcove, the pipe that came in from a rainwater barrel outside, the precarious shuttered balcony on which I was not allowed to stand. The stairs down which I was not allowed to go. The soup which I was not allowed to drink. "Two hundred years I've stirred this poxy cauldron," the witch would grumble, knotty hands so tight on the wooden ladle that they looked as if they'd grown from the same tree. "Two hundred years of boredom and slavery and for what? A mess of stupid tales, so twisted and twined you can't tell the barley from the beans or the leeks from the lentils."

"Tales?" I asked her once. "What have tales to do with soup?"

"You'll find out," she said darkly. "One day, this'll be your job."

I didn't much like the sound of that, but I was smaller than she was, so I didn't argue.

Whenever the witch went foraging, I stole the opportunity to gaze out of my high window. One day a man passed the foot of the tower, with a bundle of sticks on his back. I recognised him from the witch's stories: a woodcutter. Woodcutters were stalwart, strong and good. They killed wicked wolves and rescued girls in distress. This one walked with confidence and held his shoulders square. When he glanced up towards my window, I saw kind eyes and a sweet, shy smile. I shrank back out of sight. *Don't let anyone see you*, was one of the witch's rules. There'd never been anyone before, unless you counted spiders and swallows. My mother didn't come, not once. I imagined her at home alone, dreaming of lettuce.

The witch was quiet when she came in that evening. We shared what she had brought: a skinny chicken which we roasted in the coals, and a handful of spinach from her garden. She didn't need to bring bundles of sticks; our fire burned all by itself. I stirred the cauldron while she ate, staring at the bubbling surface of the soup. Amongst the grains and vegetables I saw things that surely didn't belong in a broth: little men in chain mail and women dripping jewels. Half-hidden by strands of cabbage and leek were crowns and swords, goblets and gauntlets, nooses and necklaces . . .

"Girl!" The witch's voice was sharp. "You're falling asleep! Pay attention!"

I grasped the ladle more tightly.

"Maybe you don't understand," the witch said. "Stirring this pot is the most important job in the whole world. Let the fire die down, let the soup cool and congeal, and something irreplaceable is lost. It is a grand task, girl."

"You said it was poxy and boring," I felt obliged to point out.

"What else are you going to do up here?" she asked, fixing me with her beady eyes. "Spin flax into gold?"

I had no idea what she was talking about, so I stirred, and imagined I saw in the cauldron a hero coming to rescue me from the tower. He would climb up to my window and carry me away to . . . to whatever lay beyond the forest. Surely it must be a better existence than this.

The woodcutter hung around. The path he took to deliver his bundles of sticks seemed to bring him to the tower at least once a day, usually at the time when the witch was out. Once he'd seen me there seemed no point in hiding, so I'd come to the window and look down. He'd smile; I'd smile back. One day he took off his hat and waved it to me, and I waved my hand, feeling very daring. The next day he brought a little bunch of flowers, red and blue and green; I opened the balcony shutters and called my thanks to him, though there was no way I could reach them.

"What's your name?" he shouted.

I hadn't decided what to call myself that day, so I smiled and shook my head. Then I spotted a familiar figure approaching, dark cloak billowing, pointed teeth gleaming in the sun, gnarled fingers carrying a cargo of vegetables for our supper.

I stood in the shadows by the window, watching. As the witch walked up to my woodcutter, her dark cloak became a pale muslin gown sprigged with violets; her pointed teeth turned regular and white. The wrinkles vanished, the hooked nose straightened, the grey hair became a cloud of fine gold thread. He was dazzled. The lonely girl in the tower, the one who had been blessed with his shy smiles and his gift of flowers, had gone right out of his head.

As easy as one, two, three, she stole him. With her arm through his and her beautiful fair head on his strong shoulder, she led him away into the forest and out of my life. The key was still in her pocket.

Time passed. I had a supply of water, a privy, work to do. Without my jailer to forage for me, I ate the only food I had: soup. When you're starving, you don't balk at the fact that something's been sitting in a pot for two hundred years.

The fire kept burning; the only fuel it needed was kind words. I tried to pretend the level in the cauldron wasn't going down, but as summer turned to autumn I could see it was. I imagined myself wasting away, dying with my eyes on the distant shadows beyond the forest, the land of the stolen future. I made myself think. I made myself observe the little things in the cauldron, the items that were not bean or lentil or barleycorn, but crown and cloak, sea-serpent and sailing ship. The soup held the ingredients for a fine story. Many stories. Perhaps, lacking the cabbages and turnips the witch's garden used to furnish, I could replace them with fantastic ideas, amazing creatures and exotic settings. I could put in love and longing and heartbreak; I could add courage and beauty and betrayal. After all, it seemed I had inherited a real job.

Seasons came and went. The forest grew thick around my tower; in the witch's garden, nettles invaded the vegetable beds and brambles choked the gooseberry bushes. I stirred the cauldron and whispered stories into the bubbling soup. I made a future for myself; I made many futures. I journeyed far, fought battles, won prizes. Sometimes I was alone in the story, and sometimes he was by my side, the only hero I had been able to imagine. I gave him a new name for every tale: Robin, Fox, Oak. But his face was always the same, kind eyes, shy smile, brown hair like autumn leaves.

My own hair grew very long. When it began to annoy me, I cut it off with the knife the witch had used for chopping vegetables. I plaited it into a rope, but it only stretched halfway down the tower. So much for escape.

The soup smelled better every day, exotic and homely both at once, like the best story in the world. Sometimes it did well enough on its own, and I could stand at my high window looking out over the trees to the distant places I would never visit except in my own head.

It was winter. The light in the window was cold and pale; its beams touched my hair, and I saw that amongst the gold there was grey. I felt my face; were those wrinkles? In my tower there were no mirrors. A picture came to my mind of a little old woman, stirring, stirring, her eyes rheumy, her hands knotted, her nose a beak in a face as wrinkled as an old apple. In a few years' time, I would *be* the witch.

"No," I muttered, my tears turning the winter forest to a vague wash of grey and blue. "I can't only live in dreams, it's not fair . . . "

Down below, someone shouted. "Anyone there?"

My heart skipped a beat. I scrubbed my eyes and ran to the balcony shutters, flinging them open.

No bundle of wood; no fine young man with broad shoulders and thatch of nut-brown hair. This traveller wore a soldier's greatcoat, and he stood crooked, as if he were carrying an injury. His hair was grey; his face was lined and weary. The kind eyes and the shy smile were still the same.

"I'm here!" My voice, so long unused except for whispering, croaked like an ancient frog's. Words fled abruptly; it had been so long. How old was I, exactly?

"I've got a rope," said Robin, or Fox, or Oak. "Catch."

He tried hard, but he lacked the strength to get the rope high enough. We were both older.

Robin looked up at me. "What now?" he shouted.

"Couldn't you climb up somehow?"

He said nothing, just rolled up his trousers to show me that, below the knee, his right leg had been replaced by a length of metal, serviceable enough for walking, but not at all suited for scaling walls. "Sorry," he said.

He stayed. I watched him every day as he built a little house in the corner of the witch's garden. I saw the smoke from his hearth fire rising as winter turned towards spring. He cleared away the nettles and brambles. He sang as he worked and I joined in, liking the sound our voices made together. He took off his shirt when he was digging, and I thought perhaps we were not so very old after all, for the sight of his muscular body was more than pleasing to me.

He asked me one day if he should try to break down the door to the tower, and I said no. It seemed to me the magic the witch had set on the place would turn back on us if we tried to go against it. Our happiness was too fragile to risk. "Wait, Robin," I told him. "Be patient."

He told me the witch was gone. The grim satisfaction in his tone silenced further questions before they left my lips. He did not ask me about the future. He gardened, and waited.

The answer, when it came, was simple. On the first day of spring, when Robin was down below chopping wood for his fire, I stirred my cauldron and saw a key floating amidst the strands of spinach and chunks of carrot.

Quick as a flash, I thrust my hand into the soup and grabbed the prize. It hurt, and I yelped. That was only right; without pain, no quest is achieved.

The chopping sounds had ceased. "Are you all right?" came his voice.

He was still staring anxiously up at the window when I came out the door at the bottom of the tower.

"You're here!" He took my hand as gently as the breeze captures a feather. His touch was more thrilling than anything in my stories, for it told me I was truly alive. I observed the lines around nose and mouth, the desperate worry in his kind eyes. He looked . . . real. He looked wonderful.

"You're so beautiful," he whispered. "I'm sorry I left you. More sorry than I can say."

"I forgive you," I said, drinking him in. "But you need to understand that I can't go off and have adventures. There's nobody else to stir the soup."

"This is an adventure," my woodcutter said.

We took hands and went back into the tower, but we left the door open behind us.

☽

poppy seeds

In a world like ours, but not quite like, there once lived a miller who had three sons. The eldest son was a fine strapping fellow, a man well able to help his father with lifting sacks of grain or other heavy work. The second son lacked his brother's bulging muscles but made up for it with his sharp wits. He could drive a harder bargain than anyone in the district, and that ability helped his father's mill to thrive, though it did not win the miller any friends. And the third son? As is the way with third sons, this one was nothing special to look at, being shorter and slighter than both his brothers, and not quick to learn the art of bargaining, nor indeed that of milling flour. When he did help, he was inclined to fill half a bag, then set it down to watch the way the sunbeams came through the windows and caught the flour dust dancing through the air, turning it to fey brightness. Or he would be entrusted to accept payment for a bag of flour, and he'd let it go for five coppers instead of ten. Why was he so foolish? Because he knew the farmer had fallen on hard times; his children had been stealing apples from the chieftain's orchard because their bellies were empty. This son was a disappointment to his father.

Now as is the way of things, the time came for the miller to decide which of his sons was to take over the running of the mill when he died, or when he got too old and tired to do it anymore. He'd have liked to pass the place on to his first and second sons to run together; but the sons did not care for that idea at all. Each wanted the mill outright. Once they knew the path of their father's thinking they began to argue. Every day it went on from dawn to dusk until the miller began to wish he'd never mentioned dying. He was half minded to tell them he was leaving it all to his youngest son, the time waster, the dreamer, just to bring an end to the shouting. But his wife counselled him differently. "Send them off on a quest," she suggested. "Let's have some peace and quiet for a bit, and they can come home when they've sorted themselves out."

This was a fine idea; the miller wished he had thought of it himself. "Where shall I send them?" he asked.

"It's usual in such quests for folk to seek a magical object," said the miller's wife. "But I don't suppose there are any such treasures in these parts." The region surrounding the mill was all little farms and quiet valleys full of grazing sheep.

"They'll have to go to the town," the miller said, thinking hard. "That's all the way through the wild wood, up the craggy mountain, over the pass and down along the shadowy valley. And back again. A long journey."

"They're big strong lads," said the miller's wife, imagining how many days of peace and quiet such a venture would bring to the mill. Her cat would come out from under the bed, where it had been cowering since the arguments began. She'd be able to take a nap in the afternoons without being woken by strings of shouted oaths. "Let all of them go off to seek their fortunes, and let each of them bring back the best treasure he can lay his hands on. And whichever of them has the prize of greatest value is the one who takes over the mill."

The three brothers set off on their journey, each carrying supplies wrapped in a cloth, for although their mother was quite happy to wave them goodbye, she would not send them out into the world without a comb, a cup, a pocket handkerchief and a packet of bread and cheese. "Farewell! Farewell, sons, and may a fair wind blow you to the land of your dreams!"

The first and second sons walked together for a while, not saying much. They went with long strides, wasting no time as they passed by the fields around their home village and headed toward the dark mass of the wild wood. Soon the third son was so far behind that he must surely be already out of the race. *Race*, thought the first son; *I mustn't forget it's a race,* and he strode out still faster.

"See up yonder?" The second son pointed ahead to the forest, where a massive rock could be seen like a crouching monster amid the deep green of the pines. "A fellow told me once there's gold buried under that rock. A great chest of gold, enough to buy a palace. A wee man hid it there long ago, so the tale goes, and forgot where he'd put it." He paused a moment, then added, "Not that I believe a word of it. Just a foolish story, that's all it is."

"Foolish, aye," said the first son, wondering how he could get up there to have a look without his brother tagging along after him. If the story was true, he could take home a treasure beyond all expectations and he need not trouble himself with the long and perilous journey to the town at all. He might be back at the mill by supper time. How pleased his mother would be!

The two brothers reached the edge of the wild wood, where nobody went if there was any choice in the matter. Many tales were told about the place, and most of them didn't include chests of gold. A pathway led ahead under the pines, soon losing itself in shadow. Strange stones lay by the path, tiny brothers of the monster rock that guarded the wee man's lost treasure. The eldest brother could almost hear them whispering to him, *This way to the gold, clever wanderer! This way to riches and freedom!* His belly churned at the thought of walking all the way through the wild wood to the other side. Nobody knew how far it was. It might take days. He might have to sleep in there, in the dark. The big rock was not so far up the hill, most likely along that smaller path that branched away to the right. If only . . .

"I'll stick with this path," said the second brother. "Straight ahead, more or less. How about you, brother?"

"I'll try the little side way over there," said the first brother, unable to believe his luck. "Up by that big rock there's sure to be a good view of the track ahead." Part of him wanted to tell his brother to wait, so they could go on together. But that would mean sharing the treasure.

"See you on the other side, then," his brother called out cheerily, and vanished into the wood.

Now you might be thinking that the third brother, the dreamer, was taking rather a long time to catch up with the others, and that was indeed so. The third brother, whose name was Derry, had seen a woman on the road, a creature all skin and bone. She'd been pulling her worldly possessions along on a little makeshift cart, but one wheel had come off and the pitiful contents lay scattered in the dirt. The woman had a child in a sling on her chest, an infant as scrawny and sad-looking as its mother.

"Let me help you," said Derry, setting down his little bag and crouching to gather up the woman's belongings. When he'd got them together, and the woman had stammered thanks as if help was the last thing she'd expected, Derry set about mending the cart for her. This might be a lad who took his time, but he spent that time looking properly, and seeing what another young man might miss. And he was good with his hands, especially when the job involved making something from nothing much. So with a twig here and a scrap of twine there, a whittled peg here and a folded piece of leather there, Derry soon had the cart as good as new. Nearly new, anyway. He loaded the woman's few possessions back onto it.

"Got far to go?" he asked, thinking she looked too weak to walk further than the next corner, let alone to any kind of decent shelter.

"Not so very far," the woman said.

Derry doubted that she had anywhere at all to go. "Here," he said, getting out his packet of food, dividing the contents in two and giving the woman half. "A bite to eat always makes the road shorter."

"Thank you, young man. Your kindness does you credit. Here, take this for your pains." She fished in her pouch and brought out a strange little figure made of twigs, perhaps a toy fashioned to amuse the babe.

Derry thanked her, for a gift should always be received with courtesy, even if it seems of no possible use whatever. "Tell me," he asked the woman, "did my brothers pass this way earlier? They must have come along this road, for all three of us are headed through the wild wood, up the craggy mountain, over the pass, and down along the shadowy valley until we reach the town. Our father has sent us to seek our fortunes."

"If your brothers are the two big fellows who passed me and my babe on the road just after the cart broke and never lifted a finger to help, then yes, I've seen them, and bad cess to them," said the woman. "Travel safe, young man."

Derry walked on, thinking it must have been two other men she saw, for surely his brothers would not be so heartless. This was the sort of lad who always thought the best of folk, even when the evidence of his own eyes should have told him different. He made his way up into the wild wood, and there on the path before him were the footsteps of his brothers, one set going straight on, the other heading off along the little track to the right.

"Which way should I go?" he muttered to himself.

"Straight ahead, and don't look behind you," spoke up a wee little voice.

The first thing Derry did was look behind him, and then in front of him, and then to either side, but the harder he looked, the plainer it was that nobody was there. Maybe the stories he'd heard about the wild wood were true. Folk said it was full of strange creatures: monsters, ghosts and figments. He wasn't sure what a figment might be, only that he'd rather not bump into one on a dark night, so he'd best get walking, and straight ahead did seem the right choice. He made good speed, and before the sun was low in the sky he was close to the far edge of the wood.

It was as he rested by the path and enjoyed a little of his dwindling supply of bread and cheese that Derry heard crying somewhere among the bushes, sad as sad could be. He'd heard that under such circumstances a man should put his fingers in his ears and walk on by, but the sound was so forlorn, he hadn't the heart to do so. So he searched by the track, and there, tangled in a bramble bush, he found a spotted dog whimpering in pain. "Hold still, little friend," Derry said, and with gentle, patient hands he worked the creature free. Just so had he often tended to the animals back home, though his family hardly noticed, so busy were they with milling flour and taking payments and shouting at one another. There was a nasty thorn in the wee one's foot, and Derry removed it with deft fingers. Then he gave the little dog a morsel of the bread and cheese, and bade it run off home.

But the spotted dog had different ideas. When Derry set off, it came right along with him, all the way to the far side of the wild wood. No amount of *go home* or *stay* would keep it back.

"You can't come with me," Derry told the dog. "I'm headed up the craggy mountain."

Up spoke the wee little voice from before. "Oh, yes, we can." Derry looked behind and in front, and from one side to the other, but nobody did he see but the dog, standing one step behind him.

"Who said that?" asked Derry. Then he felt a twitching and a wriggling in his pouch, right next to the last remnant of his bread and cheese, and up popped the stick man.

"I did," said the poppet, clutching onto Derry's shirt lest he fall to the forest floor and be lost in the undergrowth. "You wouldn't do as your brother did, and leave the wee doggie crying in the wild wood while you walk on without him?"

"Come on, then," said Derry, for although he was mightily surprised, it was more the surprise of fascination than that of terror. Derry was a dreamer, and did not fear the unknown. The wee man rode in the pouch, and the spotted dog stayed at Derry's heels, and they made their way up the steep side of the craggy mountain as the sun was setting. They climbed and climbed, and when it was too dark to go on they sheltered in a little cave on the mountainside and watched the stars appear one by one, making wondrous bright patterns on the blanket of night.

"Stick man," ventured Derry as the three of them sat on his spread-out cloak, eating the last of the provisions, "you said my brother had passed by and left the wee doggie in the wild wood. But two brothers set off ahead of me. What about the other?"

"Went off the track in search of hidden treasure," said the stick man. "You're ahead of him now."

Amazing, thought Derry. He was never ahead of his brothers; he was always the slow one, dawdling behind, taking time to look at everything, to ponder everything, to make up stories and songs as he went about his daily work. Maybe his brother had already found that hidden treasure and gone home in triumph. That didn't matter to Derry; it was nothing to him who inherited the mill. What mattered was that tomorrow he'd go over the pass and along the shadowy valley, and he'd reach the town. There, he would at the very least find something interesting. Best of all, he didn't need to walk on alone. "It's good to have friends on the journey," he told the stick man and the spotted dog. "But tell me something, stick man. If you've been in my pouch all the way through the forest, how can you know what my brothers are doing?"

"I know what I know," said the stick man, and that was all the explanation Derry could get from him.

Sleeping was not so easy on the craggy mountain, for strange noises were all around them. Things shrieked and gobbled and scrabbled. They whistled and whispered and wailed. "Don't heed them," the stick man told Derry. "When the dawn comes they'll go deep down where they belong." It was a long night, all the same. Derry had never been happier to see the sun come up.

The three companions passed along the shadowy valley, where the trees joined hands over the pathway and everything was so still, a traveller could not but expect an ogre to leap out at him any moment, or a monster to drop down on him from the high valley walls that towered on either side, near up to the sky. Though it was day, in the shadowy valley a long dusk lay over the land, and Derry nearly stepped on the dove before he saw she was more than a grey stone on the path. The bird lay limp as if dead, but when he knelt to take a closer look she turned her head to gaze at him, and the pleading in her mild eye went straight to his heart. Her wing was hurt; she could not fly.

Derry put his deft hands to splinting the wing, and the dove found a soft resting place in the pouch beside the stick man. The odd crew went on down the valley, passing into a landscape of skeletal birches and still grey tarns. On this side of the wild wood it seemed to be winter, though it was only a day or two since the three brothers had set off from the mill, and there it had been springtime. Derry walked through the valley as quickly as he could, looking out for his brothers: the one who walked ahead, and the one who came behind. But not a trace of them did he see.

"Where can my brothers have got to?" he asked himself aloud. "Maybe one has gone all the way home and the other is already in the town. Maybe both of them have found their fortunes by now."

"Answer me a question," said the stick man. "When a man sees an injured bird on the path, what should he do? Stop and help? Pick it up and carry it along with him? Or kick it out of his way?"

"You know what I'll say," Derry answered.

"Well, then," said the stick man, as if that explained everything. And try as he might, Derry could get no more sense out of him.

In time Derry and his three friends arrived in the town, and Derry made enquiries about his brothers—had they reached the place safely, and if so had they found their treasure yet? But nobody knew anything about them. Derry found shelter for himself and his friends in an outhouse behind a bakery. The baker was happy to provide a bed, a roof and a misshapen loaf or two at the end of the day in return for Derry's getting up at dawn to stoke the fire, sweep the floor and generally make himself useful.

The days passed, and Derry proved himself so reliable that the baker told him he'd be delivering a special cake on Tuesday. So special was it, the baker told his new assistant, that none but Derry's own hands should carry it. He must take the special cake to the big house on the hill.

The baker didn't bother to mention who lived in the big house: a sorcerer with a heart black as night, eyes like splinters of ice, and spells that could shrivel a fellow's manhood in a moment. It was no wonder the baker could never keep a helper for long. It was no wonder he'd been so ready to offer the position to Derry, untried and untested. In fact, the sorcerer was no secret; everyone in the town knew to stay clear of the big house. Everyone knew twelve young men had taken cakes into that house and not one of them had come out again, with or without his manhood. It was a mystery why any of them had agreed to be the baker's delivery boy in the first place. Mind you, folk did say the sorcerer had a treasure stored away under magical lock and key, and that may have played some part in it.

Derry had never been scared by tales, though he did respect them. By passing the time of day with one local or another, he discovered the sorcerer expected a cake every Tuesday morning, each one fresh, perfect and different from the cakes that came before. He wandered past the big house and had a look-see to work out how best the delivery might be made without getting in trouble. There was a big front door with heavy iron bolts across it and a knocker in the shape of a clenched fist. And there was a wee back door. A crooked pathway led up to it through a garden all tangled with ivy and thistles, and in that garden there was a mastiff with eyes as big as saucers, teeth as sharp as knives and a voice fit to wake the dead.

"What do you think?" Derry whispered to the stick man as the friends peered between the cracks in the back gate, and the mastiff lunged and bayed at them from the other side. "This way or the front way? I'd rather not be shrivelled for something as insignificant as a cake. On the other hand, those are biggish teeth."

"Your answer's a bone," said the stick man, and the wee dog yipped agreement. "My advice is, do the butcher a favour before Tuesday."

So after his day's work in the bakery, Derry took himself over to the butcher's and offered to scrub the floor clean as a whistle in return for a large meaty bone, and the butcher obliged. Derry did such a good job that the butcher threw in a couple of cutlets for his supper and a wee bone for the spotted dog, which made everyone happy.

Tuesday came, and the plan worked like a charm. The mastiff was distracted by the meaty bone; the spotted dog hunkered down to keep her company. Derry and the stick man crept up the pathway to the little back door, which was standing ajar, and went in to find themselves in a kitchen full of gleaming pots and pans, sharp shiny knives and clean empty jars and bowls. Either there was a very tidy cook here, or the place didn't get used at all. There was a strange tingling feeling in the air. Whether it was magic, or whether it was something else, they didn't stay long enough to find out. Derry set the cake—chocolate with fresh cream filling and crushed nuts—on the table. Then out they went again as quick as they could. That was the first Tuesday survived.

The next week it was an almond cake with a dusting of icing sugar. A fresh bone did the trick with the mastiff, who seemed a lonely sort of creature—the only company she appeared to have was a rabble of farm animals kept in an enclosure at the far end of the garden, pigs, ducks, chickens, sheep all in together as if the sorcerer had had a try at farming and not quite got the hang of it. Derry would have liked to go closer and check the creatures had proper food and water, but the tingle of magic was on everything and he did not dare. He set the almond cake on the table, and as he turned for the door there came a muffled shouting from within the house, as if someone were trapped down below, perhaps under the floor. "Help! Help me!" That cry set cold fingers around his heart; it curdled the blood in his veins. He stood stock still, torn two ways. Then, much closer at hand, came the sound of approaching footsteps.

"Run!" urged the stick man from the pouch, prodding Derry's stomach with a twiggy finger. They bolted out the door, down the little path, through the gate and away down the road to the bakery, with the spotted dog coming along behind. The mastiff's mournful howling followed them all the way.

That night, as the friends settled to sleep—the dog by Derry's feet, the stick man bedded down in the pouch and the dove, her wing still splinted, on the pillow by Derry's cheek—Derry was still thinking about that cry for help. The voice had sounded just like his middle brother's. He should have gone to check. He should have been brave enough. He should not have let his fear of the sorcerer's magic stop him from doing what was right.

The third Tuesday came, and the cake was a delicate lemon torte. The delivery proceeded as before: the bone for the mastiff, along with the company of the spotted dog; the quiet approach up the little pathway; the culinary masterpiece set on the kitchen table. When that was done, Derry tiptoed toward the inner doorway and listened, and sure enough, the pitiful cry came again: "Help! Get me out!" It was his brother's voice, he was sure of it. He took a step through the doorway, following the sound.

"Put me down!" said the stick man. "If you think I'm going in there you're crazy!"

Derry set the stick man down on the floor, but before either of them could take a step further a pair of hands appeared, not attached to anything in particular, and wrapped themselves around Derry's neck. The hands began to squeeze, as if they would strangle him to death. The stick man could not reach high enough to help. He would have taken on the fiercest attacker but, truth to tell, his tiny blows would likely have been ineffective. *This is the end,* thought Derry as everything turned dark around him. *Farewell, brothers. Farewell, parents. My friends, goodbye forever.*

Swoosh! In through the tall window flew the dove, which Derry had left at his lodgings, still recovering from her injury. He had removed the splint just that morning; already she could fly again. Peck! Stab! Scratch! She attacked the phantom hands with all her small strength, and before the assault of dagger-beak, needle-claws and furiously flapping wings, the hands released their grip and vanished into nothing.

"Quick!" said the stick man. "Run!"

"Not yet!" Derry gasped. "I heard my brother . . . He's here somewhere . . . "

"That would be the brother who leaves wee dogs alone in the woods and kicks injured birds out of his way?" enquired the stick man. "The brother who walks by women in trouble as if they're invisible?"

"He's my brother," said Derry, as if that explained everything. And perhaps it did.

"Help!" came the voice again, and there was nothing for it but to search all through the sorcerer's house—and believe me, it was full of strange and disturbing things—until at last they found a small grille in the floor. Clutching onto this grille were the hands of Derry's brother, who was immured in a dark chamber beneath.

Before Derry could so much as draw breath, a door opened within the house and someone came stalking along the hallway toward him. It was the sorcerer, tall and fearsome in a robe of midnight blue. Through the knocking of his heart and the shaking of his knees, Derry took in the most surprising thing of all: the sorcerer was a sorceress. Unless being half-strangled had addled his wits completely, this was a woman, and a young one at that. She looked barely older than himself, but she was at least a hand-span taller and every bit as frightening as he had imagined.

"Who gave you permission to enter my house?" the sorceress roared. "What fell charm allowed you through my magical doorway?"

There was nothing for it but to speak up and hope he could talk his way out of this. "Cake got me in," he wheezed. "And I'm hoping my brother will get me out. He's down there under your floor."

"You've brought the cake? What kind of cake?" the sorceress demanded. There was a greedy glint in her eyes.

"Lemon," squeaked Derry, still not quite recovered from his near-strangulation.

"With poppy seeds?"

"Er . . . no." Would his life, and his brother's, depend on something so insignificant as a poppy seed? This was not the way heroic missions were supposed to end.

"No lemon cake can be eaten without poppy seeds," declared the sorceress, pointing her long fingers at Derry as if she were about to cast a spell and turn him into something unpleasant. She drew her dark brows together in a ferocious scowl. "My storeroom lies along that passageway. There you will find a bag of seeds. Set aside the brown seeds and pick out the black; sprinkle the perfect quantity of black seeds onto my cake. Have the cake ready by suppertime, and I will allow your brother to live for one more day."

"But—" protested Derry, then fell silent as the stick man jabbed him in the ankle. The youthful sorceress stalked off to her spell chamber, and Derry went to the storeroom, where an immense bag of seeds stood on the floor, half as tall as a man. The seeds were all mixed up; in the dim light there was no telling black from brown. Derry was in despair.

"Do not fear," spoke up a sweet voice at his left elbow. When Derry looked to see who it was, there was the dove, perched on the bag of seeds by his side. "I will complete this task for you."

"Did you just talk to me?" asked Derry in wonder.

"It surely wasn't *me* offering to spend the rest of the day sorting poppy seeds," remarked the stick man. "Why you're bothering to save your wretched brother when we could simply walk out the way we came in, I cannot imagine."

The dove made no comment, but began to peck away at the seeds, quickly making two piles of them, one brown, one black. Each time she dropped a seed, the stick man picked it up for her. Before Derry's amazed eyes, the task was completed before there was any sign of the sorceress returning. He rushed back to the kitchen and sprinkled black poppy seeds onto the cake, just the right quantity, with a few drops of lemon juice to keep them in position—though sparsely filled, the cupboards had yielded up a useful item or two. He made a brew of tea to go with the cake, and set out a fine platter and cup and a silver cake fork all ready.

When the sorceress swept in from her afternoon of spell-casting she was not well pleased. She'd expected the young man to fail miserably, like all the others who had attempted this task—in fact, Derry's brother was the only one not yet turned into a creature of some kind. Her yard was awash with piglets, chickens, ducks, goats and the like. She was becoming quite weary of the need to find fodder for them all.

So she came into the kitchen with mixed feelings. On the one hand, it seemed a very ordinary sort of lad had outwitted her. On the other, the cake looked and smelled delicious, and lemon cake with poppy seeds was her particular favourite. Besides, the smell of chamomile from that steaming cup was deeply soothing to her frayed nerves. It was a long time since anyone had made her a cup of tea without being ordered to do so.

"Sit down!" she barked. Derry sat. The stick man and the dove were both hidden in the pouch by now. Of the little dog, Derry had seen nothing since it went off to chat with the mastiff. "Question for you," the sorceress said, breaking off a piece of cake and popping it in her mouth. "Mmm, not bad. Why do you want to save your brother? He's an opinionated oaf, selfish and rude. Why not let me turn him into livestock like all the others out there, and take yourself off home?"

It was true, Derry thought. His brother *was* an opinionated oaf. But that made no difference. "Brothers look out for each other," he said. "That's the way it is." Then, seeing something in her eyes, he went on, "Do you not have brothers or sisters of your own?"

"What's that to you?" she snarled.

"I only thought—"

"You're not here to think, you're here to deliver a cake. And now you've delivered it, so you can go."

"And my brother with me?"

"Not so fast," said the sorceress. "If I let him go, you'll be off back home before the sun rises on another day, and who'll bring the next cake?"

There was something in her voice that made Derry think twice before he answered. Powerful sorceress as she was, with a menagerie of ensorcelled men and a house full of clever tricks, she was lonely. "Can't you use your powers of sorcery to conjure up as many cakes as you want?" he asked her.

"It's not the same." Her scowl was even deeper now; without it, she might be quite a comely girl, Derry thought, if a bit on the tall side.

"What if you learned to bake?"

She turned her baleful dark eyes on him. "I am a sorceress. I do not *bake*."

"You can't have it both ways."

"If you depart, taking your brother with you, I don't suppose I will have it any way," she said.

"The baker will find a new delivery man, as he found me. Some hapless wanderer who needs a place to stay and work to keep the wolf from the door."

The sorceress was silent for a little while; she had almost finished the cake. "Tell me," she said eventually, "what work did you do before you became the baker's boy?"

"My father is a miller. My brothers and I helped him. But he sent us to seek our fortunes, and here we are. Two of us, anyway." Derry glanced around the sorceress's kitchen, taking in the shining, unused pots and pans, the glinting knives, the pristine crockery. "A mill has a good supply of flour. We have chickens and ducks too, a vegetable patch and a row of fruit trees. There would be room for your . . . creatures. And my mother bakes cakes; good ones. She would teach you."

There was a moment's astonished silence. "Your *mother* would teach *me*," the sorceress said flatly.

"That's what I said." Derry felt a sharp jab in the ribs. "I'm sure there's plenty you could teach her, too," he added politely.

The sorceress narrowed her dark eyes at him. "Either you're a fool," she said, "or you're too clever by far. I suppose you think if I go back to this *mill* with you," she spoke the word as if not quite clear as to its meaning, "I'll marry you and bear your children and keep you in riches for the rest of your life, huh?"

"Oh, no!" Derry was horrified at the idea. Him, the slow one, the dreamer, wed to this overwhelming creature? "That was not at all what I meant. Though if you are looking for a husband, my brother down there in your dungeon does scrub up quite well. And he's a hard worker. He stands to inherit at least a half-share of the mill, and it is a thriving enterprise." He hoped he had not pushed his luck too far. In the pouch someone was quivering, whether with fear or laughter Derry could not tell.

The sorceress fished a key from her pocket and threw it onto the table, next to the empty cake platter. "There," she snapped. "Send your wee man down to let my prisoner out, tell him to make himself presentable—there's a pump in the yard—then gather my creatures ready to travel. Let us inspect this *mill* of yours."

"Er . . . it's a fair walk," Derry ventured. "Out of the town, along the shadowy valley, over the pass, down the craggy mountain and through the wild wood. A long journey, especially for the piglets . . . "

"Leave that to me," said the sorceress.

So it was that, not long after, a strange party appeared rather suddenly on the edge of the wild wood, close to the place where Derry's eldest brother had gone up the side track to look for the hidden gold. There was no sign of him, but before them spread the broad sunny farmlands around the mill, and the air was mild and fresh, and the grass was green, and Derry felt happiness stealing into every part of him. The ducks, the sheep, the chickens and the piglets foraged under the trees, the little dog ran about busily, the mastiff lay down for a rest, and Derry's second brother pointed out to the sorceress where the mill was, and where the stream ran, and how the business of milling worked, and at the same time threw in a few remarks about how bonny she looked in the gown she had worn for travel, and how the shade of her eyes matched exactly the deep blue-black of his favourite flowers—when they got home he would show her where to find them, in the shade under the big oak tree. And the sorceress commented that, for a man who had never been far from home before, he had coped quite well with both incarceration and magical transportation, but that he was not to forget, even for one instant, that she had her eye on him.

So they arrived back at the mill, two men, a highly unusual young woman, and a retinue of assorted animals. The dove rode on Derry's shoulder, wary of the mastiff. The stick man peeped out of the pouch, but what he thought about the situation was anybody's guess. Since the sorceress had joined their company, he hadn't had a lot to say.

The miller and his wife received their sons with open arms, though their prospective daughter-in-law was something of a surprise. However, she had brought some very fine, healthy additions to the mill's complement of domestic creatures, and when she professed an interest in learning to bake, the miller's wife began to warm to her for all her odd manner. As for the second son, he seemed a changed man, though that may have owed a little to the continued absence of his older brother, who had not returned from his journey. Whether he was still in the wild wood somewhere, hunting for the wee man's gold, or whether he had travelled to some far stranger place, nobody knew.

The second son settled down with his sorceress wife, and pretty soon everyone at the mill was eating the most remarkable cakes this side of the wild wood, and the flour was being milled so fine and even that folk around the district said it was almost as if the stuff were touched by magic. From time to time rumours came to them about the eldest brother: that he had become a crewman on a pirate ship and was sailing the seven seas; that he was being held by trolls in an underground prison; that he had married a washerwoman with twelve children. There was no way of knowing if they were true or false.

After some while, the miller got his two sons together and said he planned to leave the mill to them jointly, since the second son was a good worker and had mended his ways, and Derry, the youngest, had surely earned something for bringing contentment to the place. But Derry was restless. One day he wrapped up a bundle with bread and cheese, and plum cake with raisins, and his knife, his cup and his kerchief, and he set off down the track again, looking for adventure, and thinking he might find his eldest brother along the way. The little dog stayed behind, having made fast friends with the mastiff. But the dove and the stick man rode along, one on Derry's shoulder, the other in the pouch. Where were they going? Nobody knew. But when they stopped for the night under the fringes of the wild wood, Derry remarked to his two companions, "I love journeying. I love surprises. I love not knowing what's around the next corner. Only . . . my brother seemed so happy with his new wife, just as my mother and father are still happy in each other's company after all these years. The sorceress was not for me; I'd have been scared to turn over the wrong way in bed. But . . . I do feel lonely sometimes. Of course, I welcome your company," for he meant no insult to his two dear friends and fellow travellers. "But a wife to walk beside me on the road, and give me good advice, and keep me warm at night would be a grand thing."

There was a bit of a silence. Then the stick man spoke up. "Just wishing isn't enough. For a dream-come-true, you need magic."

"Oh." Derry was crestfallen, for there wasn't a scrap of magic in him.

"Put a feather under your pillow tonight," advised the stick man, "and fall asleep with an open heart. That should do the trick."

Derry looked about under the bushes for a feather, but there was none to be found. "Another night, maybe," he murmured, not putting much faith in the stick man's suggestion anyway.

The dove flew up to his shoulder, then dipped her beak to pluck out a downy feather from her breast. She offered it with some delicacy. Derry thanked her, put the feather under his makeshift pillow and fell asleep thinking of love and happiness, of courage and family, of kindness and respect. Through his dreams walked his mother and father, his two brothers, his intimidating new sister-in-law, the folk of the village, and of course the wee dog, the stick man and the dove. In his sleep he thought, I'm such an ordinary man, and yet I'm surrounded by fine people. How lucky I am.

When he woke at dawn, the stick man was still tucked up in the pouch, but the dove was gone from her usual place on the pillow by his cheek. And seated beside him, as if waiting for him to wake up, was a graceful little woman clad in a cloak of soft grey feathers. Her hair was of the same grey hue, but she was young and comely, her lips sweetly curving, her eyes bright as gems. He saw in her face that she found him pleasing to behold, though, in truth, he was a plain-looking man.

"Long ago, I vowed that I would only wed a man with the courage of a lion and the gentleness of a dove," said the woman. "A man with kind hands and a humble heart. In my search for you, I have taken many forms. But now I appear before you as myself. Will you be my husband, Derry? I would gladly walk the journey by your side."

"Oh, yes!" said Derry, with happiness flooding into every part of him.

"At last," said the stick man, peeping out of the pouch.

Derry could have sung and danced for joy right there on the track, but instead he embraced his dove wife and thanked fortune for bringing him his own treasure. He did not ask how his perfect mate had taken the many forms she'd mentioned. He did not enquire whether she was some kind of fairy, though he suspected she might be. If she wanted to tell him, she would tell him in her own good time.

So they moved on together: the miller's youngest son, the dove wife and the stick man. Did they reach the pirate ship, or the cave of the trolls, or the washerwoman's house? Did Derry find his missing brother? Ah. That is another story.

☽

in coed celyddon

The forest was forbidden. Coed Celyddon was a perilous place, especially now there was a war on. Tribe fought tribe: Ector's men against Hywel's, Drustan's warriors against the Red Bull crowd from Rheged. Then there were the others, dangerous others. Pictish mercenaries had a habit of popping up when least expected, all wild tattoos and crossbows, and to the south and east was the real enemy: the Saxons.

Before he rode off to battle, Ector had given the three boys a lecture, short and sharp as always. One: keep out of trouble. Two: work hard. When these skirmishes were over, and he had that fool Hywel on his knees begging for mercy, Ector would come home and see who had improved the most at swordcraft, and archery, and riding. He liked them to compete, to challenge one another. Three: stay out of Coed Celyddon, or he'd tan their hides for them.

Cei, Ector's son, was the biggest of the three boys. He always won when size mattered, for instance in wrestling, which was not part of the official curriculum. Cei's cousin, Bedwyr, come to stay for the summer, was the smallest. Bedwyr had a talent for throwing: the spear was his favourite weapon. He might be only twelve, but grown men came out to watch him at target practice, and sometimes cheered. As for Arthur, he was in the middle: smaller than Cei, bigger than Bedwyr. Turned fourteen last midwinter day, Arthur was too young to go to battle and too old to be content with staying home. He was good at everything, best at nothing.

It came with being a foster-son, he thought: that feeling of always coming in second. He never said so, of course. Ector had been kind to him, and although Cei punched him sometimes, it was in a friendly sort of way, soon forgiven. All the same, Arthur would have liked to shine, perhaps with the sword. Not much hope of that; he didn't even have a real one of his own, only the rough practice blades the master-at-arms, Owain the Fists, gave them to work with, blunt-edged and poorly balanced. Cei had a proper sword, long and heavy, with watery patterns all along the length of it; his father had given it to him. Arthur's father never came to see him. He was away somewhere in the south, fighting battles of his own. Arthur couldn't remember what he looked like.

"Come on," hissed Bedwyr, crouching low as the three boys snaked their way up the hill through the long grass and bracken to the shadowy edge of the woods. The dog, Cabal, padded silently behind. Ector was gone on his campaign, but there were others who might see them and call them back. Cei's mother was like a dragon, and it was not for nothing Owain the Fists had earned the nickname Ogre.

They reached the trees, slipping in under sharp-toothed holly bushes to the deeper shadow cast by great oaks. Coed Celyddon was huge, dark and mysterious: the perfect place for exploring, and all the better because it was out of bounds. Each of them was armed; they weren't stupid. Hywel's tribe had been known to slip spies in right to the fringes of Ector's land. Cei bore a bow and quiver, Bedwyr carried a throwing-spear, and Arthur had a knife in his belt.

"Right," said Cei, assuming command in that way he had. "Let's find this druid."

They all knew the druid, of course. He dwelt in the heart of the forest somewhere, all alone, and came down twice a year to Ector's stronghold on the feast days of midsummer and midwinter. There were no prizes for guessing why: the fellow liked his food, and Ector always put on a good spread of roast boar, jellied eels, salmon seethed in buttermilk, pastries and fruit tarts. Strong mead flowed freely. After his third goblet, the druid could be persuaded to tell stories, wondrous tales of gods and goddesses, heroes and monsters, treachery and courage that put his audience in another world, and had them begging for more the instant he'd finished.

Afterwards, the druid sat by the fire and stared into the flames. Folk gave him a wide berth; it was common knowledge that if a druid took a dislike to you, he could turn you into a cockroach or a newt. Arthur talked to him. Arthur couldn't see the point in being afraid when it stopped him from finding out something interesting, and the druid certainly had a lot to tell. He never told his name, though. He'd say to one man it was Corr, and to another man Faol, and the next time he came he'd tell them he was called Dobhran. Those weren't proper names at all, they were animals: Crane, Wolf, Otter. Some people said the druid's real name was Myrddin or Merlin, which was disappointingly ordinary.

The druid had a knack for disappearing. Once moment he'd be sitting there having a word with Arthur, and then all at once he'd be gone. He had a hideout in the woods, a place the boys had never been able to find, though they'd tried hard enough. It was as if the branches and bushes, the twisting twigs and snapping tendrils shifted about, making a net to block the way.

"I think north," said Bedwyr. "Under the beeches, by the pond, down the hill a bit."

"I think south," said Cei. "You know where the big rock is, the one that looks like an old man with a beard? I think we should look there again."

Arthur said nothing. He was watching his dog, Cabal. Cabal was a half-breed, part wolfhound, part something really ugly. He'd been born by mistake, and Ogre had been going to drown him. Begged politely, the master-at-arms had let Arthur keep the scrawny pup. Cabal's legs were too long for his grey, hairy body; his ears stuck obstinately upwards instead of drooping elegantly, and his long tongue perpetually hung from his grinning mouth. Ogre had predicted Arthur would never make anything of such a misbegotten creature, but Arthur had known from the start that this was wrong. Cabal was a dog of high intelligence and flawlessly obedient to his master. With others he was less reliable. He'd nearly bitten Cei's finger off once.

"That way," Arthur said as the hound, sniffing frantically, headed off down a middle path, a narrow, rough track twisting and turning into the dark heart of the wood. He went after the dog, soft-footed on the uneven ground, and the others followed him without a word.

It wasn't the easiest path. It sidled past thorny bushes; it toppled into swampy hollows and clawed its way up steep, overgrown slopes studded with unexpected rocks. They rested on a hilltop by a gushing spring. There was a view from here, over the dense, purple-green blanket of the great forest toward open heath. Cei stood balanced on a flat rock, gazing southwards: there lay the region of Cumbria, Hywel's land. Somewhere out there Cei's father was even now fighting his rival chieftain: fighting, and maybe dying. Cei wouldn't be able to see anything, though. It was too far away.

"He'll be all right," Arthur said quietly. "By new moon he'll be back home large as life, full of tales about brave deeds and vanquished Cumbrians, see if he isn't."

"Of course he'll be all right!" snapped Cei, seizing his bow and heading off down the hill. "Come on, we haven't got all day."

It was Bedwyr's fault that they got separated. They were walking along a narrow track under low-branched beeches, single file, when he thought he saw something, a boar, a deer, and, balancing his spear with the instinct of a true hunter, ran off between the trees in hot pursuit, the dog at his heels. When Cabal came back he was on his own. A pox on Bedwyr. It wasn't safe for both Cei and Arthur to leave the track; they might never find their way out of the forest then, judging by the tricks it had played on them in the past. They couldn't just wait, either; what if Bedwyr was hurt, gored by a tusk, pierced by an antler? They called out as hard as they could—Cabal's voice was the loudest—but the only reply was squirrels rustling in the canopy above, and the buzz of insects about their summer business.

"You go after him," Arthur said. "I'll wait here. If you're too long, I'll run back for help. You'd better take Cabal with you."

There was a small clearing close by. He sat there on a fallen tree and tried to judge the time of day by the sunlight filtering down through the arch of foliage high above. He couldn't stay long; if there was something wrong he'd need to run all the way home and get back here with Ogre or another of the men before nightfall. Only a fool would linger in Coed Celyddon after dusk.

The light changed slowly. Time passed, and Arthur's head was full of unwelcome images: Bedwyr lying injured, all alone; Cei wandering lost, brambles tearing at his clothes, cobwebs blinding him, blundering deeper and deeper into the darkness of the woods. Cabal facing a savage boar, a ravenous wolf. This was no good; he had to do something and do it now. Arthur sprang to his feet, and at that moment there was a sound of movement along the track ahead of him. Someone was coming, and fast.

"Bedwyr?" he called hopefully. But it was not his friend who ran into sight, emerging into a patch of dappled light where the sun touched the earthen path with gold. It was Cabal, tongue lolling, tail thrashing, every part of him bouncing with energy. After him came another dog, squatter, thicker, with a short liver-brown pelt and the very same look of mischief in his eye. The two of them raced each other across the clearing, twisting and turning, rolling in play-fight, pausing to sniff and greet a moment, and an instant later bounding about again in a kind of mad canine dance. Arthur began to laugh. Who but Cabal would find a friend in such an unlikely spot? A twig cracked. His laughter died in his throat. He drew his knife without a sound; Ogre had taught him well.

There was a boy on the other side of the clearing, standing half in shadow. The boy was holding a bow; the string was drawn taut, the arrow poised for flight, aimed straight at Arthur's chest. The boy was wearing a scarlet band around his head, knotted at the back. Everyone knew what that meant. He was one of Hywel's tribe: the enemy. A spy, right here in Coed Celyddon, at Ector's very doorstep.

The boy stood still as stone. His eyes were hard; his mouth was set in a thin line. He was pale as chalk. Arthur had the knife in his hand. He could throw it; it would have to be a very good shot to do any damage before that arrow reached him. Arthur had never killed a man before, only rabbits, hunting. He looked across the clearing into the boy's narrowed eyes, and wondered how it would feel to die.

The dogs made another wild pass through the undergrowth, a mock chase ending in a complicated tumble. The two of them together flopped down on the path between the boys, mouths open, tongues lolling. Cabal rolled onto his back, grinning, and the other hound licked his ear.

Arthur looked at the red-scarfed boy, and the boy looked back. Very slowly, Arthur lowered the knife and sheathed it, putting out his two hands to show he carried no other weapons.

For a moment he gazed straight at that arrow-point, in perfect line with his heart. He did not move. Then the boy brought down the bow and put the arrow back in the quiver. There was nothing to say. They watched the dogs a moment. The two creatures were tired of play for now, and lay side by side in the leaf-mould, each watching his master.

"Come on, Cabal." Arthur clicked his fingers. The other boy gave a short whistle, and the liver-coloured dog got up and went to him. Cabal stood by Arthur's side, obedient as ever. The red-scarfed boy gave a sort of nod, and Arthur nodded back. He had the strangest feeling, as if some great change had occurred, something that would make his whole life different. Were these tears in his eyes? Impossible. At midwinter he would be fifteen. He would be a man, and a man does not weep. He watched dog and boy as they vanished back under the trees, gone like shadows, gone as if they had never been, save for the disturbance of the ground made by eight scuffling hound-feet. "Come on," he said again. "I think we'd better go and look for the others."

The forest of Coed Celyddon was full of surprises. Arthur set off, expecting a long, fruitless search followed by an uncomfortable night huddled in some chilly hollow between oak-roots. He retraced his steps, thinking to set Cabal after the others' scent and track them as far as he could before dusk fell. But the path had changed. It was not narrow and shady any more, twisting and turning, but ran broad and straight. It did not slope downwards as before, but ran up to the top of a neat, conical hill crowned with a circle of massive oaks. From within the circle a plume of smoke arose, and there was a smell of frying sausages. By the time Arthur reached the top, with Cabal a step behind, he was not so very surprised to see Cei and Bedwyr sitting on one side of a small, bright campfire, and on the other side, the druid squatting down to inspect the sizzling contents of the frying pan set on the coals, and muttering to himself. There was a tiny hut of stone, and a well, and a crow pecking at something underneath low twiggy bushes. The oaks stood dark and solid, like a ring of wise old folk watching and listening. Arthur stepped into the circle.

"What took you so long?" Bedwyr asked, accepting a sausage and wincing as it burned his fingers.

"We've been here ages," said Cei. "Where were you?"

Arthur opened his mouth to tell them, then shut it again. There was no doubt what Cei would do if he heard there was one of Hywel's tribe lurking so close to his father's stronghold. He'd be off in a flash, bow at the ready, and it would take more than a couple of dogs to stop him from shooting.

"I got lost," Arthur said. "Can I have one of those?"

They ate in silence. The food was too good to get less than their full attention. Whatever was in the sausages, they tasted wonderful. Of course, druids could do some strange things, so the tales went. They could probably make sausages out of thin air if they wanted.

The meal was finished. The druid gave them water from the well; it tasted fresh and clean, like a mouthful of sunshine.

"Can you do real magic?" Bedwyr asked abruptly, as if he'd been working up to the question for a while.

"Real magic?" the druid asked, raising his brows. He was not an old man; he stood tall and straight, his long plaited hair dark as night, his eyes so pale you couldn't tell what colour they really were. All the same, he had an old look, as if he'd been around as long as those trees had.

"You know," said Cei eagerly. "Changing things, and seeing the future, that kind of magic. Can you do any?"

"Conjurers' tricks?" the druid asked in scathing tones, and an instant later, where the crow had squawked and pecked under the bushes, a black cat lay curled on itself, watching them balefully through slitted eyes. "If that is your understanding of magic, you have much to learn. Would you see your own future? Could you gain wisdom from that?"

"Maybe," Cei said, more hesitant now. "I wouldn't mind a try."

Arthur said nothing. It was odd; the druid hadn't looked at him once, and yet he felt those pale eyes following him, intent, searching, as if they could see right inside him.

Now Myrddin, if that was his name, passed long, bony hands over the fire, once, twice, three times, and a cloud of wispy smoke, blue-tinged, arose and settled above the glowing coals.

"Look now, Cei son of Ector," the druid said.

Cei stared into the smoke, eyes wide. Arthur couldn't see a thing, but evidently Cei could; his face changed, he frowned, then grinned, and after a while sat back on his heels, blinking.

"What did you see?" Bedwyr demanded. "Tell us, go on!"

"A battle; I was in it, and winning," Cei said slowly. "A lot of blood. And later, there was . . . " He stopped, a violent blush rising to his cheeks.

"I bet Rhian the miller's daughter was in it," Bedwyr said, laughing. "Me next. Please."

Afterwards, Bedwyr was less keen than Cei to say what he had seen. He'd gone very serious and sat in silence, as if thinking hard. The future is not always as we would wish it when we are twelve years old.

"Now, Arthur," said Myrddin. "Do you not wish to look into the flames and see your own destiny?"

There was a lengthy silence.

"No," Arthur said eventually. "I don't need to. Knowing beforehand just makes it harder."

"Makes what harder?" Cei asked, puzzled.

"Doing what's right," said Arthur, thinking of the boy, and the arrow, and the dogs. "Making sure other people do what's right. Going on when it gets difficult. All those things." He looked up at the druid, who was regarding him gravely with those eyes that seemed to see so much. "I want to ask you something."

Myrddin inclined his head, waiting.

"If we stopped fighting each other, the tribes, I mean, if we made peace and helped each other instead, then couldn't we—"

"That's a stupid idea!" Cei snapped. "Make peace with Hywel's people? They're scum, every one of them. The Red Bull tribe are a bunch of oafs, Father says so. They're our enemies."

"All the same," said Arthur, "just imagine it. All the tribes together, under one leader. What a great army that would be. A force as strong as that could beat the Saxons. An army like that could drive them out and save our lands. We could do it. We're all the same kind underneath, Hywel's men, Ector's, Drustan's. Why shouldn't we do it?"

There was a pause.

"That's the worst idea I've ever heard," Cei said crossly. "Us, teaming up with Cumbrians? No leader would be fool enough to try that. It's crazy!" He tossed a handful of pebbles into the fire.

"I don't know," said Bedwyr. "It could work. Maybe not yet, but some time. My father says—"

"What would he know?" muttered Cei.

Arthur was silent. He could see it in his mind, the image bold and bright: a great strong army, all the chieftains of Britain with their banners, a tide of courage surging across the land, sweeping the invader before it. And when the last battle was over, a time of peace, a time for harvest and celebrations, good fellowship and wise rule. Who would lead them he did not know, but the time would come: he had never been so sure of anything.

"It's getting late," Myrddin observed, rising to his feet. "You'd best be off, if you don't want to risk the dragon's tongue. Now that you know how to find me, I expect to see more of you. Bring that muddle-footed hound with you. I like him."

Arthur was last to go. He bowed to the druid politely. "Thank you," he said.

"Ah," said Myrddin, "don't thank me. This is your own vision, and it is for you to achieve it, not I. I'm good for a little advice from time to time, and a sausage or two. Off you go, now."

Down the hill they went, along the track, under the beeches, over the rocks, all the way to the margin of Coed Celyddon. Of red-scarfed spy and brown-haired dog there was no sign; the only sound was the whisper of their feet in the undergrowth. First went Cei, who liked to lead. Next came Bedwyr, spear in hand, a little frown on his brow. Arthur came last, with Cabal padding beside him. Arthur's head was full of dreams. As for Cabal, being a dog, he was probably thinking of supper.

◯

juggling silver

Grandmother kept her silver plates in a row on a high shelf. They sat there looking down at us like three round eyes. Every day she took them off the shelf and polished them with a soft red cloth, and then she put them carefully back. If we climbed up, we could see our faces in them. Ulli climbed up a lot.

"Ulli, Ulli, what are we going to do with you?" Grandmother would say. "Eight years old and never out of trouble! Eight years old and still babbling baby talk! Get down off there before you break something!"

The plates were very old and very valuable. They had belonged to Grandmother's great-great-grandmother. On the rims of them were silver berries and leaves, owls and wolves, whales and dolphins. Grandmother called them the tree plate, the eye plate and the sea plate. Sometimes she let me hold them. "Careful, Sami! That's treasure you have in your hands!" She never let Ulli hold them.

Ulli was different. The other boys and girls his age ran around and played with a ball. They hunted for shells and went swimming in the rock pools. They helped their mothers to salt fish and gave their fathers a hand with tarring boats or untangling nets. I could talk to them and they'd understand me. Not Ulli. My little brother wasn't safe on the beach by himself. He'd just walk into the water and keep on going. I'd waded in and fished him out hundreds of times. Ulli didn't understand what people told him. And he couldn't talk, not the way other folk talked. All he would say was a sort of rhyme, over and over, in words that didn't make any sense: tipi api sipi oh, tipi api sipi oh. He'd sit on the bottom step outside Grandmother's hut and play with a little pile of round black stones, throwing them up in the air and catching them one, two, three, and all the time he'd be saying it, tipi api sipi. There was no point yelling, "Stop it!" Words meant nothing to my brother. Grandmother said Ulli would never be able to cast a net or paddle a canoe, not even when he grew up. All he would ever do was talk nonsense and juggle stones and get into trouble. It was just as well he had me to watch over him. Taking care of Ulli was my job.

The year I turned twelve there was a long, cold winter and by the end of it everyone was hungry. The last of the salt fish was nearly gone, and the grain was down to a scattering in the bottom of the sack. I could feel my ribs sticking out. When I looked in the silver plates, there wasn't a boy looking back, but a bony, big-eyed thing that scared me.

We were waiting for the fish to come. On the first days of spring the fish always came to the bay, enough for a big feast, and more to be smoked or salted and put away. By harvest time the storage huts would be full to bursting. That meant the women could walk over the hills to the field people's village, a long way, and trade salt fish for grain and vegetables. As long as the fish came, nobody stayed hungry for long. At the field people's market there were fine things to trade for, woven baskets and iron cooking pots and shoes made of deerskin.

But this year was different. It stayed cold. The sun hid behind thick clouds, hardly showing its face at all. I stood on the beach with Father and Uncle, looking out to sea. There were no fish, only dull, flat waters and a few screaming birds. Ulli ran about on the sand, singing to himself, tipi api sipi oh, tipi api . . . We waited there all day, and at sunset we went home hungry. Grandmother made soup out of boiled weeds, with a few grains floating around in it. It wasn't much of a meal. The grumbling in my belly kept me awake. Tomorrow, Father said. Tomorrow surely the fish will come.

But there were no fish, only grey days one after another, and pinched, grey faces. Ulli sat on the floor with a blanket over him, like a little bear in a cave.

"Tipi api," he hummed tunelessly. "Sipi oh . . . "

"Shut up!" I snapped. Everyone was cross. Everyone was hungry. Soon there would be no food left. What if the fish never came? People could not survive on stones and sand.

We would have to leave the bay, Father said, leave our houses and our boats and go inland, away from the sea. What good were nets when there was nothing to catch in them? What good were fishing boats when the seas were empty? Tomorrow we would pack up and go, while we were still strong enough for the long walk. We had no fish to give the field people, nothing to exchange for food except our one treasure: the silver plates. The plates would have to go; there was no choice. Father would break the news to Grandmother tomorrow.

The dawn light woke me. Father was still rolled up in his blanket snoring, but Ulli's bed was empty. I could hear Grandmother's voice from the hut next door, wailing and crying. "My plates! Who's taken my beautiful plates?"

Quick as a flash, before the noise woke Father, I pulled on my clothes and went outside. Where was Ulli? Not up the track that way; not down that way, but there were his small bare footmarks in the sand, heading for the beach. I ran. Ulli had never understood the sea, how dangerous it was, how hard it could pull. Ulli loved the water. I had never been able to teach him to swim.

I pelted toward the dunes, heart pounding. I was the big brother; it was up to me to keep Ulli safe. Behind me, Grandmother's shrieking voice was joined by others: Father's, Uncle's. "The plates!" they were calling out. "Who has taken the plates?"

I came up through the dunes and down onto the wide, cold beach. My chest ached; I couldn't breathe. "Ulli!" I tried to call, but the wind snatched my voice away. "Ulli!"

Down on the sand, halfway between the sea and the dunes, Ulli stood very still, his hair sticking up on end and his clothes rumpled from sleep. I halted, staring. Above my brother's head there was a flashing, silvery pattern, a shimmering flow of light like the wings of some fantastic bird. The sun was peeping between the clouds. It sent a ray of brightness down to catch the silver plates as they spun and danced in the air, as Ulli juggled and sang: 'Tipi api sipi oh, tipi api sipi oh!' It was like something out of a strange dream.

A crowd gathered around me. The whole village had been woken by Grandmother's screams. All of us stood quiet on the sand, staring at the plates whirling in the sunlight, and at Ulli's small deft hands as they threw and caught, threw and caught again.

Then I saw something else, out beyond the bay. "Look!" I shouted, pointing. Everyone looked: everyone but Ulli. The glittering plates leaped and dived, and out in the sea something bright moved in its turn, a surge of silver. A great shoal of fish was moving steadily in towards the shore where the juggler stood. Beneath the clear, green water their pale bellies glinted in the sunlight.

'Quick!" Father yelled. "The nets!"

Rubbing the sleep from their eyes, the men gathered the biggest net, waded out and cast it wide. I took my place at the edge, waiting, as the silver plates spun and danced in the air behind us. The fish swam in. There were hundreds of them.

'Pull!" called Father, and while Ulli juggled, we hauled in the catch. That morning we took three nets of plump, juicy fish. That night we slept with full bellies and smiles on our faces.

After that, the sun shone over the bay and the weather turned warm. It was a good season after all, with enough fish to see us through the cold months and plenty left over to trade. Grandmother went to the field people's village with a bundle of stiff salt fish on her back, and when she came home she brought me a new pair of shoes. And she had a gift for Ulli: three little balls of deerhide, sewn with neat, strong stitches. He threw them high in the air, one after the other. His grin was so wide it made us all laugh. The plates were back on their shelf. I didn't think Ulli would steal them again.

All the boys take turns looking after Ulli now. He still can't swim, but he splashes in the shallows while we dive and play. Maybe one day Ulli will learn to do ordinary things. Maybe he'll even learn to talk. After all, he can juggle with plates, and none of us can do that.

I thought a lot about what happened that day on the beach. One night, when we were sitting by the fire, I asked Grandmother about it. Grandmother is very old. She's so old she knows the answers to a lot of questions.

"Did Ulli make the fish come, Grandmother?"

"Hrmph." Grandmother sounded cross. Or perhaps she was trying not to laugh. "What sort of a question is that? Don't the fish come every year?"

"Yes, but—"

"But nothing," Grandmother said. "Ulli juggled. The fish came. My silver plates are safe on the shelf, and we're here by the sea where we belong. And now it's time for bed."

She still sounded cross, but when she tucked me in she was smiling.

◑

'twixt firelight and water
(a tale of sevenwaters)

~ Conri ~

A fair maid in the wildwood lies
A raven pecks her sightless eyes
Then wings into the heavens again
To shriek his song of death and pain.

I have a tale to tell. I would recite its verses while playing the harp, had not a sorceress long ago robbed me of my capacity to share my story. That may be just as well, for my tale would only make you sad. I was a bard then. I brought tears to the eyes of my listeners, made them hold their breath in anticipation, gasp in wonderment, cheer as the hero won his battle, cry as the fair lady lost her true love. In those days, I contrived happy endings. Folk like to see lovers reunited, challenges met and overcome, good triumphant over evil.

If ever my voice is returned to me, I will sing only sad songs.

I listen as my companion instructs a clutch of green novices.

"In the land of Erin dwell three races," he tells them. "First are the Tuatha De Danann, commonly known as the Fair Folk, proud and strong, noble and wise." *With a few notable exceptions*, I add in my mind. "They dwell in hollow hills and in deep forests," the druid continues, "though such sanctuaries are shrinking with the coming of the new faith. Second are the Old Ones, the Fomhoire, whom I should perhaps have placed at the start, since they have prior claim. Their shapes are many, their attitudes inscrutable. Long time and endless patience provide their solutions. They blend; they wait; they observe. The Old Ones are survivors. Last, human folk, late come to this land, short-lived, unsubtle, as moody and changeable as a Connemara shore in autumn."

Up speaks a bright young fellow, all bony wrists and eager eyes. "Master Ciarán? There are surely more than three races here. What of leprechauns? Clurichauns? What of the *bean sidhe*?"

"What about the Sea People?" another novice chimes in.

"And there's those wee things that drink the milk straight from the cow," pipes up a red-cheeked lad who, from the looks of him, has but recently replaced his hayfork with a druid's staff.

"True," says my companion, unruffled as always. "There exists a fourth race, a fifth, a sixth; perhaps more than we will ever know. Set them aside for now and consider another variant. Ask yourself what may ensue when the pure blood of the three races is mixed and blended, creating something new. Imagine a being with human passions and frailties combined with Fomhoire endurance, say, or human stubbornness alongside the pride and craft of the Tuatha De. Imagine an individual with the Old Ones' long memory and the Fair Folk's facility in magic; picture a warrior of superb skill and courage, who possesses the ability to become rock, water, earth, tree in a heartbeat.

"Such blends are not common. The three races of Erin seldom have congress with one another, and such alliances rarely produce children. When there is a slipping across boundaries, a union between old enemies, and an infant is born of that coupling, chances are the child will be something exceptional. The bravest heroes and the darkest villains are oft products of such unsanctioned pairings."

The tutor pauses, his mulberry eyes seeing something beyond this grove, beyond this forest, beyond this summer day. I, too, contemplate. Hero or villain? If I still had my human tongue, I could answer for him. My companion walks the path of light. Here in the nemetons, his vocation is to teach, to guide, to set the feet of the young on right ways. His choice brought him some peace of mind. Some. He has suffered losses as painful as my own. The shadow of death lingers in those dark eyes even as he leads the young brethren in a prayer.

Hero or villain? It depends. I was once hero of my own tale, loved by a girl with star-bright eyes and hair like a soft shadow. I had youth, talent, a path before me. And then; and then . . . Had I a human voice, I would turn the fresh faces of these young druids pale with horror. I would shout and scream my story to the treetops, I would sit by the pool and let my tears fall into the still water, one and two and three. I would whisper her name to the wind, I would teach it to skylark and thrush, to sparrow and nightingale, and they would sing it abroad, an anthem, a lullaby, a love song, a dead march. Oh, if I had my voice again, there would be such a tale to tell. And in that tale, perhaps I would be hero and villain both.

I glimpsed her first 'twixt lake and fire
My heart took wing; soared high and higher
Lóch was her name. The moon above
Smiled down, pale witness of our love.

Ah, that night! She stood reed-slender, the fire's glow warming her face, and behind her the bright moon danced on the waters of the lake. My heart gave one great leap and I was changed forever. But I get ahead of myself. First I must tell of a day some years earlier: the day when I watched my mother bringing her new son home to the Otherworld.

I was hiding. At thirteen, I was in more fear of her than I had been as a little child. By then I'd begun to understand the darkness she carried within her, a weight of bitter resentment so tightly woven into the fabric of her that it was plain nothing would ever shift it. She'd been away. Three years it had been, three wonderful, peaceful years without her. I'd spent them making verses, practising the harp, and hoping beyond hope that she'd never come back. With her gone, folk had begun to befriend me. I had started to believe it might be possible for one of my kind to follow the paths of light. Yes, even a son of hers.

I was hiding high in the cradling branches of an oak. I watched her pass below, every part of me on edge, willing her to be only a phantom, only an evil memory. But she was real, as real as the little boy she carried in her arms, a red-haired mite of perhaps two summers. I knew at a glance that he was hers. Her son. My replacement.

It was her habit to summon me after one of these trips out into the human world, and her summons came as soon as she'd left the child with a pair of local cottagers, then returned to our own realm. She stood in the shadow of the oaks, eyes cool as I approached. "Conri," she said. Her tone hardly differentiated me from a grain of dust under her foot.

"Mother." I knelt before her, since that was the way she liked it, making my voice respectful.

"I don't suppose I can hope you spent the time of my absence working on the elements of your magical craft."

It was not a question, and I did not offer an answer, merely gazed at the ground, wondering how she would punish me.

A sigh. "I've had a reversal, Conri. A serious reversal that needs attention. Look at me!" The voice suddenly sharp as an axe. I raised my head. She was young today, auburn hair cascading over her shoulders, figure shapely in a gown of soft green. Her mouth was set tight. Her eyes probed deep inside me. I could think of nothing to say that would please her.

"You've wasted the time fiddling about with your music. Yes?"

"Yes, Mother." I set my jaw firm and held her gaze as my belly twisted in fear.

"Pah!" An explosion of annoyance, then a click of the fingers. Pain shot through my arms and hands, crippling, crushing. I crumpled, screaming. Around us in the high trees of the Otherworld, a host of birds echoed my cry. "Stupid boy! With your parentage, you could have amounted to something. You are useless! Useless! A weakling!"

I forced myself back up to my knees. The agony was fading. I glanced at my arms, half-expecting that every bone would be broken, but they looked much as usual. My breath wheezed in my chest. I said nothing at all.

"Never mind that." Mother's tone had changed again. "It's of little account now. Despite the reversal, I have not returned empty-handed. I have a weapon. A fine weapon. Or so it will become, when suitably polished. Conri, I have work for you."

"Yes, Mother," I croaked.

"There's a child. A boy. I've left him with human folk, right on the margin between that realm and this—you know the cottage in the forest, close by the place they call Hag's Head in the human world?"

I did not tell her I'd been watching as she passed her baby boy over to strangers. "Yes, Mother," I said.

"Folk might come looking," she said. "Human folk. The child is too small to be brought to our realm as yet; he requires a tiresome degree of feeding and cleaning. He'll stay with these cottagers for a year or two. I've set a ward over him, of course. But you will watch, also. There will be a certain degree of ill will towards me, I imagine."

"Are not human folk too weak to break these wards, Mother? They have no magic."

She smiled thinly. "These are not your common or garden human folk," she said. "They'll be rather determined, I fear. Conri, you must tell me immediately if you see anyone loitering close to the cottage, or in the woods nearby. And I need to know if my son's guardians become at all careless. I don't anticipate that will happen. They understand the importance of this task, and the punishment that will befall them if they do not fulfil it to my expectations."

"Your son," I said, making my tone suitably surprised. "So I have a little brother."

"Hah!" There was neither affection nor amusement in the sound. "A half-brother, but you'd be wise not to regard him as kin. You will not approach him, Conri. The child is mine only. As soon as he can listen and obey, I will commence his training. He will be subtle; clever; powerful. Ciarán will be my sword of vengeance."

It sounded ridiculous. That little scrap, not long out of swaddling clothes, the instrument of her fell power? Time passed. I watched as his carers tended to him, as he learned to run and to climb, as he began to talk. I watched him solemnly investigating all he discovered. I saw him gazing into tranquil pools; I observed him sitting so quietly the birds came up to perch on his toes. He was still a very small boy when I saw him bring a ripe plum down from high in a tree, right into his hand. Not long after, he sang a fox out of the bracken to lie down by him, obedient as any pet dog. My brother; my clever little brother. The cottagers tended him well, but they had no time for play. I wanted to show him how to catch a ball; how to make a little house in the woods; how to tease minnows into his hand. I wanted him to know he had a brother.

I reported regularly to my mother. "Nobody has come looking for him. Nobody at all." Of the magic, which Ciarán explored further with every passing day, I said not a word.

In time, inevitably, she discovered to her fierce satisfaction that this second son possessed all the potential the first had failed to exhibit, and she began his training. My job as overseer was at an end. I found myself at once relieved and saddened. I was free now to pursue my music. I did so within both worlds, for I could pass for a talented human bard provided I was careful not to reveal my eldritch gifts. Those were meagre enough beside my tiny half-brother's.

I was selfish to step away from him. I knew how cruel she could be; I had experienced her training at first hand. She would not understand the frailty of a small child. She would not care what damage she inflicted. I told myself I could do nothing about it. She was a sorceress, powerful and without conscience. I was a half-and-half. My only assets were a good singing voice and nimble fingers. I reminded myself of this when occasionally I chanced upon my mother and the child working together. My brother's small face had become pinched and pale; his eyes, so like our mother's, were smudged with a bone-deep weariness. I saw her punish him. He took it stoically and tried harder to please. The joyous, instinctive magic he had used as an infant was quite gone. She taught him other skills.

Yes, I was both selfish and a coward. I avoided the clearing where they were accustomed to work, an Otherworld place beyond the eyes of Ciarán's human guardians. I tried to be blind to what she was doing to him. In the human world I found a master harper, a solitary man who made time for me, and I stayed long months with him, learning new skills and sharpening old ones. Ciarán was a prickle on my conscience, but I ignored him. Any attempt to intervene would see us both punished.

I was nearly seventeen; I guessed my brother would be four or five. I went to a Beltane fair and played my harp for dancing. At dusk a great fire was lit on the lakeshore. All knew the forest nearby held portals to the Otherworld. On such a night doors might be left ajar, and lovers who wandered into the woods for a little dalliance might find themselves on a longer journey than they'd anticipated. A perilous spot. Still, that was the traditional fair ground, and there we were, a little merry with good mead, a little dizzy from dancing, a little amorous, as befitted Beltane. At least, the human folk were—I remained detached, concentrating on playing and singing. I reached the end of a jig, looked up and across the throng, and there she was. The firelight glowed on the perfect curve of her cheek; it put a warm glint in her lovely eyes. The breeze blew strands of her dark hair over her brow, and she pushed them back with a graceful hand, smiling. Behind her, the moon shone on the trembling waters of the lake. She was looking at me.

In a heartbeat my life was changed.

With arms entwined, all summer long
We danced to our own secret song
We shone with love's transforming flame
And then—oh, then—the autumn came.

I forgot my mother. I forgot the small shoulders that now carried the weight of the sorceress's expectations. Lóch loved me, and I was new-made. We wandered the forest paths hand in hand. I made sure we kept away from portals to the Otherworld.

We were young, but we made plans. I could earn a living as a bard. Thanks to my maternal line—who would ever have believed I might gain some good from being *her* son?—my skills were already superior to those of human musicians, and I would have no trouble finding work. Lóch wanted a baby. We imagined her, a girl, always a little girl, with dark wisps of hair and eyes the colour of lake water. We would travel north. Lóch's grandmother, who had looked after her since she was an infant, could come with us. We would be a family.

There was no need to spell out my ancestry. My sweetheart had sound instincts, and she saw from the first that I was something unusual. I would not talk about my mother. I would have spoken of my father, but I knew nothing about him. When I'd asked my mother, as a child, she'd said, "It doesn't matter who he was. He fulfilled his purpose. Not especially well, as it turned out." I had seen in her eyes that I must not ask again.

"We'll live wherever you want," I told Lóch as we lay on the grass one warm afternoon. "Just not here." The tide of desire was strong between us, the denial of it a painful pleasure. Her fingers traced delicate patterns on my arm; mine rested against her stomach, the soft sweetness of her body only a thin layer of fabric away. We had sworn we would not lie together until we were married.

We planned to be hand-fasted at Lugnasad, after the prayers of thanks for the season's bounty. Once wed, we would go, away, away, free of the burden of my mother, free of the anxiety and fear and pain she seemed to bring with her no matter how obedient I was to her commands. The freedom that beckoned was not only the opportunity to be with my love as her husband, and to tread a new path with her beside me. It was my chance to be unshackled from my mother's dark ambition.

"Conri," said Lóch, raising herself on one elbow to study my face. "You look so sad sometimes. So troubled. What is it, dear heart?"

"Nothing," I said. "I'm trying to remember the words of a ballad, but the rhyme's eluding me." I sat up and tickled her nose with a blade of grass until she was helpless with laughter, and the shadow was forgotten.

Lóch's grandmother liked me, but she wanted us to wait. We were so young, she said, too young to see anything but an easy future. The prospect of leaving the cottage where she had brought up her orphaned granddaughter, and the friends she had in the district, and everything familiar, was frightening to her. Well, she was old by human standards, and I almost understood how she felt, but I knew we must leave. If we stayed close to this forest we would be within my mother's reach for all of our lives.

My musical skill was not the only thing I had inherited from my mother's line. I would live far longer than Lóch; I would continue to look young as she gradually aged. I dismissed this, certain my love for her was strong enough to withstand any test. Like many folk of mixed heritage, I had the ability to turn the minds of human folk one way or another—charm, one might call it, though not a charm in the sense of a spell, more a gift for choosing the right tone, the right words, the right look of the eyes to persuade a person to a certain way of thinking. I never used it on Lóch. She chose me for myself, for the man I was. I shied away from all magic, for I wanted to be human, not fey. But when Lóch's grandmother put her foot down, determined that we should wait at least a year to be sure of our minds, I used it on her. It was not long before the old woman was saying the plan was a fine one, and of course we were old enough, at seventeen, to be wed and journeying and thinking of a baby. So the hand-fasting was set for Lugnasad. We'd be married as soon as the harvest ritual was over, and straight away we would head north to a place where there were some cousins of Lóch's dead father. We packed up the cottage; there was little enough in it.

"What about your things, Conri?" Lóch asked. "Clothes, tools, all your possessions?" She had never asked me where I lived. I thought perhaps she did not want to know. Of recent times I'd been sleeping at the cottage, chastely on a bench while Lóch and her grandmother shared the bed.

I was about to reply that the only possession that mattered was my harp, but I realised it was not quite true. I had a little box, back in the Otherworld, with objects I had collected through the uncomfortable years of my childhood, treasures I had taken out at night after the day's failures and punishments were over. Holding and stroking each in turn, I had been comforted by their familiarity. I did not want to leave that box behind. Besides, Lóch was right about clothing. In the human world one had to consider such activities as washing and mending. Before I was quite done with the Otherworld, my mother's world, I must make one last trip back.

Ten days before Lugnasad, on a morning of bitter wind, I slipped across the margin and fetched my box from the cave where I had hidden it. I took a cloak, a pair of boots, a favourite hat. I spoke to one or two folk, not saying I was leaving, and discovered that my mother had gone away to the south. Nobody knew if it was a short trip or a long one. I breathed more easily. With luck, she would not return until Lóch and I were far away.

I emerged into the human world close by the cottage where Ciarán and his keepers lived, a low, secluded place nestled at the foot of the crag called Hag's Head, and surrounded by rowans. Why did I choose that way? Who knows? As I passed the place I heard a sound that stopped me in my tracks. It could have been me weeping like that, in little tight sobs as I tried to hold the pain inside, so nobody would hear me and know how weak I truly was. I found that I could not walk on by.

He was scrunched into a hollow between the rocks, arms wrapped around himself, knees up, head down. The bones of his shoulder, fragile as a bird's, showed under the white skin, through a rip in his tunic. His hair was longer now, and the hue of a dark flame. He heard me coming, soft-footed as I was, and every part of him tensed.

"Ciarán?" It was awkward; he did not know me.

The small head came up. The dark mulberry eyes, reddened with tears, fixed their stare on me. He was like a little wild animal at bay, quivering with the need for flight. And yet not like, for there was a knowledge in those sad eyes that chilled me. My brother was too young for this.

I squatted down at a short distance, putting my belongings on the ground. "Did she hurt you?" I asked.

Not a word. She had threatened him, no doubt, to keep him from speaking to passers-by.

"Ciarán," I said quietly, "my name is Conri. We both have the same mother. That makes us brothers."

He understood; I saw an unlikely hope flame in his eyes. Impossibilities flooded through my mind: *we could take him with us, we could hide, perhaps she would never find us.* And then, cruellest of all: *I should not go away. I should stay for his sake.*

"Conri." Ciarán tried out the sound of it. "When is my father coming?"

The hairs on my neck rose. Surely he could not remember his father. I'd seen how little the boy was when she brought him here: too young to understand any of it. But then, this was no ordinary child.

"I don't know, Ciarán." *Don't ask if you can come with me.* Already, so quickly, he had a grip on my heart. Why in the Dagda's name had I passed this way? "I have to go now."

"Will you come back?"

I drew a shaky breath. There would be no lying to this particular child. "I don't know." It was woefully inadequate. "Ciarán, I have something for you." I reached across and picked up my treasure box. My brother edged closer as I opened the lid. It was a meagre enough collection, but each item was precious to me. What to give him?

"Here," I said, picking out a stone with swirling patterns of red and grey, a secret language ancient as myth. "I found this up in the hills beyond the western end of the lake. Earth and fire."

His fingers closed around it. "Thank you," he whispered. "Goodbye, Conri."

"Goodbye, little brother." Morrigan's curse, tears were starting in my eyes, and they trembled in my voice. The longer I stayed, the worse this would be for the two of us. I gathered my belongings, turned my back and walked away.

Eight days until Lugnasad and our wedding. There was no point in looking backwards. I could not save Ciarán. Even if Lóch had not existed, even if I had been prepared to sacrifice my own life for my brother's sake, and stay where she could find and torment me daily, the sorceress would never have allowed me a part in his future. If Ciarán was to be her tool, she would not want his edge blunted by weakness, or his true metal tarnished by love. I could do nothing for him.

So there was a thread of sorrow and regret in the shimmering garment of our happiness. All the same, Lóch prepared for the ritual with bright eyes, and both she and her grandmother professed themselves ready for the adventure that lay ahead. Lóch and I embraced under the shelter of the trees, our bodies pressed tight, desire making our breath falter. Our hearts hammered one against the other. Our wedding night could not come quickly enough.

Six days until Lugnasad, and both Lóch and her grandmother had gone to the far side of the lake to bid farewell to an old friend, a crippled woman who would not be coming to the celebrations. They would be gone all day. I planned to spend the time practising the harp, for we'd been busy of late and I had neglected my craft. With the two of them to support, and perhaps soon a babe as well,

I'd need to maintain my technique and keep on making new songs. Folk soon weary of a bard who repeats himself.

I worked all morning and by midday I was growing thirsty. I decided to go down to the local hostelry for a cup or two of ale. While I was sitting there minding my own business, a man came in. I looked at him once and I looked twice, for there was something familiar in that face. The fellow was quite old, with many white threads in his dark hair. His face was a map of experience. Despite his years, there was a strength in every part of him, like the tenacity of a wind-scourged tree. He wore plain traveller's garb, a grey cloak, well-worn boots of best quality. A broad-brimmed hat; a dagger at his belt. No bag. I studied the face again, and this time knew where I had seen it before.

The traveller looked around, then approached the innkeeper.

"Ale, my lord?" The innkeeper had sized up the newcomer and was greeting him accordingly.

"Share a jug with me," I put in quickly, indicating that the traveller should come to sit at my table. "I'll pay."

The traveller's grey eyes narrowed, assessing me. My mother's words came back to me, sharp and clear: *These are not your common or garden human folk. They'll be rather determined, I fear.* Then the man walked over and seated himself opposite me.

I waited for the ale to come. I did not ask any of the questions he might have been expecting, such as *Where are you headed?* and *Where are you from?* Instead, for the time it took for the innkeeper to bring the jug, I let myself dream. What if this strong, sad-looking stranger was *my* father, come to fetch me? What if he had been looking for me all these years, seventeen whole years, and now he was going to bring me home, and I would meet my family, and Lóch and I could live in a place where I truly belonged?

"Are you from these parts?" the man asked diffidently as I poured the ale.

"Close by." I wondered if he glimpsed my mother in me. I wondered if he was as good at guesswork as I was.

"Been here long?"

"All my life. My name is Conri."

"Mm." He acknowledged it with a courteous nod, but did not offer his own in return. After a moment he added, "Why would you buy me a drink, Conri?"

My heart thumping, I said, "You're a stranger in these parts. I imagine you may be here for a particular reason."

"You imagine correctly." I could almost see his mind working. He needed information, but speaking to the wrong person might put his whole plan in jeopardy. "What kind of trade do you ply?" He glanced at my hands.

"I'm a musician. Soon to be wed. We'll be travelling to live with kinsfolk in the north."

He nodded. This answer seemed to satisfy him. "Know all the locals, do you?"

"Most. Are you looking for someone?"

"A child. A boy."

"I see." I traced a finger around the rim of my ale cup, thinking he must indeed be tenacious if he thought to pit his human skills against her uncanny ones, his honest strength against her overweening ambition. "A small boy or a bigger one?"

It was in my voice, no doubt: the knowledge. The fear. When he spoke again his tone was hushed, so nobody else could hear, and there was an edge in it. "He'd be five years old by now. Red hair; pale skin; unusual eyes, the colour of ripe mulberries."

"Your son?" I kept my own voice down.

"Never mind that. Have you seen him?"

I thought of my mother's wrath. I thought of Ciarán with my gift in his hand and his eyes full of shadows. "There is a child who meets that description living nearby," I whispered. "But there are . . . risks. High risks, my lord." Oh, how his eyes came alight as I spoke! The selfsame look had kindled on my brother's small face when I told him we were kin, and died when I bade him farewell.

"How do I know I can trust you?" Ciarán's father asked.

"I might ask you the same question," I said. "But I will not. I think the two of us want the same thing: for the boy to be safe. Where would you take him? How could you keep him out of danger?"

He looked at me. I saw the strength written in his face, and the suffering. "If I tell you," he said, "those who seek to harm him can get the answers from you and hunt him down. So I will not tell. But there is a place where he can be protected, and I will take him there. His father and his brothers will keep him safe."

"Brothers?" I echoed, somewhat taken aback to think there were more of us out there.

The stranger glanced towards the unglazed window of the inn. I had thought this a solitary journey, a father's lonely quest to claim his lost son. But this man was no fool. He'd brought reinforcements. The two of them were standing out the front waiting for him, youngish men made very much in his own mould, with pale, intense faces, keen eyes, unsmiling mouths. Weaponry of various kinds hung about them. The father hadn't needed to carry a pack; each of his sons bore one. His sons, but not hers. There was no touch of the uncanny on these hard-faced warriors.

"Half-brothers."

It was not a question, but I thought it needed an answer. "I only have one half-brother," I said. "Promise me he will be safe, and I will show you where he is." Fear dripped through me like ice water. "But understand the danger, for all of us."

"Oh, I understand." His voice was like iron. "You are her son?"

I would not answer so direct a question. "I will show you," I said. "The best time is early morning, not long after dawn. You must be prepared to leave quickly and travel swiftly. At present she is not here, but she may return at any time. Weapons such as those your sons bear will not help you in this struggle."

"Come," he said, rising to his feet.

The two sons were wary; everything about them spoke distrust. I bore some resemblance to my mother, and while I did not know their story, I imagined she had wrought havoc amongst their family. Unsurprising, then, that they did not warm to me. But they did their father's bidding, and a plan was made. We would camp out in the woods overnight, close to the cottage. We would move in before dawn and take him. They had horses stabled nearby, and could travel swiftly. And they had one or two other tricks, they said, but nobody told me what those were.

I prayed that my mother's visit to the south would be a lengthy one, though I knew Ciarán's training would call her back soon; her methods required that the student not be allowed time to mull over what she was doing to him. If she discovered this plan, all of us would be caught up in her fury. By Danu's sweet mercy, it was a risk indeed.

"We must make a pact of silence, Conri," the nobleman said when the four of us were out of doors, under the trees, working out how it would unfold. "Neither I nor my sons here will mention your name, whatever pressure is applied to us. None of us will say how we found the boy. In return, you will not speak of what happened. You will cover our tracks as best you can. You will do all in your power to avoid laying a trail. If you love your little brother, and it seems to me that is so, you will do what you can to ensure he is not hurt."

Not hurt? Ciarán had already been hurt so badly the scars of it would be with him all his life. "I will honour the pact," I said. "As I said, I'm to be married at Lugnasad. We won't be making our home here."

"I wish you joy," he said quietly. "Now take us close to the place. We must remain in cover until it's time."

I wondered what Lóch would think when she came home and found the cottage empty. I'd have to invent a story to cover my overnight absence. It felt wrong to lie to her, but she could not know the truth. If this worked, if Ciarán escaped, my mother would be brutal in her efforts to track the perpetrators down. The thought that her touch might reach my sweetheart curdled my blood and froze my heart within me. *Let the sorceress stay away. Let us be gone when she returns.*

I think Ciarán knew. His eldritch abilities were exceptional. As the first dawn light touched the leaves of the rowans, a small form slipped out the cottage door, a hooded cloak concealing his bright hair. He moved across the open ground as swiftly as a creature evading predators, which, in a way, was exactly what he was. I glanced at the father's face, just once, and saw the glint of tears. The nobleman squatted down as the child approached us where we stood under the trees. Ciarán stopped two paces away, a tiny, upright figure, preternaturally still.

I think the father was intending to re-introduce himself, to reassure, to explain quickly the need for silence and flight. After all, his son had been a baby when they last met.

"Papa?" The small voice was held quiet. The child understood that this must be covert.

"I've come to take you home, Ciarán." The grimmest of warriors could not have kept his tone steady, under the circumstances. "We must go now, and as quietly as we can. Shall I carry you?"

Ciarán shook his head. He put a hand in his father's, as if they had been parted only from twilight till dawn, and they set off side by side. At the rear, uneasily, came the two brothers and I.

It felt as if I scarcely breathed while we made our way out of the forest and along the lake to the place where their horses were stabled. I waited at a distance while they retrieved the beasts; the fewer people saw me in their company, the fewer could make a link if my mother came asking. They mounted. Ciarán was seated before his father in the saddle.

"Thank you," the nobleman said gravely. "I understand what you have risked for him. I am in your debt."

"Ride safely," I said. "I don't suppose we will meet again. Goodbye, Ciarán." I saw, looking at him, that while he was my mother's son, a child with more than his share of the uncanny, he was also a human boy of five, scared, excited, almost overwhelmed by what had happened. "The blessing of Danu be always on you, little brother."

He allowed himself a smile. "And on you, Conri," he said, and they rode away. Perhaps Ciarán's father did not understand that an ordinary human man could not break a sorceress's protective charm, however strong and determined he might be. But I understood, and I recognised in that moment that without the innate talent of the child himself, this rescue mission could never have been accomplished.

Lugnasad morn: the dawn of our wedding day. The cottage had been promised to a local family down on their luck; they had paid only a token sum for the use of it. The grandmother had traded her house cow for a creaky cart and an ancient horse. I doubted either would last as far as our destination, the place where these cousins lived. Nonetheless, as soon as the hand-fasting ritual was over we were heading north. We would make camp by the wayside, and our wedding night would be spent under the stars.

Lóch sent me out of the house while she put on her finery. It was a surprise, she told me with twinkling eyes. I had seen her gown already. In a tiny cottage, there is little room for secrets. But I kissed her and went outside anyway. We had a small supply of good hay we'd kept aside to give the horse a strengthening meal before we started out. I'd take that down to the field, not hurrying over it. By the time I got back Lóch would be ready.

One moment I was standing by the dry-stone wall, feeding the horse by hand. The next I was flat on my back, held immobile in the grip of a spell. I could not move so much as my little finger. I looked up and into my mother's eyes.

"*Where is he?*"

There was only one feeling in me, and that was terror—not for myself, not for Ciarán, who should be well away by now, but for Lóch. I didn't make a sound. I couldn't have told my mother what she wanted anyway. The charm she had set on me made every breath a mountain to climb. Speak? Hardly.

"Where is he, Conri? Tell me! *Vanished in the night,* his keepers said. A child of that age does not wander off on his own." Her face was a spectral white, her eyes wine-dark. Her voice scourged me. "Speak, Conri! What did you see? Who came? Which way did they go?"

I lay mute, staring up at her like a dullard who cannot understand plain words. With a very small part of my mind, the part I was able to shield, I willed Lóch not to come out and look for me.

"What is the matter with you, wretched boy? While you tend to horses like a feeble-minded farm hand, and no doubt waste day after day on your endless hummings and tinklings, my son has disappeared from under your nose! You fool, Conri, you stupid, treacherous fool! Tell me! You must know! Tell me who has taken him!" She relaxed her spell a little; she wanted me capable of speech.

If I lied, she would recognise it instantly. If I told the truth she would be off after them in a moment. My silence could win them precious time. I lay there, looking up at her, and spoke not a word.

"Come." My mother clicked her fingers. Now I could move. I could move in one direction only, and that was after her. A good thing. She led me away from Lóch, away from the grandmother, away from the cottage and into the forest. She led me, a dog on an invisible chain, across the margin and into the Otherworld. We stood in the shade of the oaks, the sorceress and I, and in my mind I offered an apology to my little brother, and another to his father, and my regrets to the two hard-faced men who were Ciarán's half-brothers. I had not particularly liked them, but I had respected them. I had seen the bonds of family there, a phenomenon previously unknown to me. I hoped those bonds were strong enough to withstand a sorceress's fury.

"Very well, Conri." My mother's face was calm now. She knew I could not run, not with her spell on me. She knew how easily I had bent and broken before her punishments in the years of my growing to a man. "I can ensure you never set your fingers to the harp strings again. I can turn you into a twisted, crippled apology for a man. I can do this in the space of an eye blink. There is one way you can save yourself, and that is by telling me what you know. Now, Conri. Right now."

My heart thudded like a war drum; my skin broke out in cold sweat. She didn't know about Lóch. Somehow, all summer long, she had been so engrossed in her new project, honing her human weapon, that she had taken her eyes right off me. She had not seen that I had fallen in love. She had threatened my hands; she had threatened my body. She had not used the threat that I most feared. Oh gods, if only I could be strong, both Ciarán and Lóch might be spared my mother's wrath.

I drew a deep breath. "I know nothing," I said. "Nothing at all."

I expected pain, and she delivered it. I put my teeth through my lip; I bloodied my palms with my nails. At a certain point I lost control of my bladder, ruining my wedding clothes. The sun rose higher. The Lugnasad ritual would be starting, and Lóch would be cross with me. I tried not to think of her. The most probing, the most penetrating charm my mother could devise must never find the small, safe place where my dear one was hidden, deep in my heart.

My mother must soon come to believe I had nothing to tell her, surely. I had never held out so long before. Always, eventually, I had delivered what she wanted once the punishment reached a certain level. Back then, I had not had Lóch to think of. Or my brother. I was starting to understand about family. As I writhed, I allowed hope in. *Soon she'll give up on me. She'll leave me here and head off to wherever she gave birth to him, and I can creep back over the margin. Lóch will forgive me. We can be wed tomorrow . . .*

The sun rose higher still. The harvest ritual would be over; the folk of the village would be celebrating with mead and games. Lóch would be upset, worried.

Through the tears and blood and sweat I saw a change in my mother's eyes. She stood very still, so still that only a person familiar with all her moods, as I was, would have realised what fury possessed her. "You know something," she said. "You have lied to me; you have held something back. I cannot wait any longer, Conri. Someone's taken my jewel, my treasure, my son. Not his father; I left that man fit for nothing but dribbling into his beard. It will have been one of the brothers. They'll have taken him back to Sevenwaters, thinking to hide him in the nemetons. Fools. Not one of them can outpace me, outride me, outwit me."

I thought of Ciarán. Might not my exceptional little brother and his formidable kinsmen stand strong even against her? *Hold your silence, Conri.* I was almost beyond speech anyway. My lip was split; my jaw was on fire. Every part of me hurt. I was glad Lóch could not see me.

"I knew you'd never amount to much," my mother said, and one elegantly-shod foot came out to deliver a casual kick in the ribs.

And then, ah then, when she might have headed off on her quest and left me lying, a pathetic bundle of rags and bloodied, filthy flesh splayed amongst the hard roots of a great oak, I had to open my mouth, didn't I? I had to speak. Fool. Bitter, hopeless fool. "In the end," I whispered, "Ciarán will turn against you. He will defeat you. I know it." And I did, though how, I could not have said. Not magic. Not the Sight. But deep in the bone, I knew.

Looking in her eyes, beyond terror, I believed she would kill me. I was wrong. I believed she would find Lóch and destroy her. I was wrong there, too. What my mother did was set a *geis* on me.

"Conri son of Oonagh," she said, raising both hands so the full sleeves of her robe spread out like wings, the fine blue fabric rippling in the forest breeze, "you will pay the price for your disobedience!"

I was starting to feel very odd, as if the aching in my joints, the nausea, the burning and stinging and tearing sensations had been only a prelude to the grand tune of the day. Now I itched all over. My skin began to sprout like a field of new-sown wheat, save that this crop was night-black. My lips pushed forward, tightened, hardened; my throat began to close up. My limbs shrivelled. *A twisted cripple of a man* . . . She was doing it. She would make me a man unfit to wed, unable to earn a living . . . *Lóch loves you, Conri. Hold onto that. She will love you no matter what kind of monster you become.* Gods! I was shrinking, changing, my clothing falling off me, my feet becoming . . . my feet becoming . . . claws . . .

"From this day forth, Conri, take the form of a raven! You will live in this bodily shape, but your mind will not change. Every moment you will understand what your life might have been, had you not chosen to defy me!"

Raven. I was a raven. A dazzle of colour assaulted my eyes; all was light. Tiny sounds came clear to me from high in the canopy: chirp, rustle, whisper. I turned my head one way and the other, and the dizziness made me stagger on my splayed bird-feet. No wonder my skin itched so. I had sprouted feathers.

"Fifteen years will you live thus, as a wild creature. When those fifteen years are done you will regain the form of a man. You'd best live solitary, Conri. For should any man or woman know who you are, should anyone at all recognise you as the man who dared thwart me, or as my son, or as Ciarán's half-brother, or as the fellow who used to play the harp in these parts, should anyone know you and call you by your name before those fifteen years are up, you will be condemned to stay in that form—" She paused, the word *forever* trembling on her lips. Perhaps the knowledge that we were kin stopped her; or perhaps she simply wanted to make this more entertaining, as is the nature of *geasa* generally. She was nothing if not inventive. "Until a woman agrees to marry you in your bird shape," she said. And after a pause for reflection, "A woman of *that* family. The Sevenwaters family." There was an unpleasant smile on her lips, a smile that told me how likely such a means of salvation must be. "None of them would ever agree," she added. "Not after what I did to them. The shadow of it will hang over generation on generation. Make sure nobody knows you, Conri. Fly away, foolish musician, fly far, far away. *And never meddle in my affairs again.*"

Cursed to remain in raven form
I left Lóch on our wedding morn.
No word could speak, no story tell.
My life became not heav'n, but hell.

My mother could hardly have pronounced a crueller *geis* if she had known all about Lóch and our plans for the future. Fifteen years. In fifteen years' time, Lóch would be well past the safe age for childbearing. In fifteen years, her grandmother would be gone. For all that time I'd be incapable of providing for anyone but myself. Worse still, I had no way to explain to Lóch what had happened; why I had vanished on our wedding day with not a word, not a sign, not a clue. I could not even watch over her. There were only two people in the world, barring my mother, who I believed might recognise me in the form of a raven. One was my clever little brother. The other was the woman who loved me. If I were ever to be a man again, and if Lóch were ever to be my wife, I must keep out of her sight for fifteen years.

I stayed close, but not too close. And so I watched as it unfolded, the disaster I had brought down on the one I loved. The cottage was already promised; the cow was already sold. Lóch and her grandmother waited a while for me, relying on the hospitality of friends. The grandmother thought I had bolted, suddenly frightened of the responsibilities of marriage. Lóch refused to believe it. Some harm had come to me, she said; but I was strong and courageous, and eventually I would make my way back to her. I would have wept at that, if I could.

When others were growing weary of housing the two of them, they took up the old plan and headed north. I followed, unable to do more than keep an eye on them, but finding it impossible to leave. Lóch looked sad and tired; the grandmother was stoical, tending to the horse, finding firewood, saying little. I made an error, coming too close one day when I saw Lóch weeping by the fire, her head in her hands, her lovely shining hair lank and lifeless across her shoulders. She had taken off her boots. Her feet were red with blisters. Perched on a branch nearby, I was startled when she raised her head suddenly and looked straight at me.

"You again," she said, and smiled. I was possessed by the longing to wing down and alight beside her, to feel the gentle touch of her hand, to offer what comfort I could. But I saw in her eyes that I had already come too close. My broken heart cracked anew as I spread my wings and flew away, away, where there was no chance at all that she would see me. I could offer her nothing at all.

Fifteen years. Lóch and I were seventeen when the *geis* was set on me; its term was almost our whole lives again. My imagination, trapped inside my bird form, ran riot with what could happen in such a time. I was a bard; I conjured up tragedies of a grand and entertaining nature. Well, I have said already that my tale was a sad one, and that much was true. Grand and entertaining, no. Just full of helpless, useless tears.

From this point on, it is short enough to tell. The early years passed. Lóch's grandmother died within two winters of my transformation, carried off by an old people's sickness, a cough, a loss of appetite, a quick fading. They had given up the search for their kinsfolk when the horse could not manage the distance, and had instead established themselves in a tumbledown hut abandoned by earlier tenants who perhaps feared the encroaching forest with its shadowy strangeness, its mysterious night time noises. Lóch eked out a living. She turned her hand to whatever tasks the season demanded, helping local farmers with haymaking or pear-picking or minding children. I could not leave her; it would have been like cutting out half my soul. I lived in the woods near her little house, making sure I saw but was not seen. I learned the habits of a wild creature. Sometimes it seemed to me I was losing myself, becoming more raven than man, until I saw Lóch coming home, a slight, purposeful figure, thinner now, the gentle curve of her cheek turned to a sharper line, her gaze watchful. On her own, living so far from other dwellings, she had an eye out for the perils one might expect in such a situation, and once or twice I saw her drive off a foolish fellow with her pitchfork. She was waiting for me. Four years on, five years on, she was still waiting.

I never saw my mother. I tried not to think of her, but bitterness grew in me with every passing season. I wondered if she had found Ciarán, or whether my silence, maintained at so great a cost, had won my little brother freedom and a place in the heart of his family. I felt some pangs of jealousy. Under the circumstances, that was not unreasonable. I began to understand how resentment and fury could drive a person mad. I did not want any insights into my mother's mind, but they came to me anyway. If I had possessed the means to destroy her I would have done it without a second thought. The wide-eyed bard who had fallen in love with a girl between firelight and water was no more. The raven was a different creature. With every passing year, some of my mother's darkness crept into my spirit.

You could imagine, I suppose, various endings to the tale of Lóch and Conri. I have said already that it did not follow the path of *happy ever after*. I watched her; she waited for me. By the time ten years had passed, Lóch had cleared a good-sized area around her cottage and established a garden, in which she grew not only vegetables for her own use, but a variety of herbs. She had taught herself certain healing skills, and received frequent visits from folk in search of simples. My love had a circle of friends and was no longer alone. She had admirers, too, men whom I hated for the way they looked at her, but she refused every offer of marriage. I dared not come close enough to hear what she said to them, but I imagined it. *I will not wed. I'm waiting for my sweetheart to come home.* After ten years, folk must have found this more than a little odd.

It happened in summer, late in the afternoon. Lóch had been working in the garden, and I watching her from a position high in the boughs of an oak, well screened from her sight. I loved the lines and curves of her body in the practical homespun she wore. I could see how time was changing her, but for me she would always be the perfect creature I had seen that very first night, the fire on her face, the moon at her back, the woman who had looked at me and made my heart hers in an instant.

Lóch had a work table outdoors, a place where she could enjoy the sun while preparing vegetables for the pot or herbs for drying. I gazed down from my branch, and it seemed to me every movement she made was a poem, and every glance from her weary eyes was a song. She lost her balance, her ankle turning as she trod on a stone. The knife in her hand slipped. I heard her cry out, and I saw the blood flowing from her arm, a crimson stream, welling, spurting . . . Lóch snatched up a cloth, pressed it against the red tide. The cloth filled with blood, the stream dyed her gown, her face went ashen pale. She fell to her knees, too weak to hold the staunching rag in place. So quick, oh, gods, so quick . . .

I flew to her, bird-heart rattling in bird-breast, dark wings beating a panic song, shock driving the *geis* right out of my consciousness. I tried to help her. I tried, I tried. Where were my human hands that could press the cloth hard against the ebbing life? Where was my human voice that could shout for help? Where was my human strength, so I could pick her up and run to the nearest house? Gone, all gone. Nothing I could do would save her.

Lóch lay where she had fallen, her sweet features filmed with sweat, her skin pale as moonlight. With a fold of cloth held in my beak, witness of my futile attempt to stem the flow of blood, I stood by her right shoulder, my bird-eyes fixed on hers. *Beloved. Oh, beloved.*

She tried to speak; her lips moved, searching for words. I remembered the *geis* then, and cared nothing at all for it. Lóch was dying; I could not help her. I had failed her. If she was gone it mattered nothing whether I lived or died, whether I was bird or man. Without her I had no life. In that moment, all I wanted was that she look at me and know me, know that I had kept faith all these years, as she had. Know that I had not deserted her; know that I loved her still.

A film was creeping over her eyes; her breath faltered. *Oh, Lóch. Don't leave me. Don't leave me all alone. I love you. More than the moon and stars, more than the pure notes of the harp, more than the whole world. Lóch. Lóch, my love.*

She snatched a rasping breath. The dying eyes turned on me, sweet and steadfast as always. "Conri," she whispered. "I knew you'd come." And she was gone.

There was a long time in the wilderness. Heedless of danger, caring nothing if I lived or died, I came close to starving myself, and closer to killing myself by other means, but the fey part of me made that a harder task than it might have been. As for the *geis*, it was no longer of any significance. I'd be a bird forever. What did that matter? I had nothing. I had nobody. I was less a raven than a festering mass of bitterness and sorrow, and if I became a man again, I did not think I would be a man worth knowing. So I wandered, and the years passed. I never took a mate; I never kept company with other ravens, for wild birds shunned me, sensing my difference. All feared me: man, the predator. Hah! If only they knew what a helpless, hopeless creature I truly was. If Lóch had not loved me, she would by now have been happily wed, with children half-grown and a man who could warm her bed and provide for her. Loving me had destroyed her.

I do not know what changed in me. Perhaps it was visiting the hill where once I had picked up a stone patterned in red and grey: fire and earth. Perhaps it was seeing a man with his two little sons, walking on a lake shore and laughing. I remembered that I was not quite alone. If my sacrifice and Lóch's had not been in vain, somewhere in the north I had a brother. Ciarán would be a man now, close to the age his sombre half-brothers had been when they came for him. I remembered the name Sevenwaters. I considered the bitter, cynical, hopeless creature I was now, and knew I could not bear to live on like this, summer after summer, winter after winter, for all the lengthy span allotted to a half-and-half like myself. If I did not manage to make an end of myself, I would live far longer than the lifetime of an ordinary man. So would Ciarán. I went to find him.

"Ready to go?" he asks now. So lost have I been in my reverie that the lesson is finished, the novices have departed without my noticing, and Ciarán is watching me quizzically, his travelling bag strapped up and ready in his hand. Today we head off into the forest for a few days' solitude. It is our habit to make these quiet journeys from time to time. Ciarán gathers herbs, prays, meditates. I keep him company, making myself useful when I can.

We've been together many, many years. His father brought him safely to the nemetons but died not long after, and Ciarán was raised by the druids. A choice was made to let the boy forget what little he knew of his origins. He grew up unaware that his father had been lord of Sevenwaters. In time, that proved costly indeed.

Ciarán became a fine man; a better man than I ever would have been. He had his own share of sorrows. Love drew him away from the druid path awhile. What our mother did to him and his sweetheart was crueller than the punishment she meted out to Lóch and me. Ciarán rose above it. My brother; my strong, clear-headed brother.

"Come, then," he says. I fly to perch on his shoulder, and together we walk off into the forest of Sevenwaters.

☽

~ *Aisha* ~

"Go," my father said. "Go and find out for yourself."

It was fair enough. I was a woman grown, and though there were certain expectations I had not fulfilled—by my age, a woman was supposed to have a husband and children—my life so far had contained more than its share of adventures. I could always rise to a challenge. I was my father's daughter, wasn't I? He'd done both, the adventures and the family. It was family we were discussing now, the shadowy, mysterious part of it that was away to the northwest in Erin. I'd travelled to many places, but never there.

"I will," I replied. "And you can come with me."

Father laughed, his eyes crinkling up. He had my smallest half-brother, Luis, on his knee and was whirling a wooden rattle. The baby reached for it, shrieking with delight. "Me? I'm an old man, Aisha."

In years, perhaps he was. He didn't look old, save for the touch of snow in his dark hair and those smile lines on his sun-browned skin. "Is that what Mercedes says?" I asked, knowing my stepmother said nothing of the sort. Mercedes was a few years my junior: my father's third wife, and mother of his youngest children. Ours was a noisy, busy establishment that saw a constant stream of visitors, mostly folk from the village wanting Father's advice on matters of law or religion or the care of sick animals. He had become a father to all of them since we settled here. His seafaring days were done; in that sense, perhaps he was old, but there was a vigour about him like that of an aged olive tree, hardy, tough, his roots sunk deep in the land. And fruitful; the children kept coming. The place was full of toddlers and animals—Father had never learned to resist the pleading eyes of a homeless dog.

"Never mind that," he said now. "You go. Sail on the *Sofia* when Fernando next takes her to Dublin. You're an enterprising girl, Aisha; you can make your own way from there."

"And what do I do when I get to Sevenwaters? March up to the front door and say, Good morning, I'm your—what, great-niece?

Second cousin? Sorry my father couldn't come; it's only been forty years."

"Closer to fifty," Father said, lifting Luis up against his shoulder. "Just as well I taught my children Irish. At least you'll be able to introduce yourself. Tell them your father's a doddering ancient who has trouble hobbling as far as the front door. Tell them whatever you like."

I wondered, for the hundredth time, why the bonds of family had not drawn him home in all those years. With his ships loading and unloading in Dublin regularly, he could easily have gone. Sevenwaters was not so very far north of that port, provided one could negotiate the borders between Norse and Irish territories, which were under ongoing dispute. But while Father had a hundred stories of his boyhood, and a hundred more about heroes, monsters and warrior women, he never talked about what might have become of his kin since he last saw them.

"I don't want to know, Aisha," he said, reading my thoughts on my face. "Every time I got news, in those first years after I left, it was bad news. My brothers dying, one after another, all uselessly. The borders shrinking; war and madness. Besides, I like the sun. It's always raining in those parts. And I'd miss Mercedes and the little ones." After a moment he added, "I suppose Conor may be still alive—your druid uncle. It's been a long time. And my nephew may still be chieftain at Sevenwaters; he was only a lad when my eldest brother died. But they'll be strangers to you, despite the tie of blood."

It was hard to think of my father's family as strangers. They were in the most enthralling of his stories, the one that told of a disaster that had nearly destroyed them all. It included a wicked stepmother—when I thought of Mercedes, this made me laugh, for my father's rosy-cheeked, smiling young wife was as far from that figure as I could imagine—and a transformation wrought by magic, six brothers turned into swans and saved only by their sister's courage and endurance. My father had been one of them. I knew those boys from the inside out. I knew the intensity of their anguish; I felt their terror; I understood their guilt. I knew them up till the point when the ordeal was over and my father, Padriac, who was the youngest of them, decided to walk away from Sevenwaters and never look back. And yet they were not real.

They were characters in a story, like Cu Chulainn the great hero, or Emer who was turned into a fly. The notion of meeting them in the flesh felt very strange. They would be old now. But perhaps they were like Father. I only had to look into his eyes to see the boy there, the same who had once splinted the legs and salved the wounds of injured creatures in Erin, and who still did it here in Xixón, far from the shores of home.

"You must miss it sometimes," I said. "You must miss them."

"My life is rich, Aisha," said Father, patting his son rhythmically on the back. Luis was hungry; the rattle of pots and pans from the cooking area told me Mercedes was preparing a meal. "I've made my home wherever I travelled. And you are your mother's daughter, my dear. A restless soul; an adventurer. So go, and go with my blessing. When you come back, I'll be ready to hear the tale."

I owed it to both of them, to Father who had always trusted me, no matter how wild an adventure I attempted, and to Mother who had perished at sea while working as his first mate, to go ahead with the plan that had sprung from nowhere. Two months later, I was stepping off the *Sofia* in Dublin, where my general appearance caused bystanders to gawk and whisper behind their hands. What went relatively unremarked in Galicia was clearly the height of exoticism in this town of wheat-fair, pale-skinned Norsemen and slight, dark Irish. I'd offered to give Fernando a hand with the unloading, but he'd declined, saying I'd only attract crowds that would get in his way. So I wished him well and headed off on my own, telling him I'd pick up a lift home when next he made landfall here.

There were one or two incidents by the wayside. Not every traveller in Erin is a respecter of womenfolk, but I'd had plenty of practice at fending off advances of various kinds; there were years and years of dented skulls and bruised privates behind me. At a wayside inn I arm-wrestled a local farmer for a jug of ale and ended up sharing it with him and his friends. I didn't talk any more than I needed to. Demonstrating my fluent Irish would only mean all sorts of questions, and idle curiosity bored me. With Father's map in my head and a sailor's sense of direction—I'd captained the *Sofia* for Fernando more than once—I headed north to Sevenwaters.

I reached the edge of the forest at dusk. I had seen plenty of forests in my time, back home in Xixón and in other parts of the world on one voyage or another. Hot, damp forests full of bright birds and howling creatures. Cold, crisp, empty forests where snow bent the boughs of fir and spruce, and bears lay in winter dreams. This was less forest than blanket of darkness, lying over hill and valley in mysterious, shadowy silence. I decided to camp overnight and go on by daylight. It wasn't just the brooding quiet of the place, the sense of its being somewhere out of ordinary time and space. There were guard posts to north and south, well-manned even at this hour. Likely the whole forest was ringed by them. I didn't suppose those guards would put an arrow through me first and ask questions later. But they might well try to apprehend me. I hadn't decided yet how I would introduce myself to my father's long-lost family, but I knew I didn't intend to walk into their hall with a spear shoved in my back and some man at arms announcing that he'd caught me spying.

It was a cold night. I made no fire, but slept rolled in my blanket. Soon after dawn I packed up and set out into the forest. Somewhere in these woods there was a lake, a big one. Beside the lake was a keep, and in that keep lived the family of Sevenwaters, my father's kin.

Father had warned me about the paths through this forest, both directly, when he knew I was coming here, and indirectly, through the stories he'd told over the years. I'd never been sure whether to believe the implication that eldritch folk made their homes here alongside the human ones. In the tales there were two other races of people in Erin, both of them ancient. Understanding between the various groups was quite unusual in other parts of the land, but at Sevenwaters they all lived more or less side by side. When a person told tales about cows with wings and giant serpents that spewed up precious stones, it did lead one to assume that he was given to flights of the imagination. On the other hand, Father was the most practical of men, whether removing a thorn from the foot of a dog or talking over trade matters with Fernando and me. Besides, there was one especially uncanny story in his past that I had come to believe must be true, the one about him and his brothers being turned into swans. So perhaps he was right about the paths through the Sevenwaters forest changing of their own accord from one day to the next. It was to keep out strangers, he had explained. Many was the traveller who had gone astray somewhere in this tangle of pathways, only to come to light years later as a little pile of bleached bones. But I would be all right; I would find the way. I was family. For me the paths would lead where they should.

I considered this as I headed further into the dense and murky woods. It was all right in theory. The difficulty lay in the fact that I looked nothing like Father. Since stepping off the *Sofia* in Dublin I had seen no woman, and few men, as tall as I was; I had seen nobody, male or female, with skin as dark as mine. My features were not those of an Irishwoman. I took after my mother's side of the family. How would these uncanny forces—supposing they did exist—pick me out as my father's daughter when all the outward signs suggested I was as out of place here as an olive in a bowl of grapes? It was supposed to be less than one day's walk from the forest's edge to the keep of Sevenwaters, depending on where one started. Since I was heading for a lake, I'd find a stream and follow its course. I'd watch out for markers—rock formations, notable trees, ponds, clearings—and with luck I would reach my destination before nightfall.

It was a pleasant enough walk, for the main part. The woods were not as empty as they'd seemed in that odd dusk light, but full of birds and other creatures about their daily business. I saw no uncanny folk, but I spotted a deer, a wild pig and a wary fox. I found a stream and, after refilling my water skin, I followed its course as best I could. Here and there the waterway lost me, gurgling among tumbled rocks netted with brambles. The day passed, and the massed trees stretched ahead. By morning light I had admired the myriad greens of their foliage, the patterns of sun and shade, ever-changing; I had enjoyed walking to the sound of rustling leaves and calling birds. Now, in late afternoon, they were starting to look more like guards, an army of dark trunks blocking my way. I found I was longing for open ground.

I walked on, sure I was heading due west, yet uneasy, for there was a sameness about this row of leaning beeches, this stone somewhat resembling a toad, that suggested I had passed this way before. I was not the kind of traveller who walked in circles. There was a true direction in me; I had never been lost. Under my breath

I uttered one or two choice epithets, keeping to Galician, though with only the wretched trees to hear me I might just as well have cursed in Irish. This was ridiculous. If I didn't find a better path soon I'd be spending the night in here. All right, I had a blanket, I had food and water, I had slept in far less comfortable places in my time, but I grappled with the sense that the forest of Sevenwaters was shutting me out. Or in.

"My grandfather was a chieftain of Sevenwaters," I said aloud, finding myself faintly ridiculous. "If I can't come in, who can?"

I expected no reply and I got none, save for the mocking *kraak* of a raven as it flew to alight on a branch nearby. The creature turned its head to one side, assessing me. Was I imagining things, or did it have a particularly inimical expression in its eye? As I looked up, it flew a short distance away, then alighted and peered at me again.

"Would I trust a bird with eyes like those to show me the way?" I muttered. "Not for an instant. But as I'm headed in that direction anyway, by all means tag along."

The light was fading fast. The thick canopy and the filtered sun had made me misjudge the time of day. With hardly a clearing to be found and the broad, leaf-strewn paths of this morning completely absent, the wise choice would be to make camp the next time I came upon some rocks that might provide shelter, and accept the fact that I would not reach the keep today.

There were, of course, no rocks. I was starting to believe Father's stories now, and wishing I had asked him for better directions. As for the wretched raven, I didn't like the look of it at all. It seemed altogether too knowing for a wild creature, and it wouldn't go away.

"Rocks," I said, slithering down a muddy incline bordered by stinging nettles. "An outcrop, perhaps a cave, that's what I want." I eyed the bird with distaste, wondering if ravens made good eating. I suspected this one's flesh would be as tough and bitter as the look in its eye. I slid to a halt, digging my walking staff into the ground. "Or then again . . . "

We had emerged at the edge of a small, circular glade. It was a patch of light in the dark forest, and in its centre the stream flowed into a neat pool circled by flat stones. A campfire burned on the stones, and by it sat a man, cross-legged. His back was as straight as a child's, his hair a striking dark auburn, his eyes a peculiar shade of mulberry. He looked around my own age, and was clad in a long grey robe. As I stood at the edge of the clearing, waiting for him to speak, the raven winged its way over and landed on his shoulder. I winced, imagining those claws digging in.

The red haired man rose gracefully to his feet. His garb seemed that of a religious brother of some kind, though I saw neither cross nor tonsure. All he wore around his neck was a white stone strung on a cord.

"Please, warm yourself at our campfire," he said courteously. "We see few travellers here. Have you lost your way?"

I moved forward, feeling not only his gaze but that of the bird. "Thank you," I said. "Lost my way? Not exactly." I studied the pair more closely, wondering if there was anything uncanny about them. I wasn't sure how one could tell. There was a neatly strapped bundle over near the trees and a blanket spread out, as well as cooking gear and some other items—corked jars, a little book, a bundle of rowan twigs, a sheaf of herbs. I saw no weapons. "I'm heading for the keep of Sevenwaters. It can't be far from here."

"Less than a mile as the crow flies," the man said. "But dusk is close. I'd advise you to wait until morning, then we can walk on with you and show you the way. You're welcome to camp here, if you wish."

Not a word about who I was or the nature of my business. I liked that. On the other hand, it showed a remarkable lack of caution. What was to stop me from sticking a knife in the fellow's back and making off with all his worldly goods?

The raven gave a *kraaa*, which I interpreted as: *Don't flatter yourself, we can overpower you with our eyes shut*, or something to that effect. I shot the bird a look of dislike. "Unusual pet," I commented, putting down my pack and lowering myself to sit beside it.

The red haired man almost smiled. "Fiacha is an old friend," he said. "Far more than an ordinary raven, as you can perhaps see for yourself. My name is Ciarán."

That startled me. I scrutinised his features anew, seeking signs of my father. This was a handsome man, strong-jawed, the planes of his face well-defined, the eyes deep and watchful. Ciarán. There was a Ciarán in the tales of family, a half-brother born of a sorceress, who had been spirited away from home and had not returned until after my father was gone. The sorceress had been one of those others, the ancient races I was not quite sure I believed in. If this was the same Ciarán, his mother had come close to destroying my father's family. But no, this could not be the man; he was far too young.

"I'm a druid," he said. "The nemetons where my kind live and work are not far from here. Fiacha and I are spending a few days alone in quiet meditation. A respite from my teaching duties. I am responsible for the novices."

"Then I've interrupted your time alone."

"As to that," Ciarán said, organising a cook pot, water, beans, herbs with a deftness obviously born of long practice, "my visions have been troubling. I want no more today. I would welcome your company, if you wish to remain with us."

I asked no questions until the supper was cooked and we were eating it by the fire. Night was falling in the forest around us; birds sang their last farewells to the fading light. The raven, Fiacha, sat hunched on a tree stump nearby, his unnerving gaze following every mouthful from bowl to fingers to lips. If he was hungry, why didn't he fly off and catch something?

"Do you know the Sevenwaters family well?" This seemed a safe way to broach the subject.

Ciarán glanced up from his meal. "I do."

"You mentioned that you are a druid. Can you tell me if there is a man called Conor among your number? He would be old, over sixty by now."

A silence. Then he said, "Why do you ask?"

There seemed no particular reason to hold back, so I came right out with it. "My father's name is Padriac. He's Conor's youngest brother. I would be interested to meet Conor, and perhaps the current chieftain and his family. That's if I get to the keep. Father told me family can find their way in this forest, but I can't say it's been easy."

"You are Padriac's daughter?" A smile of delight and wonderment transformed Ciarán's sombre features. "Then you will most certainly find your way. In any case, Fiacha and I can guide you to the keep, as I said earlier. No hurry. For now, let's enjoy our meal and the quiet of this place, and perhaps exchange a tale or two. I did not know your father. He left Sevenwaters when I was an infant. But Conor is still here. My brother is chief druid, in excellent health despite his years, and much respected. He will most certainly want to meet you."

My mind was working hard. *My brother.* "Forgive me," I said, "but does this mean you are indeed the same Ciarán who was born to the chieftain of Sevenwaters and a . . . a . . . " I seldom found myself short of words, but this was delicate.

"I am that Ciarán. My father was Colum of Sevenwaters. My mother was one of the Fair Folk." He spoke plainly, as if this knowledge were in no way extraordinary.

It went some way to explaining why he looked so young. Father's tales had taught me the Tuatha de Danann were a long-lived race and kept their youthful looks into old age. Observing the calm expression on Ciarán's face, the relaxed, graceful hands as he passed me a chunk of bread, a wedge of cheese, I considered the likelihood that along with her longevity he had inherited his mother's facility for magic. A druid. Were druids something akin to mages?

"You spoke of visions," I said. "What kind of visions?"

"It is part of our discipline to practise the use of still water—a scrying bowl, or a pool—for this purpose," Ciarán said. "We may see past or present; we may see a possible future. We may be shown what might have been. Or nothing at all. Some folk have a latent ability. Several in the family have a strong natural gift. We do not always use water. Images may be present in the smoke from a fire, or we may see them after fasting, a vigil, a time of bodily denial. Unspoken truths may visit us in sleep."

I shivered. He sounded so matter-of-fact. I watched him as he passed a slice of cheese to Fiacha, who snatched it from the outstretched fingers and swallowed it in a gulp. "How long has the bird been with you?" I asked.

"Long. Fiacha has seen me through many trials. Folk think him ill-tempered. He has his reasons for that. Time after time he has aided me in the cause of good. He has worked with me to battle the forces of darkness. And indeed, to quell the darkness within. Our mother . . . never mind that. Let us exchange a tale or two. May I know your name?"

"Aisha. It is a name from my mother's country. He brought her here once, he said, when his sister was dying. But they didn't stay.

Father was changed by what happened to him when he was young. He wanted to live his own life, far from this place."

Ciarán nodded gravely. "I, too, went away," he said. "I made a choice to return. I have my brethren. I have the family, though I do not dwell among them. I have Fiacha. I have my memories and my visions."

He was a man of such controlled demeanour, it was only the slightest break in the mellow tone, the very smallest change in the eyes that hinted at suffering, regret, a depth of sorrow I had no hope of understanding. As Ciarán spoke, Fiacha flew across to perch on his shoulder again, almost as if offering comfort.

"Clearly your father wed and had at least one daughter," Ciarán said, entirely calm again. "Is he in good health?"

I grinned. "Robust health. Thrice married, and a father of many children, the newest a babe not long out of swaddling. Beloved in his home village; owner of a significant trading fleet that is mostly managed by my half-brother these days. My stepmother is a woman of four and twenty. She loves Father dearly. He made a good life for himself."

"And taught his children to speak Irish like natives."

"He said the stories wouldn't sound right in Galician."

We sat in silence for a while. I felt suddenly edgy. I had plenty more questions to ask, but it seemed to me there was something unspoken, something weighty that the druid knew, and the bird knew, and I didn't. I held my tongue. The fellow had been perfectly courteous and open, and there was no reason at all to suspect him.

"What of you, Aisha?" Ciarán asked. "Have you a family of your own, a husband, children?"

Kraaak. The sound conveyed a desire for the conversation to take some other turn, or to cease so we could all sleep.

"It's uncanny," I murmured. "That bird speaks a language I can almost understand. No, I have neither. I've never felt the need or the wish for a husband, and as for children, the kind of life I lead hardly has room for them." As I spoke, I thought of Mercedes and her many sisters, cousins and aunts. At all times of day and night there tended to be a bevy of women in our house. If I had produced a child or two, there would have been no shortage of doting substitute mothers. "I don't really want them," I said, making myself be honest and thinking, not for the first time, that darkness and a campfire encourage all manner of confidences between strangers.

Ciarán nodded. "A child is the most precious gift of all," he said quietly. "But you cannot understand that until you have one of your own."

This idea was familiar from the little talks I got from Mercedes and her kinswomen, lectures that had become increasingly frequent as I approached the age at which I might as well give up thoughts of motherhood. I had not expected it from Ciarán. Nor had I expected him to say it the way he did. "But you're a druid," I blurted out.

"I was not always a druid. Nor was Fiacha here always a raven."

This was getting beyond the acceptable borders of oddity. "What did you say?"

"That is a tale for another day," Ciarán said. "Let us have something else instead. Has your father told you the saga of the clurichaun wars?"

He was an expert storyteller. While I had heard the clurichaun tale before, Ciarán had his own version, droll and witty, and I was soon captivated. I told a tale in my turn, about a princess and a drowned settlement. He told another, and all too soon it was time to settle by the campfire for the night. I fell asleep still smiling. The raven roosted above us, a deeper patch of shadow.

The next day we struck camp and walked on, and as we walked we told more stories: the voyage of Bran, Cruachan's cave, the dream of Aengus. The prince who kept his dead wives in a closet; the spurned lady left to starve in a tower, her ghost thereafter scratching at the window every night and keeping the household in terror. Fiacha punctuated our tales with his hoarse cries. Time was not softening his evident disapproval of his master's new travelling companion.

Dusk fell on the second day, and we still had not reached Sevenwaters.

"I thought this was only one day's walk," I said as Ciarán stopped in a comfortable camping spot. A rock wall sheltered a patch of level ground, and there was a pool among stones, much like the one by which we'd camped the previous night. "I'm sure that's what my father said."

"Sometimes it takes a little longer." Ciarán was calm. Out came the cook pot, the bunch of herbs, the flint and tinder. "Could you gather some dry wood while we still have light?"

I busied myself collecting fallen branches and piling them nearby. I watched him building a fire, and after a while I asked, "Will we reach Sevenwaters tomorrow, do you think?" He seemed a good man, but I could not help being a little suspicious. If he had told the truth about his identity, he was half fey. What if he was guiding me, not to the home of Father's kinsfolk, but down one of those tracks spoken of in the tales, leading to the Otherworld? There were stories of people getting trapped in that uncanny realm for a hundred years. I might relish adventures, but the prospect of such a journey was a little too much even for me.

"Perhaps," Ciarán said in answer to my question. "If not tomorrow, then the next day. If not the next, then the one after. Are you in a hurry, Aisha?"

"No," I said. "But I'm perplexed. *One mile as the crow flies*, I think you told me. It seems you've chosen quite a circuitous path, Ciarán."

He smiled. "The path is as long as the stories we tell," he said. "It is as long as it needs to be. Don't concern yourself; we'll reach our destination at the right time."

I could think of no appropriate answer. It would be sheer folly to strike out on my own; I had no choice but to stay with him. The evening passed. We sat by the fire and told more tales, wondrous, grand, surprising and silly in their turn. I achieved a minor miracle by coaxing Fiacha down from his branch and onto my shoulder. I could feel his claws through my woollen tunic.

"Come, then," I murmured, holding my lure—a piece of the cheese the bird so liked—between my fingers. "Come on, I'm not so bad." The raven sidled down my arm, step by cautious step. I thought he would snatch the prize and fly off, but I kept talking to him quietly, as I had seen my father do with wild creatures, and he stayed there long enough to eat the morsel from my fingers. I reached slowly across with my other hand; brushed the soft breast feathers. The bird fixed his bright gaze on me, and my heart went still with the strangeness of the moment. Then, in an eye-blink, he was gone back up to his perch.

"Ciarán?"

"Mm?"

"Do I remember correctly, that you told me Fiacha was not always a raven? What did you mean by that?"

"Ah." My companion settled himself more comfortably by the fire. "I imagine your father has told you many tales of Sevenwaters. You know what I am and can guess, perhaps, what my mother's line has given me. I could tell you a story, a remarkable and sad one. You might find it easier to believe if I did not use words, but showed you instead."

My skin prickled. "Showed me? In pictures?" I could not imagine how this might be achieved by night, in the middle of the forest.

"In a vision. If you are open to it, I can reveal the story to you in the water of this pool. Indeed, that would be entirely apt, since the tale begins between firelight and water."

Fiacha ruffled his feathers, moving restlessly on his branch.

"Why is he doing that?" I asked, eyeing the bird. "Does he not want the tale told? Or is he merely complaining of hunger or a sore belly?"

"He thinks he does not want the tale told," Ciarán said, apparently taking me quite seriously. "But there is no doubt that this is the time to tell it. I would guess you are afraid of very little, Aisha. There is no need to fear this. The challenge lies not in the tale itself, but in the choice it reveals."

"A choice for whom?" I was intrigued. I had always prided myself on meeting whatever challenges came my way.

Ciarán did not answer my question, but moved to kneel by the pool, stretching out a long hand towards me. "Will you try it?" he asked. Fiacha turned his back on us. He could hardly have made his disapproval more plain. "You'll need to sit beside me, here, and keep hold of my hand. Fix your gaze on the water, and you will see what I see. It may take some time. Be patient."

It did not take long at all. Images formed on the surface of the pool and in its depths, and while I held Ciarán's hand I could see them quite clearly. I thought I could hear voices, too, though here in the glade all was quiet. Perhaps they spoke only in our minds. It was indeed a strange tale, and a sad one: a big brother and a little brother; a malevolent mother and a courageous father; true love turned to sorrow and loss; an ingeniously cruel curse. It was a tale that fitted neatly around the one I already knew of Sevenwaters, the story of the Lady Oonagh, who wed my grandfather and turned his sons into swans. Conri's was a tale fit to bring a strong man to tears. When it was done, and the pond showed no more than a ripple or two, we sat for some time in complete silence. Glancing at the bird, trying to imagine what might be in his thoughts, I met a glare of challenge. *Don't you dare feel sorry for me.* It came to me that I had been told this tale for a purpose.

"A choice," I said flatly. "You're offering me the choice to marry a raven."

Ciarán stretched his arms and flexed his fingers; he had become cramped, sitting so still to hold the vision. "Offering, no. Setting it before you, yes. I thought it just possible you might consider it."

"No man would want a wife who wed him out of pity," I said.

The raven—Conri, if it was indeed he—gave a derisive cry. The sound echoed away into the darkness under the trees.

"Is it pity you feel?" Ciarán asked.

"For the bird, no. He's a wary, prickly sort of creature, and I wonder what kind of man he would be, if it were actually possible to reverse this—*geis*, is that the word?—by going through with a marriage. Who would perform such a marriage, anyway? What priest could possibly countenance such a bizarre idea?"

"The one you see before you," Ciarán said. "Performing the ritual of hand-fasting is one of a druid's regular duties."

I felt a chill all through me. He could do it; he could do it right now, tonight, and if the peculiar story proved to be true, I could free a man from a life-long hell set on him simply because he'd wanted to protect a child. And I'd be saddled with a husband I didn't want, a man who'd likely prove to be just as irritable and unpleasant as the raven was. I wondered if I had in fact fallen asleep in the forest, and would wake soon with a crick in my neck and the nightmare memory fading fast.

"What possible reason could I have for agreeing to do this?" I asked, then remembered something. "Wait! Did you actually know I was coming? Did you guess who I was? He came to find me. Fiacha. He led me to you. Don't tell me—"

"Nothing so devious, Aisha. I did not know who you were until you mentioned your father. I had seen you in a vision, earlier, approaching this place. I sent Fiacha out to find you, thinking you might need help. Perhaps some other power has intervened to aid my brother here, for your arrival seems almost an act of the gods."

I thought about this for a while. Reason said I must give a polite refusal. A small, mad part of me, a part I recognised all too well, urged me to be bold, to take a chance, to do what nobody else in the length and breadth of Erin would be prepared to do. That impulse had led me into some unusual situations in my time. I'd never once failed to extricate myself safely. I considered the story itself and the odd bond between these two half-brothers. "I have some questions," I said.

"Ask them."

"First—is it safe to speak his name now? To acknowledge that I know who he is?"

"Quite safe. That part of the *geis* died with his beloved Lóch."

"Then tell me, how did you learn Conri's story, and when? Was it like this, in a vision?"

"Some of it was revealed to me in that way. But I knew already what had become of him. She told me. Our mother. There was a time when I went back to her. A dispute with my family drove me from Sevenwaters. There were aspects of our mother's craft I wanted to learn. She welcomed me, little knowing the depth of my loathing. She gloated over what she had done to Conri; she thought herself ingenious. It was another reason to destroy her."

"She's gone, then?"

His mouth went into a hard line. "She is no more."

"Ciarán . . . " I hesitated.

"Mm?"

"What she did to Conri—it was very long ago. Haven't you tried to undo the *geis* before? There must have been other unwed girls in the family over the years."

He grimaced. "It seemed too much to ask. As you can see, he himself has mixed feelings on the matter."

"Can you . . . can you communicate with Conri?"

"You mean speaking mind to mind, without words? Alas, no. We have an understanding; it has developed over the years and has served us well enough. But I cannot ask him what he wants, Aisha. I can only use my own judgement. He needs to do this. And I want it done. He's my brother, and I owe him. I cannot put it more simply than that."

"Then why now and not before? If it seemed too much to ask those other women, why is it all right to ask me?"

Ciarán regarded me with his dark mulberry eyes. "You seem . . . formidable," he said quietly. "A woman travelling all alone with perfect confidence; a woman of wit and intelligence, balance and integrity. Strong; brave; whole. If anyone can do this, I believe you can."

"You don't even know me."

His lips curved. "You think not? We've exchanged many tales as we walked, Aisha. We've passed through the forest of Sevenwaters together. Besides, I am the son of a sorceress; I have abilities beyond the strictly human. I believe my assessment of you is accurate. If I did not, I would never have suggested this course of action. Would I trust my brother's future to a woman who was doomed to fail?"

The situation was nothing short of ridiculous. I considered the possibility that Ciarán was actually completely mad, one of those wild men who are supposed to wander about the woods and commune with the trees, and that the next thing he might do was strangle me or have his way with me, or both.

"Why do you smile?" he asked.

"I'm wondering what he's like now," I said. "Conri. In the vision he was just a lad, barely become a man. He hadn't even—" I broke off as a new thought struck me. Conri had been transformed into a raven on his wedding day. If I did what Ciarán wanted, I'd be acquiring a husband who was not only elderly, but also inexperienced in the art of love. The prospect hadn't much to recommend it. "There would be rather a large gap between our ages," I said. My mind quashed this objection instantly with an image of Father and Mercedes dancing together by lantern light. Tenderness. Passion. Complete understanding. A pang of some hitherto unknown emotion went through my heart. Longing? Yearning? That was crazy. My life was a good one, a complete one. I did not need this complication.

"He was a good looking boy," Ciarán said. "He's likely to be a well-made man. And he is the same kind as I am: my half-brother. I expect that in physical appearance Conri will seem no older than five and thirty."

"And he'll come complete with an ill temper and a load of bitterness on his shoulders."

"It's not as if there's been no cause for that," said Ciarán mildly. "And once he is a man again, it may change. You could change it, Aisha."

"And if I can't bear the fellow?"

"A hand-fasting can be made for a finite period. A year and a day. Five summers. Whatever is deemed appropriate." After a moment, Ciarán added, "I must be quite honest with you. To be sure of meeting the requirements of a *geis*, one might need to make permanent vows."

"I need time. Time to think." By all the saints. Was I actually considering this? What had got into me?

"Of course." Ciarán looked as if he'd be quite content to sit here by the fire all night if necessary. "You'll be tired," he added. "Take all the time you need. He's waited many years; a little longer can make no difference."

A little longer. Or much, much longer. If I said no, Conri might be condemned to stay in bird form more or less indefinitely. The raven seemed bitter and warped. What would he be like in another twenty years? I began to realise what a good man Ciarán was. A good brother. They both were.

"You may prefer that we lead you straight to the keep in the morning," Ciarán said now. "I can introduce you to Sean and his family: his wife, two unwed daughters and a very small son. And Conor; I could take you to meet him."

There was something he wasn't saying.

"But?"

"It just occurred to me," Ciarán said with unusual hesitancy, "that if we performed the hand-fasting *before* you went to meet the family, your explanations would be much easier. You arrive with your husband, the two of you receive a delighted welcome. Conri is accepted as a member of the family without question. There would be no need to speak of his past or of his parentage. It seems you have travelled widely, Aisha, and met many folk from different lands. The fact that you were wed to a man of Erin would hardly provoke questions. Appearing as a single woman travelling alone, then suddenly acquiring a husband more or less from nowhere, surely would."

"Do these people know about Fiacha?"

"They know him only as a raven."

I stared into the fire, trying to imagine how it would be to walk into the keep of Sevenwaters as a married woman. I could not picture it. Instead, I saw young Conri facing his mother, holding his nerve against the onslaught of her cruelty. That boy with the lovely voice, losing himself. And the raven by Lóch's side, watching her die.

What Ciarán had just suggested would be too much for Conri. It would be too soon. Once the transformation was done, he'd need time, space, quiet. I'd seen the way Father tended to abused animals, how he gentled them, waiting until they were ready to take the first steps forward. Gentle was not a word folk used when describing me. But I supposed I could learn.

"If I agreed to this," I said, "I wouldn't take him straight to meet the family. It's been a long time for him. We'd be best on our own awhile. He needs to mend. Until that's begun, he should see only you and me, I think. I know how to fend for myself in the woods, Ciarán. All we'd need would be shelter and quiet, until he's healed." Out of the corner of my eye, I saw that the bird had turned around. He was looking at me.

"You have the time for this?" Ciarán asked.

I had told Fernando I would catch up with him next time the ship came into Dublin. It could equally well be the time after, or the time after that.

"There's no point in agreeing to something if I'm not going to do it properly," I said. "I'd be foolish if I expected a man to step out of such an ordeal with no damage at all. And if I'm to be his wife, it's up to me to help him get over it, I suppose. I should make it quite clear"—I glanced over at Fiacha, who had gone so still he resembled a carven effigy of a bird—"that I never planned to settle in these parts. That doesn't change. I can stay awhile. As long as he needs. Then he'll be coming back to Xixón with me. He should meet my father." It was quite difficult to surprise Father; in that, he was like me. But I was sure, *Here's my husband. Not long ago he was a raven,* would startle even him.

Ciarán had gone rather pale. I think that up until now he had not given real credence to the possibility that I might say yes.

"I suppose," I added, "it's not so much a husband I'll be getting as an adventure."

◯

~ Conri ~

My frail bird body shudders. I watch my brother as he readies himself for the hand-fasting ritual, and there's so much in me I think I might split apart. Lóch, sweet, lovely Lóch, forever lost. And this woman, this tall black woman with the clear eyes and strong jaw, a woman like a shining blade, a woman as unlike my sweetheart as anyone could be; why is she doing this? She almost frightens me. *Lóch, dear heart, I'm sorry. It should have been you by my side. Lóch, don't hate me for this.*

"Are you ready?" Ciarán asks.

I cannot answer, but the woman—Aisha, her name is—nods her head. At the last moment, she reaches up and tweaks a corner of her elaborate head-cloth. The cloth unwinds; a cascade of hair descends, black as night and glossy as silk. Even my ascetic brother gawks at her. Suddenly, despite her height, her garb that might be a man's—long tunic, woollen hose and boots—despite the strength and challenge in her gaze, a warrior's look, Aisha is all woman.

She turns her dark eyes full on me. "Conri," she says, quiet as a breeze in the grass, "I'm sorry your hand-fasting cannot be as you once dreamed. I did not know your Lóch, but I am certain she would not want you to spend the rest of your life this way. I can never replace her. But I can offer you a new kind of life. I can offer my best effort."

Sheer terror churns in my gut. I don't want this! Why would I want my life back without Lóch? If this works, what will I be, so many years on? A wrinkled greybeard with the mind of that young lad who thought himself man enough to wed and be a father? What if Ciarán speaks the words and I become a creature with a man's body and a bird's mind? What if I turn into a monster? I never asked for this, I never expected anyone to do it, I don't want it . . .

"Are you ready, Conri?"

I look at Ciarán's face, high-boned, steady-eyed, calm as still water. I do not look at Aisha; there is no need. I feel her presence beside me, strong as oak, fearless as Queen Maeve herself, beautiful as the keen flight of an arrow or the piercing cry of the pipes. I want this. I want it from the bottom of my heart. I want it as the parched earth wants rain. I want it as a man wants sunlight after long winter. I want it with every wretched, bitter, cynical corner of my body.

I cannot give Ciarán an answer, so I stretch my wings and fly to Aisha's shoulder. She flinches, then straightens, ready for the challenge. Her strong mouth softens into a smile.

"We're ready," she says.

Ciarán paces steadily, casting a circle in the clearing. He greets the spirits of the quarters, asks the gods for a blessing, then moves to stand before us in the centre. We are on the stones between the campfire and the pool. Aisha and I face north, Ciarán south. The star-jewelled night sky forms our wedding canopy.

As my brother begins the hand-fasting, a deep stillness seeps through me, a peace I have seldom known before. It is something like the sensation a bard feels when a song is done; when the music lingers on the air and in the heart long after the final measure.

"Under sky and upon stone," the druid says, "'twixt firelight and water, I ask you, Conri, and you, Aisha, to make your solemn vows of hand-fasting. Aisha, repeat these words after me." The mulberry eyes meet hers and I feel the smallest shiver run through her body. I edge along her shoulder until my wing feathers brush her cheek, black on black. And she says it, phrase by phrase, word by sweet word, she says it.

"By earth and air, by fire and water, I bind myself to you. Until the stars no longer shine on us, until the earth covers our bones, until the light turns to dark, until death changes us forever, I will stand by you, Conri, my husband."

She does not shiver now. Her voice is the note of a deep bell, strong and steady.

Ciarán draws a breath. Looks at me. His eyes are suspiciously bright. "Conri, best of brothers. Repeat these words after me. *By earth and air, by fire and water . . .* "

Oh gods, oh gods . . . The change is quick. My heart has barely time to hammer a startled beat, my wings hardly manage to carry me down from Aisha's shoulder before my body stretches and lengthens and thickens, my features flatten, my vision alters with sickening speed, pool and flames, man and woman, stars and dark branches swimming and diving all around me. Stone under my cheek; stone under my chest, my belly, my limbs . . . a man's limbs.

Aisha is kneeling beside me; I feel her hands, sure but gentle on my back, my shoulder. I have forgotten how to use this body. I cannot move. *Repeat these words after me . . .* I struggle to my hands and knees, Aisha helping me. I think I might be sick. I am sick, retching up the meagre contents of my belly onto the stones. Aisha scoops up water, cupping it in her hands. I drink. The skin of her palms is lighter than the rest of her, the hue of fine-grained oak. Her fingers are long and graceful.

I stand. Her arm rests lightly around my shoulders, supporting me. I draw breath, open my mouth, utter a croaking sound.

"Take your time," says my brother quietly. "*By earth and air . . .*"

I understand, through the nausea, the dizziness, the utter wrongness of this clumsy man-body, that the *geis* cannot be fully undone unless I can play my part.

"By . . . by . . . ah . . . " A paroxysm of coughing. The two of them wait for me, quiet, confident. "By earth . . . and air . . . "

"Good, Conri," whispers Aisha. "You're doing fine."

"*By fire and water,*" says Ciarán, and I see that he has tears rolling down his cheeks.

"By fire . . . and water . . . I bind myself . . . "

It comes more easily with each word. A harsh voice, for certain, no bard's honeyed tones, but a human voice. I stumble through the vow. I owe it to my brother for his long care and for his belief in me. I owe it to this woman, this stranger, to honour the sacrifice she's making for me. So, turning to look into her lustrous dark eyes and seeing not a scrap of pity there, only joy at the remarkable feat we've accomplished tonight, the three of us, I finish it: 'Until death changes us forever, I bind myself to you, Aisha, my wife." *Dearest Lóch; goodbye, my lovely one.*

Ciarán takes a cloth strip from his belt. Aisha extends her right arm, I my left. We clasp hands, and my brother wraps the cloth around our wrists.

"By the deep, enduring power of earth; by the clarifying power of air; by the quickening power of fire; by the life-giving power of water, you are now joined as husband and wife. By the mysterious, all-encompassing power of spirit, you are hand-fasted until death separates you one from the other. I give you my solemn blessing, Conri, my brother." He touches my brow with his fingertips and

I feel a thrill of power run through me. "I give you my solemn blessing, Aisha, my sister." He touches her in her turn, and I feel her tremble.

My knees are weak. I'm still dizzy and sick, my eyes unwilling to accept the change. Aisha holds me up while Ciarán speaks the final prayers, closes the circle, then moves to add wood to the fire and get out his little flask of mead. My knees give up the struggle; Aisha only just manages to stop me from falling. She settles beside me on the stones, her arm around me in comradely fashion. It feels good. It feels remarkably good.

Ciarán pours mead into cups. For a while, the three of us sit in utter silence.

"Don't look at me," I say eventually. "This was your crazy idea; yours and hers." I glance from the sombre, pale Ciarán to the silent Aisha. Before either of them can speak a word, I burst into tears. I sob and shake like a child, my head clutched in my hands. Aisha kneels up and wraps me in her arms, cradling my head on her shoulder and humming under her breath. *Gods, oh, gods . . .* The worst of it is to be so helpless, so feeble, so unmanned before this woman, this extraordinary woman who surprises me at every turn.

"Weep now, Conri," she says in a murmur. "Weep for Lóch; weep for your young life lost; weep for what could not be. Weep all night if you need. Weep until those sad tears are all gone, husband. And in the morning, know the good gifts that you have. The most loyal of brothers. A wife who will stand by you forever and always tell you the truth. We will not long be strangers, Conri. Family, at Sevenwaters and in Xixón. When you are ready, we will go to meet them."

Still the tears flow; I cannot stop them. This does not mean I do not hear her.

"The sunrise and the moonrise," says Ciarán. "The forest and the lake. The stars in the sky. The flight of birds; the secret paths of fox and badger. The company of friends. The wisdom of elders. The laughter of children; perhaps, in time, your own children."

"We'll see about that," Aisha puts in dryly, but there's a smile in her voice.

"A song by the campfire," says Ciarán. "The notes of the harp."

That stirs me to speech. "No," I hiccup against Aisha's shoulder. "Not that."

"Hush, Conri," says my wife. "Hush, now. It's a long road ahead, and we must learn to walk before we can dance. I've one more thing to say to you."

I manage a sound of query.

"You're a much finer specimen of manhood than I was expecting," she tells me. "I think it possible my father may approve."

Ciarán splutters on a mouthful of mead; he's a man who rarely laughs. I lift my head. Before I can wipe my streaming eyes, Aisha's fingers come up and brush the tears from my cheeks, sweet as a mother tending her child. But different. Quite different.

"I might see if I can keep a sip of mead down," I say in a whisper. "Long time since I . . . "

"Here," says Aisha, holding out the cup. "Tomorrow is a new day. A new dawn."

I can barely speak, but I must. "This is a gift beyond measure," I say, taking the cup. She knows I'm not talking about the mead. "I'm not up to much just now, and I may never match it. But I'll do my best."

Raven no more, I came to rest
Then set forth on another quest.
What might I be before the end?
Brother, husband, father, friend?

My brother's patience shielded me
And Aisha's courage set me free.
'Twas hope that saw me come at last
Out of the shadows of the past.

As I take up my harp again
I do not sing of death and pain.
In my song, love and courage rise.
These are the gifts that make us wise.

☽

gift of hope

Hampshire was not Jamaica, Sophia thought with a grimace. It was all very well to have fat sheep and wide acres for grazing. But Netherstowe was bitter cold; so cold that if she stood by her bedchamber window much longer she might turn into a large icicle. Shivering in her winter gown and woollen shawl, she stepped back and drew the damask curtains closed.

It had been a shock when Father got the letter. Uncle Joseph, a bachelor and childless, was dead. Suddenly they were not only owners of the sugar plantation whose lush, palm-fringed acres had been Sophia's home for her full seventeen years, but also custodians of the rich estate of Netherstowe. They would return to England, Father had announced. There were matters to be seen to, tenants to be dealt with, decisions to be made.

Sophia had imagined everything soft and green, and it was. She had pictured the mellow stone house looking out on a vista of lake and woodland. This, too, was accurate. What she had not expected was downright rudeness.

She had walked out one afternoon, down by the beech woods. There was a small cottage, and a tired-looking woman pegging out sheets. Children played in the mud; chickens scratched for worms.

"Good morning," Sophia had said. The woman had given a wan smile, but made no reply. The cottage had seemed rather run-down, the amenities less than folk deserved. Although there was unrest in Jamaica, all their own workers had been adequately fed and snugly housed. "Is there anything I—we can do to help you?" she'd ventured. "Shoes for the children? A basket of food? I'm sure my father—"

"Play Lady Bountiful elsewhere." She'd whirled around in surprise to find a young man standing there. He was big and dirty-looking, and he carried a great load of wood on his back. His eyes were impossibly blue and openly hostile. "O'Reillys don't accept charity."

Feeling a blush of mortification turn her cheeks crimson, Sophia had fled. Later, she'd asked her father who they were. A cursed breed, he'd told her. Bog Irish. Thought they had some claim to the land; too much trouble to throw them off.

"Does the young man—what is his name?—work for us?" Sophia had queried. "He did not seem in the least respectful. And what do you mean, cursed?"

"Finn O'Reilly? Works well enough when it suits him, cutting wood, tending to horses. But I'm told he can't be relied on. Bone lazy. As for the other matter, they say that family's been cursed for generations. Always in trouble. Too proud to take help when they need it and too poor to pull themselves out of the gutter. Maybe that's all the curse is: foolish pride."

"You should give the man a fair chance, Father." Sophia had surprised herself by springing to the defence. "You do not know him yet."

Now, alone in her room after supper, Sophia thought of the blue-eyed giant in the woods. He had not had the look of a lazy man. His wife had seemed exhausted. His children had been barefoot. If it was cold here, it would be bitter indeed in that ramshackle cottage.

She threw another log on her fire. She had put out the lamp, and the bedchamber walls danced with shadows. Despite the rosy glow of the flames, the room held a sadness, as if it had witnessed long hours of weeping. If Sophia had believed in ghosts—which she did not, such things being no more than imagination—she would have thought an uneasy spirit dwelled here.

A piece of wood fell smouldering onto the mat, and there was a shower of sparks. Sophia grabbed for the fire tongs to lift the log to safety, and her hand knocked against the flower-bordered tiles of the hearth. Something moved. She secured the log, then looked closer. Under her fingers a tile had shifted, showing a delicate crack at the hearth's base. Sophia lifted the tile away, and then the loose brick behind it. Her heart thumping, she reached inside the tiny hiding place and drew out a packet wrapped in what had once been a kerchief of fine blue silk. Inside were a little book bound in pale kidskin, its pages yellowed and fragile, and a small box of pressed tin. Which should be first? With an odd sense that someone was looking over her shoulder, Sophia opened the book and, by firelight, began to read.

January 6, 1805. It is not at all a happy new year. I am to wed our neighbour, James Harvey of Netherstowe, before the month is out. Father gives me no choice. Colm is away at the horse sales and I cannot reach him, for Father will not let me out. I have nowhere to turn. Mr Harvey has a strange smile. He frightens me. I would gladly be poor as a church mouse, if only I could wed my sweetheart.

January 10. I am crushed. I tried to stand up to Father in the matter of James Harvey, and he would not hear me. His financial affairs are in ruin; it seems Mr Harvey can settle them. In return, our neighbour is to have the management of all our farms, and the cottages. The last part of his payment is myself. Mr Harvey beats his dog. I have seen it. I have been fitted for my wedding gown. I am still slender; nothing shows. They set me before the mirror and I shut my eyes, not to see.

January 15. I am in joy, and in terror. Colm is returned. Last night I saw him from my window and ran downstairs, but Father made me go back. Later I left a message in the secret place. I hope and pray Colm will find it. We must meet so I can give him the news face to face. I cannot let him believe I am content to wed another. Once he knows of the child, surely he will find a way for us to escape.

The next entry was blurred, as if tears had smudged the neat lines of writing. Sophia strained to read it.

February 12. I am Mrs James Harvey of Netherstowe. The name clangs like a funeral bell. Colm is gone to sea, signed up for His Majesty's navy. Perhaps he found my note. I will never know if he waited for me. My father blocked my escape, and now my secret can never be told.

"Poor sad girl," Sophia murmured. "I wonder who she was? Perhaps the diary will tell."

April 29 1806. Colm is lost. There was a fire. The ship went down. It is as if I myself am dead. Little James thrives. My husband dotes on him, for which I thank God. Colm never knew the truth. If I had been able to tell him, he would have stayed by me and never lost his life so cruelly. Now I must live a lie, for my child's sake.

Next were patchy entries: a birthday, a visit, veiled references to her husband's cruelty. And then, dotted with tears, an entry that made Sophia's spine tingle.

July 5. Colm is alive. Saved from the shipwreck, and at last returned home after long illness. I would hardly have known him; his face is burned, his form hunched, and he is full of a terrible bitterness. I dare not go down to the cottage, though I long to wrap my arms around his poor shoulders and kiss away the hurt. I cannot go. I will do nothing to jeopardise our son's future. My husband says Colm is cursed, because he is an O'Reilly. James has let the cottage fall into disrepair and will not find Colm employment. But I can help. I have what Mother gave me when I married. I saved it for my daughter, to give her the choice I did not have: not to be locked in a loveless marriage. But it seems to me there will be no daughter. My mother's gift will be the O'Reillys' salvation. As soon as I shake off this wretched cough, I will go outside and hide it in the secret place. Somehow I will let Colm discover it for himself. He would never accept charity from a Harvey. I can at least buy happiness for him and his folk, though I myself can have none.

Sophia turned the page, but there was no more writing. It was the end of the diary. She looked on the flyleaf. There was a faint inscription: Sarah Jane Warburton, her book. "Poor Sarah," she whispered.

Next morning she went to the churchyard. The mossy slabs, the broken angels took her back through the years until at last she found it: SARAH JANE HARVEY, 24.11.1788 – 23.7.1806. ALSO HER HUSBAND JAMES HARVEY, 1775 – 1847. Sarah had died that very same month, and left her diary to hold its secret for three generations. The little box had remained hidden in the hearth. Sarah had died without doing what she had so longed to do, and the O'Reillys had laboured under the curse all those years.

Sophia searched further. This was more difficult, for the gravestone she wanted was in the far corner, choked with rough grasses and a nettle or two. She pushed them aside, wincing. COLM O'REILLY, 1786 – 1820. He too had died young, but he had not spent his life alone. There was a wife, Elizabeth, who had outlived him by thirty years. And there had been sons.

There was no time like the present, Sophia told herself. Wrongs should be righted. If there was a curse, it was up to her, as a descendant not only of poor Sarah but of the dreadful James Harvey, to lift it once and for all. She marched up to the cottage, her heart pounding, and rapped on the door. Children's voices could be heard; the door opened a crack.

"Might I speak to your father, please?"

Round eyes peered up at her. "Me Da's dead, Miss."

Sophia gulped. "Could I see Mr O'Reilly, please?"

"Who is it, Paddy?" It was his voice, the tone brusque. Clutching her small bag tightly, Sophia walked inside.

Though lacking in any luxury, the cottage was clean and tidy. The woman peeled potatoes at the sink. Three children milled around her skirts. Finn O'Reilly sat at the table. Much to Sophia's surprise he seemed to be reading a large book and making notes on scraps of paper with a scratchy pen. He glanced up, frowned, and moved the book away. But she had seen the title: *Berger's Introduction to Anatomy*.

"You are studying?" she queried, seating herself uninvited.

He muttered something, clearly much embarrassed.

"He'll be a fine doctor one day," the woman said in tones of weary pride. "Not bad for a lad who taught himself to read. Right proud of him we are, aren't we, Paddy? The cleverest uncle in the world, you've got."

"Enough, Nora. The young lady's not interested in O'Reilly business. Probably thinks I should be out chopping wood for her father. Besides, one book doesn't make a doctor. Deluded, that's what I am. O'Reilly's curse."

"Yes," agreed Sophia, "you would need to go to London, would you not, to medical school? A long and costly training, I should think."

"Why are you here?" Finn O'Reilly snapped.

"I have something for you to read; a change from anatomy. It's a diary. Not mine—an old one, written by a lady long gone. I know she would want you to see this. And I have something else, which I found hidden with it. This is still locked; I haven't looked inside. She left the key for you."

"We don't accept charity." Finn spoke more quietly now, his eyes on the pressed tin box she had placed on the table.

"Read the diary." Sophia got up to leave. "This belongs to you and to your family. Goodbye now, and good luck with your studies."

She kept herself busy for a while, and heard no news. She avoided the cottage. One cold, bright morning she was out walking and heard footsteps behind her. She turned. It was Finn O'Reilly, but so changed she'd scarcely have known him save for the remarkable blue eyes. He was clean-shaven, his hair washed and brushed, fair as ripe barley. He wore a grey suit, neat and plain, and his boots were polished.

"Miss Harvey," he said quietly.

"Good morning, Mr O'Reilly."

"I—I should thank you. I'm not good at these things. Your—your gift has allowed a remarkable change for us. I'm on my way to London; they have accepted me for training. Thanks to your discovery, I have been able to provide for my sister and her children. Her husband died at sea; part of the curse, perhaps."

Sophia found that she was blushing; she could not imagine why. "The curse is lifted, Mr O'Reilly," she said softly. "And you must thank Sarah, not me. Her gift, whatever it was, could not be put to better use. She was not able to make poor Colm happy, but it would gladden her to see how she has helped his descendants."

"It was strange indeed to learn that the owners of Netherstowe are, in a way, O'Reillys themselves. It seems we two are cousins of a sort. Distant cousins."

Sophia smiled. For some reason, she was glad the connection was no closer.

"Don't you want to know what was in the box, Miss Harvey?"

"Sophia, please. After all, we are relations. And I do know. Hope. I shall hope too, Mr O'Reilly."

"Please call me Finn. What shall you hope for?"

"That you will do very well at your studies, and in time return to Hampshire to practise your profession."

"I'll be back at Christmas for a visit. I thought I might try to find their secret place; Sarah's and Colm's."

"I'll help you," said Sophia.

January 6 1885. Dear Diary, today I start this record in memory of brave Sarah, who lost her sweetheart but left him a legacy of hope. Finn is gone back to London. I still feel the clasp of his fingers on mine, warm, strong and sure. And I have this little book he gave me, to set down my thoughts while I wait for him. My gift to him was a set of pen nibs, for it seemed to me his handwriting might be the better for them. I think my father may be persuaded that a country doctor is a suitable match for his daughter, given time.

My little room feels warm and bright tonight. Sarah is still here, I think; but now she smiles.

◗

letters from robert

My Dearest Clarinda,

The Delphine *is at anchor off the coast of Madagascar, a hot land teeming with monkeys and exotic parrots. The air is rich with the scent of a thousand spices. Five days ago, we encountered a tribe of fearsome savages. Our men fell like ninepins under their wicked assault and I count myself fortunate to have sustained only a minor hatchet wound. I hope you are keeping well. I count the hours until I can return to Midford and kiss your sweet hand once more. I miss you more than I can say.*

Your faithful Robert

Holding Robert's letter to my cheek, I imagined I could smell cardamom and cinnamon, nutmeg and cloves. My sweetheart's life far surpassed in excitement anything in the popular novels the ladies of Midford dissected over their afternoon tea. No wonder Robert was such an infrequent visitor. His seafaring adventures must render our sedate little township entirely tedious for him.

Letters from Robert were, if not as rare as hens' teeth, then something very close. A ship might dock bearing three at once, each from a different port, then nothing at all for months. It tried my patience dearly. Since Father's death I had lived alone save for my housekeeper, Maud. Father had left me everything, so there was no need for me to seek a living or a husband unless I chose to.

I unfolded another letter, almost a year old. There had been fewer missives lately, and it concerned me. What if something dreadful happened and I never got word? Robert came from a prosperous Sydney family—his father was a man of law—and he had promised that, when we were married, he would take me to visit them.

The first time I met Robert, his ship had docked at Fremantle and he had taken the steamer upriver for the Midford Spring Fair. I had been dancing with Edward Blake, proprietor of Blake's Booksellers. Robert had cut in, a dashing figure, and poor polite Edward had had no choice but to relinquish me. And once I looked into Robert's bold eyes, I was dazzled . . . There was only one man in the world for me.

My dear Clarinda, I read, *the* Delphine *is off the coast of Jamaica, in seas full of pirate ships and monstrous whirlpools . . . I miss you very much . . .*

There was a polite tap on the door of my reading room and Maud ushered in a visitor, Edward Blake. With his wire-framed spectacles and neat white shirts, Edward seemed born to be a clerk, but he had risen higher. His business was importing and distributing books. He despatched orders all over the Colony. Edward was Midford-born and chose to run Blake's Booksellers from a modest shop.

Success had not diminished his meekness. In matters of the heart, I thought, he was a man who would always step back for a rival.

"Good afternoon, Clarinda," he said. "Those are well-worn letters," he added as I refolded the one I had been reading and returned it to its ribbon-bound bundle. "One could make Robert's adventures into a book: a Penny Dreadful."

"That is a little unkind," I said. "Just because his life, beside yours and mine, is so very full of excitement . . . "

At my nod, my guest proceeded to seat himself.

"Will you take tea?" I kept my tone cool, for his suggestion had irritated me. Edward and I were old friends. I was often in his shop, being a keen reader, and he was a regular visitor to the house. Maud admitted him without question; all Midford knew he was the soul of propriety. Edward would never attract gossip to me.

"Yes, thank you," he responded. "I have brought something for you."

He passed me a little book. "Tales of a lady adventurer in darkest Africa," he told me. "I'm afraid I read it first myself. Every time Lady Josephine described her exploits, be it riding camels, haggling in bazaars or fending off bandits, your image was in my mind." Edward did not blush often. When he did, as now, it was most obvious, since he was an auburn-haired, fair-skinned man. "Don't take offence, please, Clarinda. I know how you love the idea of adventure."

I did like hearing of exciting deeds, that was true. Robert's letters thrilled me. But actually doing those things was another matter. I didn't even like horses. It was fortunate I was a banker's daughter and not a farmer's. I preferred my camels in other people's stories.

"Have you heard from Robert lately?" Edward enquired after Maud had brought in the tea. He gazed out of the window, balancing a fine china cup and saucer in his big capable hands. In my garden the stocks were putting on a vibrant display and their sweet scent wafted in on the southerly breeze.

"Of course!" I snapped, wishing that southerly would bring the *Delphine* back home quickly. After his last leave, Robert had not even wanted me to travel to Fremantle to wave goodbye. "I want to remember you here in your garden," my beloved had whispered. "A flower among flowers. We'll be married on my next leave, I promise."

Edward was fixing me with a penetrating look, the one he used on customers who tried to quibble over prices.

"Well, if you must know, I haven't had a letter for six months now and I'm worried. I know the posts are erratic, but . . . "

Edward set down his cup and reached for my hand. "What is it? You can tell me."

"I wrote to his father." My voice was a whisper; I had not intended to confide this. "I had no address, but I sent it care of the Law Society. The letter came back marked *addressee unknown*. Oh, Edward, I am fearful some ill has befallen Robert. What if he was killed by pirates and the news caused his poor dear mother to die of a broken heart and his father to go into a decline so that he could no longer practise as a man of law? What if Robert was imprisoned by bandits or marooned on a wild island with only coconuts for sustenance?"

"Coconuts make fine eating," Edward observed. His grip on my hand was warm and reassuring.

"Don't you dare laugh at me!" I glared at my old friend, though in fact I felt somewhat better for his being here with me.

"I could make enquiries." Edward spoke with some diffidence. "I have to go to Fremantle next week. The shipping records may provide details of the *Delphine*'s whereabouts. Only if you wish it, of course."

I stared at him. I had not realised it would be so simple to ascertain my betrothed's location; to find out how much longer I must wait. To my surprise, I realised I did not really want to know.

"There's no need to put yourself out for me, Edward," I told him crisply.

"As you wish." He rose to his feet. "You should be out enjoying yourself. How long does Robert intend to keep you waiting? Until you're a wrinkled old woman?"

Sudden fury seized me. How dare he? I rose to my feet. "Goodbye, Edward. I thought I could count on your good manners, but you have proven me wrong. You are no longer welcome in my house."

I held onto my dignity until he was gone. Then I put down my head on my desk and wept.

Another letter came while Edward was away.

My dearest Clarinda,
We are moored off the coast of Greenland. Snow-white bears as big as houses stalk our ship along the ice banks that border this frozen waterway. One of our crew has lost all his fingers to frostbite. I miss you more than I can say . . .

On his return from Fremantle, Edward did not come to see me. He was a correct sort of man, and I had ordered him out of my house. In my turn, I avoided the bookshop. I read the exploits of Lady Josephine until I was sick and tired of camels. I did not read Robert's letters again, but I tried to imagine my life once he and I were married. What would he do in Midford? We were decidedly short of savages, bears and whirlpools. But if he maintained his maritime career I would hardly ever see him.

Maybe I would grow old without ever dancing at the Spring Fair again. If I had children, I might be bringing them up on my own.

I shed many tears. I slept with the Greenland letter under my pillow. I wished Edward would come so I could ask for his advice and be comforted by his . . . reliability.

Maud heard gossip which she brought to me with some reluctance. It concerned Robert. Rigid with offence, I summoned Edward to the house. The moment he arrived I confronted him with it. "Have you been spreading vicious stories about my betrothed?"

"I am saddened that your opinion of me has sunk so low," said Edward. "But the gossip comes from Fremantle, and others brought it, not I."

"Tell me the truth, Edward. I expect no less of you."

He sighed. "The *Delphine* docked at Fremantle three months ago and left a week or two later for Sydney. The word is that Robert has a wife and child there, Clarinda. I am afraid he has been telling you nothing but lies. The letters are pure fantasy. I have had my suspicions for a long time, but I could not bear to tell you, knowing how much you love him." He looked utterly wretched.

"It can't be true!" I heard how shrill I sounded, but could not moderate my tone as a lady should. "What about Madagascar and Jamaica and Greenland? And if he lied about that . . . " I covered my face with my hands.

"I took the liberty of writing to a colleague about Robert's father," said Edward. "Nobody in Sydney's legal circles has heard of such a man. I wish it were not so."

I took my hands from my tear-stained face and stared at him. "You do?"

Edward's cheeks went pink as a petunia. "I hate to see you hurt. But, since I cannot lie to you, I am obliged to add that I am much relieved that you are not to wed Robert. You can do so much better."

Even in my grief and humiliation, I assessed this remark. "I am four and twenty, Edward," I said. "Past my best. And I am now the laughing stock of Midford. I shall never be able to show my face in town again."

"It occurs to me," Edward said, "that there is another approach to the problem. Imagine the town gossips are our savage bears and the Spring Fair our whirlpool to be navigated."

At the Spring Fair I wore a tight-waisted gown and matching bonnet in rose silk. Edward's well-tailored suit was complemented by a rose-coloured cravat. I held my head high. Edward did not blush once. We joined in the dancing, raising more than a few eyebrows among the older ladies. Perhaps they expected me to be in mourning for my reputation.

At a certain point a young man tried to cut in. Edward looked down at the interloper. "The lady is with me," he said in a tone as assertive as the roar of a Bengal tiger. The young man vanished more quickly than snow in springtime.

"One savage bandit down, one hundred more to go," observed Edward.

I smiled. His arms around me were not simply those of the only man in Midford whose reputation rendered him above gossip. They were the strong reliable arms of a man content to be the hero of his own story.

☽

jack's day

The waves wash in at my feet, lapping against the rocks that cradle me. The sun is making its slow dive into the inky waters of the Indian Ocean. No surfers linger at the Point.

I'm starting to feel chilly and thinking a glass of red would go down nicely. But something holds me. A voice whispers, *Don't go yet, Beth. Stay with me a while longer.*

The wind stirs my hair, intimate as a lover's breath. Oh, Jack. If you'd stayed longer with me, how different things might have been. You could have seen all our son's milestones: the first ride without trainer wheels, the first day at school, the first football match. The first girlfriend—I'm glad she didn't last—and the first holiday with his mates. Goals kicked, exams passed, graduation day . . . "You might have had a daughter, Jack," I murmur as the sun touches the water. I imagine a little girl with his curls and dimpled chin. "You might have had the dog you always talked about. You might have coached Rick's team and gone fishing on the weekends. We might have grown old together, loving each other a bit more every day."

Gulls fly over me, their harsh comments mocking my flight of fancy. Might have, could have . . . what's the point of that? Suddenly the beach feels empty, the rocks too big, too dark, the ocean immense and powerful. My footprints make a track down from the dunes and along the sand to this, my thinking place. A lonely track.

The sun's setting. Time for the ritual. I stand, lift my arms, hold my head high. I think about the two of them, Jack and Bill, mates serving together in a war most of the country didn't understand. Jack was a shooting star, one of the SAS's youngest, lauded, decorated, sent off on one secret mission after another, doing things he never talked about, though I saw them slowly darken his eyes. Bill was a plodder, an infantryman, three tours of duty in a hell-hole of swamp and jungle and snipers in the dark, till the day they wheeled him off the transport with a head full of monsters and one leg blasted to nothing. Jack never came home.

I whisper into the wind. "Happy Birthday, Jack. I love you. I miss you." A last sliver of gold flashes at the rim of the world and is gone. The beach is full of shadows. Time to go home.

The driveway's empty, the house deserted. Inside, I take a quick look in the fridge. Outside, magpies exchange evening warbles. The sound of a car, passing, fading. Jack's photo on the wall: CORPORAL JOHN MILLER, SASR. Sunset hair under the sandy beret. Sea-blue eyes, bright as diamond and hard as steel. FEBRUARY 1940 – AUGUST 1966. I wonder what you'd have been like now, Jack. I wonder if you could have borne the time when it all had to stop. How would it have been to wake to a day with no rushing adrenaline, no life-or-death choices? I wonder if you could ever have slowed down.

Old grief stirs in me; old weariness wraps around me, a familiar garment. It was hard in those first months after Jack was killed, with Rick a tiny baby and my Mum sick. I hadn't known a person could be so tired and still go on. But you do. Help comes from the least likely places. The kids grow up, and you look back and think, maybe I didn't do such a bad job after all.

I put on the kettle, get out a mug, pop in a bag of Earl Grey. Turn on the TV news to swallow the silence. Catch a glimpse of myself in the mirror and chuckle. Look at me, Jack: picture of a lonely old woman, drinking tea in the dark. At least it's not whisky.

Light flashes across Jack's handsome features as a vehicle turns into the car port. Another pulls up behind it. Doors slam; kids chatter. They're here! Sally marches straight in, dumps a laden platter on the table and switches on the light. "What are you doing sitting in the dark, Mum?" My daughter-in-law casts her eye over the empty table. "You didn't forget the salads, did you?"

As Natasha comes in the door, carrying a wriggling baby and an immense pavlova, I open the fridge and start getting out the food I prepared this morning, before the heat of the day. Nat's older kids, well trained, set the table. I hear clinking sounds as the men unload bottles from the cars. By the time Rick and Matthew join us, the meal's ready. A summer feast; a celebration.

I glance at Jack's stern image. We're a tribe, I tell him. There's your son, Captain Richard Miller, SASR, enjoying his leave, pouring wine and promising his niece and nephew he'll play beach cricket in the morning. If he has shadows in his eyes, he's learned to deal with them. There's the daughter you never had, and there's her man Matthew. There are my beautiful grandchildren. I hope that doesn't make you sad. I hope it makes you smile.

"Tom called us on Skype last night," Sally's saying. "He's looking well. Sent his love. We don't know when he'll be home."

I ask no questions. She and Rick have just the one son: Private Thomas Miller, twenty-one this year and on his first overseas deployment. Back in the sixties, when Jack went away, I played a lot of mind games. Made crazy bargains with God. I pray Tom's girlfriend never has to go through what I did.

"I'm glad Tom's well," I say, but I feel the weight of it all.

After we've eaten we sit and talk awhile, exchanging our news. Rick proposes a toast to the father he never knew; we raise our glasses. To Jack! Happy Birthday!

The girls do the dishes. Matthew and Nat gather up their yawning kids and head for home, a five minute drive away. Sally and Rick are staying the night. We linger over our last drinks, not saying much. Beyond the fly wire, the shrill sound of cicadas overlays the wash of the waves.

"Shame Dad couldn't be here," Rick says, glancing at me. "You all right, Mum?"

I nod and we say our good nights. Later I stand on the veranda in my pyjamas, letting the sea breeze cool my skin. A familiar sound breaks the quiet, the engine of an old Holden ute. Headlights pierce the night. Home so soon? My heart clenches tight. What's happened?

The car lights go off, and he's opening the door and getting out, awkward with the prosthesis. Blue jumps down and bolts ahead to greet me with a doggy kiss. And here's Bill, limping towards me with a big smile on his tired face.

I throw my arms around my husband, loving the warmth of him, the roughness of his work-worn hands, the way he lays his cheek against my hair, still so tender after all these years.

"I wasn't expecting you back until Monday!" I say. "What happened? What about the boys?"

"The boys will cope without me this once," Bill says. "I know you said it didn't matter if I wasn't here for Jack's Day. But it felt wrong, somehow. And . . . well, I missed you."

I stand on tiptoe and kiss him; he smells of wood smoke. He's been at the annual reunion, a bunch of vets out bush, taming their demons and sharing the stories nobody else ever gets to hear. Bill doesn't need it any more, not for himself. But he has to go. He's the one who makes it all happen: organiser, chauffeur, counsellor and best friend. The brother they always wanted; the comrade they don't lose.

"Hungry?" I ask as we go inside. "Your daughter made her special pavlova."

Bill shakes his head. He's standing in front of Jack's photo, looking into his old friend's eyes. I expect him to wish Jack a happy birthday; that's our ritual. But what he says is, "You saved me, Beth. You know that? You pulled me out of the swamp." His voice is hushed in the stillness of the sleeping house.

I lay my hand against his back. "You saved me," I tell him. "I've been so lucky, Bill." Without him Rick would have had no father. There would be no Natasha, no Matthew, no laughing children in my life. I'm blessed with the best husband in the world, a man who lost so much and still had love to give. "I'm glad you came home."

☾

far horizons

The novels were doing well. *Dawn* had covered Kate's uni fees, *Goddess* had paid the deposit on Sean's flat and *Whisper* had helped set Bella up in her graphic design business. My publisher had just offered me a new three-book contract.

The children took me out to lunch to celebrate. Over the second bottle of chardonnay they went serious.

"Mum," declared Kate, "it's time you spent some money on *yourself.*"

"I do," I protested. "I've just had the gutters and downpipes replaced."

"Oh, Mum," said Bella, "you know what we mean. A chic hairdo, a pair of killer shoes, something for *you.*"

"A wolfhound," suggested Sean. "A harpsichord. Riding lessons."

"I might *like* those things, but I don't *need* them."

Finances had been tight for a long time since the divorce. When there'd been funds to spare—not often—they'd always gone on something practical: textbooks, dental treatment, car repairs. We'd managed, the four of us, thanks to good management and our shared sense of humour. I'd been amazed and grateful when my new career as a romance novelist made me, if not filthy rich, at least comfortably well off.

"Get the hairdo anyway," said Bella. "You're starting to look grandmotherly, Mum. Here, I've got a discount coupon for Ennio's. They've pencilled you in for two-thirty."

☽

Ennio gave me a severely stylish cut and softened my natural silvery grey with subtle highlights. Looking in the mirror I felt an odd sensation, as if I were a balloon about to float away on an adventure all its own.

Walking to the bus, I spotted a poster of pale minarets against a dusky sky, and another beside it of a teeming market full of brassware and vivid carpets. The name of the shop was Far Horizons.

"Nothing venture, nothing win," I muttered, stepping inside and taking a numbered ticket. There were lots of people waiting: three girls in low-slung jeans; a white-haired man calmly reading a book; older couples armed with maps and travel guides. I was dying for a coffee.

I leafed through the books and magazines. BOOMERS A LOOMING BURDEN ON HEALTH SYSTEM, screamed the *Bulletin*. I put it down and picked up the daily paper. SKIN: SPOILED AND SELFISH, the headline read. Scanning the piece I learned that SKIN stood for "Spend the Kids' Inheritance Now."

The queue progressed as sales staff called customers in turn. It was clear Far Horizons preferred to employ attractive people in their twenties, in keeping with their specialty: adventure travel. Their brochures featured athletic, glowing young things, and the staff matched. Perhaps I'd make it to the desk to discover I was too old and selfish to travel as far as Geraldton, let alone Turkey.

I flipped through a gossip mag. SIXTY IS THE NEW TWENTY was blazoned over pictures of ageing celebrities, nipped and tucked and botoxed into weird images of their younger selves. On the next page, I read BOOMERS MONOPOLISE THE HOLIDAY MARKET. I sighed. Maybe I should be spending my money on a tea cosy or a pair of fluffy slippers.

"They say we baby boomers live in our own little world," the white-haired man said, reading over my shoulder. He'd slipped his book into his pocket, but I could see the title: *Byzantium*.

"I'm about to squander my children's inheritance on a trip to Istanbul," I said, looking up to meet a pair of twinkling blue eyes in an interesting face, well worn and full of character.

"Really?" The blue-eyed man smiled. I placed him as a retired teacher. His wife might be the woman in the beaded cardigan, leafing through the brochures. Or maybe the smart blonde in her thirties. Older men did attract younger women.

"Have you heard of Stannard Travel?" he went on. "Specialist in historical tours. There's one coming up with a focus on Byzantine architecture. Got a spare brochure somewhere . . . " He delved into his pockets, releasing a shower of coins, papers, keys and other debris.

The girls in the queue giggled, exchanging whispers. The man's face reddened as he stooped to gather up his belongings.

"I suppose we're typical boomers," I said, kneeling to help him. "We want the adventures we didn't have as kids. The far horizons. Really we should just sit quietly in a corner and get on with our knitting."

Mr Blue Eyes gave a snort of laughter. I was glad I'd made him feel better.

I rescued a little plastic photo sleeve. A grey-haired woman gazed out with such love it made my heart flip over. How wonderful to have someone who felt like that about you.

"My wife, Laura," he said.

"She's lovely," I said.

"Number twenty-three!" called a Far Horizons staffer.

"That's me," he said. "Best of luck with your travels."

"You too." I watched him go to the desk, his back very straight. Maybe he was not a teacher, but a retired soldier. I flipped out my notebook and jotted a description for future reference. The lined face, the sensitive eyes the colour of . . . gentians, that was it; the excellent posture. The fact that he had blushed. In the story, I would make him an ex-mountaineer, or an ex-fighter pilot . . .

I was still scribbling frantically when a voice cut into my thoughts.

"Number twenty-seven?"

I got up with a start, scattering my own belongings all over the floor. The ex-mountaineer or fighter pilot was nowhere in sight.

"Can I help?" The girls in jeans came over to pick up my notebook, pen and glasses case. I thanked them. They'd probably been laughing earlier about their boyfriends, or work, or school. I had to stop reading articles about baby-boomers. They were making me paranoid.

"Twenty-seven?"

Fifteen minutes later, with my credit card burning a hole in my wallet, I walked out of Far Horizons. The sales assistant hadn't been at all patronising. It had turned out she loved Turkish history too.

As for Stannard Travel, I'd asked for a brochure. Maybe I'd add their Byzantine Turkey tour to my itinerary. I'd probably get to see a lot more with a group. If the retired whatever-he-was and his wife were anything to go by, the company would be congenial. And if it would have been nice not to be travelling as a single, never mind that. My life was complicated enough these days without some man to be fitted in.

Outside Far Horizons, I almost tripped over a huge grey dog that was sitting quietly under the minaret poster. On a small table beyond this apparition stood a steaming espresso. There was a coffee shop right next to Far Horizons—how had I managed to miss that before?

"Please join us." It was him, Mr Blue Eyes, seated on the other side of the alfresco table, the dog leash looped around his chair. "But maybe you don't like dogs. Timur, say hello nicely to the lady."

"Timur?" I queried, reaching to scratch the hound behind his oversized ears. "After the Mongolian warlord? I guess I was right about you the first time, when I placed you as a history teacher." A moment later, I felt a flush rise to my cheeks. I was talking as if he was an old friend, and I didn't even know the man's name. "Good boy, Timur," I muttered to cover my embarrassment.

"Do sit down." Blue Eyes didn't sound put out, just curious. "The coffee here's quite good. May I order one for you?"

"Thank you." It had been longer than I could remember since a man had offered to buy me coffee. It was a good feeling. "Espresso, please."

I sat down. Timur rested his long shaggy snout on my knee as if I were his long-lost buddy.

"So," said my human companion, "what was the second time?"

"What second time?"

"When I wasn't a history teacher." He signalled to a hip wait-person in black.

"Oh, dear. Now I'm going to embarrass myself. You were either a retired fighter pilot or a mountaineer. It's the posture, mostly. You've the look of an outdoor man."

"A fighter pilot? After you saw me drop my personal belongings all over the floor?"

"I did say retired." I smiled at him and received a charming grin in return.

"Sorry to disappoint you. I'm afraid I'm an accountant. Semi-retired; I do a little consulting work here and there. My name's Bill Stephenson, by the way." He reached out a hand to shake mine; his grip was strong and warm. "I did much better at guessing your occupation," he went on.

"Really?"

"Romance novelist," Bill Stephenson said, deadpan. Then, before I could summon a reply, he added, "My wife adored your books, Ms Summer. I know them cover to cover."

"You read romance?" I asked in disbelief.

A kind of shadow came over Bill's face. "Laura died last year," he said. "Breast cancer; it was a pretty slow process. She liked me to read aloud. A good distraction from the pain. We only just made it to the end of *Whisper*."

The arrival of my coffee allowed me a breathing space.

"I'm so sorry," I managed as the wait-person departed. "How sad."

"It's taken a long time to start coming to terms with it. A lot of soul-searching. Reading's helped. I have to admit that, on my own, I do favour history over romance. Of course, a novel that combined the two effectively would be irresistible, don't you think, Ms Summer?"

"Funny you should say that." There had been an idea bubbling away in my mind ever since I'd seen the minaret poster: a sweeping romantic epic set in Byzantine Turkey. "By the way, Felicity Summer is a pseudonym. My real name's the far more prosaic Althea Brown. Call me Althea, please."

"It's an enchanting name, eh, Timur?" The dog grinned agreement, drooling on my best wool skirt. "As for the outdoor man, my main form of exercise is walking Timur. I keep planning to do more. When you're on your own, it's easy to put it off."

We talked about swimming and bushwalking. Over second coffees we exchanged family information and dissected the latest Tim Winton. The light was fading; the wait-person began wiping down tables. Bill was scribbling something on one of his many scraps of paper when my mobile rang. It was Bella, talking so loudly my companion could surely hear every word.

"Where *are* you, Mum? I thought you were going straight home after the hair salon, but I got the answering machine. I need you to come round and help with—"

"I'm having coffee with my accountant," I said primly.

"Who's that laughing in the background?" My daughter's tone was full of suspicion. "Mum? Where are you, really?"

A man passed with a terrier at his heels. Timur erupted into a frenzy of barking.

"Mum!" shrieked Bella. "Sean wasn't serious about the wolfhound! When we said do something for yourself, we didn't mean do something silly and irresponsible."

"I'm on a sort of date," I said calmly. "With a retired fighter pilot and a ferocious hunting dog." Bill was laughing too hard to write. The wait-person stared at us as if we were crazy.

Stunned silence from the mobile. Then Bella said, "You're joking."

"Not at all," I said as Bill finished writing his phone number and slid the paper across to me. "Didn't you know baby boomers have no sense of humour? It's all right, Bella. Trust your mother. I'll be over later to help you with whatever it is. Then I'm starting a fitness campaign. Lots of walks. And then I'm going to Turkey." I glanced over at Bill's mischievous blue eyes, his comfortably lived-in face, his kind smile. "And then . . . Who knows?"

☽

tough love 3001

This story is dedicated to the eight participants in the 2004 Tough Love critique course held at the Katharine Susannah Prichard Writers' Centre in Western Australia.

*It's also dedicated to Neil Gaiman,
a prince among storytellers.*

"Ground rules," I said, suppressing a sigh of exasperation. The buzz of eight Unispeak Translators died down and a small sea of eyes, bulging, faceted, retractable, feline, globular, turned in my direction. There was a silence of complete incomprehension.

"Ground rules allow us to maximize the value of our limited number of sessions." The sigh came out despite me. Of all the groups I'd been given for Tough Love since they brought me here from the 21st century to run it, this was the motliest crew of students I'd ever clapped eyes on. I suspected the short course they'd come from all over the galaxy to attend would be just long enough to make a slight dent in the shining armour of false expectations each of them wore today. Who the hell were they? What did they imagine they would get out of this? Not for the first time, I pondered the wisdom of quitting a tenured position at the University of Western Australia for this. I had burned my bridges. Time travel being what it is, there was no going back. The *Intergalactic Voyager* did have state-of-the-art teaching facilities. It did have a bar stocked with every alcoholic drink this side of Alpha Centauri. Its students, on the other hand . . .

An attenuated, multi-ocular creature was saying something. The Unispeak model I have is the V28: it's programmed to convey style as well as meaning when it translates. This voice was genteel and nervous.

"You mean, keep left? Wash hands after using the facilities? No walking on the syntho-turf?"

I found a smile. "Those are rules, certainly. We might start with something about respecting one another's work, or not interrupting."

They considered this awhile. The one who had spoken quivered her antennae anxiously.

I said, "Perhaps we could go around the circle, and everyone could think of one ground rule."

Silence. For a bunch of individuals who were supposed to be writers, this was not a promising start.

"Be on time?" I suggested. "Wear pink socks?"

They looked blank; I had baffled them. A few seconds passed, then a creature of robust build with a mass of tentacles began to quiver uncontrollably, emitting a series of guttural sobs. "Ah—ha—ha—ho—ho!" my Unispeak translated. "Very good! Pink socks! I so adore the humour of the absurd! May I contribute?"

"Be my guest," I said, marker pen at the ready. I make a point of using antique technology (repro, that is) for my Tough Love classes. The students find my pens and whiteboard as fascinating as I would quills and parchment. I could see it was going to take more than a few coloured Textas to get this lot's creative juices flowing.

"Um," said Tentacles, "let me see now. Be courteous to the teacher? Bow on entry?"

I wrote, *Be courteous* on the whiteboard. They could all read English; it was a requirement of entry to my course. Unfortunately, some of them were anatomically incapable of speaking it. "Thank you," I said. "Bowing is perhaps too culture-specific. Any more?"

"Even when bored witless, one should not sleep in class," offered a participant whose appearance was markedly slug-like.

I wondered if the Unispeak had been programmed with a sense of humour; insouciance touched with ennui made this voice sound like those old recordings of Noel Coward. "Indeed," I said, writing it on the board. "You won't be getting much sleep at night, either. I'll be setting you daily writing and reading tasks, and you'll all have a piece ready for critique by your allocated session." I wrote, *Do your homework.* "Now," I said, turning to face their expectant eyes, "we're going to go around the circle and introduce ourselves."

There was a ripple of movement which I took to indicate agreement.

"Good. I'm Annie Scott, and as you know I was head-hunted from the early 21st to run this course. Back then I was a university lecturer in creative writing and literary criticism. This is quite similar."

A collective sigh; the eyes rolled, blinked, flashed in what I decided to interpret as appreciation.

"Your turn," I said, glancing at Tentacles, who seemed the boldest.

He gave his name. Even via the Unispeak it was unpronounceable. "Difficult, I know," he said politely. "You may call me Dickens, if you prefer. I am a fervent admirer of that great writer, Charles Dickens."

"Dickens. Right," I said.

The introductions went on. Dickens had started a trend for literary pseudonyms. By the time we were around the circle we had Brontë, the one with the antennae; Seth the slug; Saramago, whose maniacal grin displayed three rows of pointed teeth; terribly tall, one-eyed Atwood; and Winton, who was vaguely humanoid. Two retained their own names: K'gruz and Armahalon. Armahalon had just sung us a formal greeting of a profoundly cerebral kind when I realised there was a ninth chair in the circle, and that it, too, was occupied. The table at which my students sat had obscured this final attendee; only the tips of its ears could be seen above the edge. I moved closer and peered down, trying not to seem rude. Eight students was standard. That was all they were paying me for.

The creature sat quietly. It was pea-green and slightly fuzzy, like a cheap velour toy. There was a look about it that suggested a dog, or perhaps a corporeally challenged elephant, or one of those things you used to see in wildlife documentaries clinging to trees and looking helpless. The ears were enormous, fragile and wing-like. The eyes were liquid and mournful. I had no idea whether it was an aspiring writer or some trendy kind of lap-pet.

"Er . . . " I ventured, "whose is this?"

The students peered down, and the little creature turned its forlorn gaze up at them.

Atwood shuddered. "I'm here to critique, not to be shed on," she murmured.

"If we're talking lap-pets," Saramago put in, "give me a Zardonian bog-troll any day. Best alarm system in the Galaxy. And they keep your feet so warm at night."

"What will we discuss today, Teacher?" asked Seth in a voice like a bubbling mud pool.

"Call me Annie, please. Tomorrow we'll start critiquing one another's work. Today we'll practise on a piece by an established author, to ease you in. Critiquing is like walking on a wire. Some writers are utterly delusional about the nature and quality of their own work. Be honest, but temper your honesty with compassion. When someone critiques your writing it can feel as if they're hurting your beloved child."

"Ah, yes," enthused Dickens, swirling his tentacles in a show of agreement. "Beloved child, yes. Better if we tell soothing lies?"

"You must tell truths expressed with understanding and kindness," I told him.

K'gruz was wearing a full body protective suit with a filter mechanism; his Unispeak appeared to be hard-wired directly into his head. The voice emerged from a speaker. "I cannot be kind about Saramago's work!" K'gruz exclaimed. "He writes by hand, and he uses green ink secreted from his own disgusting glands. How can one take such a writer seriously? The presentation is entirely unprofessional. As for his *oeuvre* itself, it stinks more richly than the filth with which he sets it down. The concepts, the themes, the woeful lack of punctuation . . . where can I start?" If K'gruz had possessed eyebrows, at that point they would have arched extravagantly. As it was, he managed an expressive shrug that made his suit and its contents ripple.

I opened my mouth to intervene before Saramago decided to use his teeth, but the ladylike Brontë cut in.

"Ink? Ink is nothing! There is no point to any of it if we cannot divine a *resonance*, a *truth*, a *transcendence*, a—"

"Don't kid yourself," growled K'gruz. "Your own work is nothing more than an inflated piece of fluff, hardly good enough for a quickvid on a short hop interplanetary transit of the less salubrious kind. You're in no position to question literary—"

"Friends, friends!" Seth was trying to make peace. "Ground rules, please—" but nobody was listening. Saramago was snapping his teeth, Brontë's antennae were trembling with indignation, Armahalon had one foot on the table, revealing scythe-like toenails that were none too clean, and Winton was leaning back in his chair, laughing hysterically. Atwood was taking notes.

"Excuse me—" I said.

"Class, please—" I cried out.

"Stop acting like a bunch of spoiled infants!" I yelled.

"Alas, teacher," Dickens spoke in my ear, "I fear this Tough Love is no more than a battleground for exhausted ideas."

Under different circumstances I'd have complimented him on his turn of phrase. Things were getting nastier by the second. Saramago had sunk his teeth into the nearest available object, which was Brontë's hand; she was emitting little shrill cries of outrage. K'gruz was fiddling with a dial on his protective suit, from which a thin stream of evil-smelling yellow vapour was hissing forth. Seth and Armahalon were locked in an embrace that had nothing at all to do with inter-species attraction. Even Winton was getting in a random uppercut here and there. Atwood's digits were tapping away overtime on her Personal Recording Device (PRD). She had the new model, the one that communicates direct with a Unispeak and reads your work back to you in your language of choice. So much for green ink. I was being paid a fortune to run this, and my class had degenerated into a whistling, shrieking, punching, gasping free-for-all.

<<onceuponatimeinakingdomdfarfaraway thereliveaprincessinatowerofglass>>

The stream of sound pierced my skull at a decibel level designed to induce rapid-onset insanity. It was clear from the sudden stillness and agonised expressions of the others that it had hit them the same way.

<< a w i c k e d s o r c e r e r h a d l o c k e d h e r u p a n d
t h r o w n a w a y t h e k e y h e r o n l y c o m p a n i o n s
w e r e t h e l i t t l e b i r d s o f t h e f o r e s t r o b i n w r e n j a y
o w l t h r u s h a n d s w a l l o w a r e w e d o n e n o w ? >>

The agony ended. Wincing, we took our hands off our aural receptors.

"Who did that?" I asked shakily. It had been the most unthinkable kind of interruption, a violent mind-assault of the kind generally employed only in situations of military interrogation. I hadn't thought I'd need to put *No torture* in the ground rules.

Eight sets of eyes swivelled towards the handbag-sized creature, which turned its liquid gaze on me and spoke in a tone now mellow and musical.

"Sorry, Teacher. I considered you a damsel in distress, and was compelled to attempt a rescue."

I wrote *No mind-blasts* on the whiteboard. "And your name is?" I snapped.

"Ne'il." The word was delivered on a mournful, falling cadence. A neat glottal stop divided it into two clear syllables.

"Neil?" asked Atwood. "Who Neil?"

"O'Neil?" suggested Seth. "Eugene O'Neill?"

I waited. Very probably, Green Handbag had stolen a march on me.

"Wait a minute." Brontë was scratching her head; it was an impressive sight. I had never seen such flexible antennae. "He forced a story into us with his beastly mind-blast. A *fairy tale.*" She glared at Ne'il accusingly.

"Ne'il Gae-munn," he said, making a little song of it.

"Neil Gay-mun?" Winton echoed. "Who the heck was he?"

I saw the shudder go through Brontë's whole body; the cold disapproval enter Armahalon's eyes.

"Some of you know Neil Gaiman's work, I see." I ignored the chill in the air and went on gamely. "This is quite a coincidence, unless, of course, our friend here has psychic abilities. The story we're going to look at now is one of Gaiman's. It's coming through on your PRDs now; please read it silently and we'll discuss it when you're finished."

There was a mutinous quality about the ensuing silence. After a little, Brontë spoke. "This exercise is a waste of time for me. I can't comment on this kind of thing. I don't understand the conventions."

"If I had known we were going to discuss *genre* fiction," Armahalon delivered the offending word with brittle distaste, "I would never have enrolled for the class."

"I, too, am a literary writer," Dickens put in apologetically.

"This is for children," growled K'gruz. "Stepmothers, dwarves, magic fruit . . . It can have nothing at all to do with an advanced class in literary criticism."

I waited.

Seth was a fast reader; he was already well into the story. "For children? Oh, I do not think so," he said. "It is a dark tale. Unsettling."

"I need coffee," Saramago declared, rising to his feet. "Call me when we get to—"

"Sit down!" I said. "I'm in charge here. Read the story. Ne'il, why aren't you reading? You are a participant in the group, aren't you?"

He smiled beatifically, and I imagined Yoda saying, *Old am I.* "I know the tale," he said. "*Snow, Glass, Apples*, yes?"

"All the same—"

"By heart," he said. "Is not that the home of all good tales: the heart?"

"Some would disagree with you," I told him in an undertone, for the class had been hooked by the story and was reading avidly now. "Some would say the intellect. Or even the soul."

"Mmm," Ne'il said, his eyes luminous. "Or the balls?"

I looked at him.

"Or anatomical equivalent," he said, glancing around the table. There was perhaps one and a half sets of testicles between the lot of us.

"Good joke," I whispered. "We're seriously lacking in humour here. Do you think I can teach this lot to laugh at themselves? Can they find their own hearts, and one another's?"

"If hearts they have," Ne'il said, grinning, "find them we will."

○

It was a gruelling few days. Each student was different. Each was compelled by dreams, hopes, delusions; each was full of insecurity and prejudice, envy and bias. They knew their stuff, that was, the narrow personal corridor of fiction writing each had decided was worthy of his or her in-depth study. Some had real talent. Dickens had written a huge novel of 19th century London, full of sly humour and unforgettable characters. Saramago surprised us with a piece in which comparative religion was studied through father/son relationships. I was impressed that a being with so many teeth at his disposal was the intergalactic equivalent of a humanist. Brontë's work was light-weight, Armahalon's impenetrably deep. Winton spent his nights in the bar and turned up late for class until I called him a slacker. The next day he brought us a delicate piece of short fiction, a gem of stylistic simplicity.

"Ah," Ne'il said. "You are a storyteller."

☽

By the second day they were forming reluctant bonds. By the third day they were going to the bar en masse to down the brew of their choice and argue late into the night about Eliot Perlman's use of the second person and whether magic realism was just a particularly pretentious form of genre fiction. By the final day most of them had seen their own work with new eyes. Brontë was the exception; she hugged her piece defensively, refusing to change a single word. Atwood was restructuring her picaresque epic into a verse novel. K'gruz had reduced the number of breast references in his manuscript from fifty-four to twelve, and found synonyms for *pert* and *perky.*

Ne'il had submitted no written work at all. Every night as the members of Tough Love 3001 gathered in the *Intergalactic Voyager*'s smoky watering hole, he would sit amongst them and tell a story. They were tales of dragons and heroes, of hardship and quest, of self-discovery and heartbreak. They were myths, legends, sagas and fairy tales. They were, without a doubt, genre fiction. From the moment the diminutive green narrator opened his mouth to the time when he said "and they lived happily ever after", not a soul in that bar made so much as a squeak, a rustle, a sigh. Ne'il had them in the palm of his hand, or anatomical equivalent.

☽

At the final class, I thanked them for their dedication and hard work and was able to say quite truthfully that I was sorry the course was over. They offered grave compliments in return: they had learned much, they would never forget me, they would be back next year.

"Where's Ne'il?" I asked, seeing the ninth chair was empty. "Has his shuttle left already? He didn't say goodbye."

"Alas, we do not know," said Dickens. "Perhaps he has exhausted his fund of tales. All good things come to an end. Annie, we wish to present you with this gift in token of our appreciation."

I'd been rather hoping for a bottle of wine or perhaps a flask of the powerful *k'grech* they brewed on K'gruz's home planet. This silver-wrapped parcel was more the size and shape of a cake, or maybe a hat. I tore off the ribbon and the shiny paper and choked in horror.

It was a handbag. It was fuzzy and green, velour-like in texture, and had a cosy rotundity of form. The handle was constructed from two large, ear-shaped flaps knotted together.

"We made it for you," Armahalon said in his humming tones.

"We made it all together," said Saramago, showing his teeth.

"I've never liked fantasy," observed K'gruz. "All those dragons and women in gauze and leather. It's so . . . so . . . "

I clapped my hands over my mouth, wondering if I could make it to the gleaming toilet facilities of the *Intergalactic Voyager* before I spewed up my breakfast all over the floor. Stars spun before my eyes; my knees buckled.

"Dickens, fetch water," a familiar voice murmured somewhere close by. "Our attempt at humour has misfired. Annie, do not cry."

"You should read more non-fiction, Annie," said Atwood drily. "Didn't you know Ne'il's species shed their skins every full moon?"

I opened my eyes. There beside me on the floor was Ne'il, or at least I assumed it was he; his new skin was a delicate shade of mauve.

"It's closer to lilac," he corrected, smiling. "See, you taught them to laugh."

"That wasn't funny!" I snapped as my heartbeat returned to normal. "I thought—"

"Ah," said Ne'il, "you forgot my name. Is not the sweetest of fairy tales tinged with darkness? Such duality lies at the heart of all experience: light and shadow, safe reality and fearsome imagining, fruitful summer and fallow winter. Has not the most charming of Gae-munn's work a tiny touch of horror?"

"What?" gasped Brontë. "Fantasy *and* horror? You mean there's such a thing as—*double-genre?*"

"Never mind," I said. "Write your stories, dream your dreams, work hard and come back next year if you can. And if I don't see you again, live happily ever after."

The bag was heavy. When I got back to my room I discovered it held three squat mini-flasks of top quality *k'grech*, guaranteed to blow out the drinker's eyeballs. My students had passed with flying colours.

☽

wraith, level one

I've never believed in heaven so I'm gobsmacked when it happens. One minute I'm half asleep in the back of the car, wondering if Dad will let me have a go with his new fishing rod when we get to the holiday house, then Mum hits the brakes and everyone screams, and the next minute we're lining up at these humongous gates carved with cherubs and stuff, and having our names written in a book by a guy in a white nightie who tells us to call him Pete. We're dead: Mum, Dad, Sarah and me all together. Everything else is gone—home, friends, school, that fishing holiday I was looking forward to—and instead here we are getting rewarded for being nice, not naughty. Some reward it turns out to be.

Thing is, it's dead boring up here. The stuff I like doing—surfing, skating, playing armies in the bush, chilling with my mates, listening to Triple J's Hottest 100—they don't have any of that. There is music, but it's this antique stuff, harps and flutes and tinkly bells, and you can't turn it off. And people don't *do* anything, they just float around smiling. Mum and Dad seem to think it's the best holiday they've ever had, and for some reason Sarah scores wings, so she's cool with it, flying around with a bunch of other girls and comparing feathers. Maybe she got some kind of credit for reading all those books about fallen angels. But me? Pretty soon I'm ready to sell my soul for five minutes on a BMX at the park. Only I guess I *am* a soul now, which is pretty weird.

So I'm at breaking point, pretty much, thinking this could be for, like, ever. I float up to the gates to see if I can do something about it. Pete's there with his big book, but there's no queue right now. Pete's smiling like everyone else here, but underneath the smile I bet he's bored too. What a job. But at least he's *got* a job.

I tell him my problem and he chuckles, like he's heard it a zillion times before. The smile starts to look real.

"Uh-huh," he says. "Can't take the eternal peace and tranquillity, right?"

"Right," I say, pleased that he's listened. "Why aren't there any other kids my age here? I mean, it's going to be mostly old people, I get that, but I can't be the only twelve-year-old boy who ever died in a car crash. Where are they all?"

Pete's starting to look like Santa on a Christmas card now, all grin. "Out on assignment," he says. "Secret missions."

"You mean, like, James Bond kind of stuff?" No way.

"I mean, like, supernatural kind of stuff. Hauntings. Manifestations. Visitations. Weird knockings at midnight."

"You're kidding!" I stare at Pete; he stares right back. "You're not kidding. Wow! Can I be one of those guys that rides around with his head under his arm?"

"Ah—not so fast. You need qualifications before I send you back down there. And Headless Horseman is a Level Three manifestation. No running before you can walk."

Bummer. Looks like I'm doomed to eternal floating. "What qualifications?"

"Good eyesight," Pete says. "Good balance. Plenty of energy. And a mission."

Double bummer. How am I going to prove all that now I have no body to speak of? I mean, it's there, I can see it, but I'm kind of transparent like everyone else up here.

"We do keep an eye on the Living." Pete's sounding sympathetic now. "Armies in the bush; BMX riding; skateboarding; I think we can assume you qualify on the first three criteria. And you came to me of your own accord, that's a plus. There's the mission, of course. Any ideas?"

"Don't you assign the mission?"

He shakes his head. "Not the first one. That's your opportunity to prove yourself. A chance to show you can do something worthwhile. If you pass, you're on the payroll. In a manner of speaking."

"Wow." My mind goes completely blank for a bit, then fills up with all the fantastic stuff I could do as a ghost: rattling chains at midnight, making dogs meow, writing surprise messages on school blackboards. I have a feeling Pete won't want me spooking little old ladies or causing accidents. "Is there a, whatsit, a Code of Conduct?"

"We follow the old principle, *Do No Harm*. There's to be no direct contact with the Living. They may see the results of your actions, but you mustn't speak to them or appear to them in your own form. That causes no end of trouble for everyone. No going back to reassure your family that you're existing happily in the Afterlife. They'll find out soon enough."

Right. So those meetings where people pass on messages from the dead—séances, that's the word—must all be fake. Interesting. The part about family doesn't matter to me, since my family's up here already. But there is someone I want to see.

"How about friends?" I ask. "If I make absolutely sure they don't see me?"

"As I said, no direct contact. No talking to the Living. No manifestation, and no getting inside people's heads—Inhabiting is a Level Four skill. Try that without the proper training and you'll find yourself in floating mode for all eternity." Pete looked very close to winking, but his voice was stern. I could tell he meant every word.

"How do I get back down there?"

"Once I've approved your mission it's as simple as a click of the fingers. Good luck, Matthew."

I have no trouble choosing my mission, and Pete okays it. I have—had—this friend, Sean. We were in Year Seven at City Beach Primary together. Sean wasn't my best friend—guys don't have best friends like girls do. We just had our group, five of us, and we did things together, like going to the beach after school or playing in the bush. Sean was sort of in the group and sort of not. He was mainly *my* friend, and the others let him come along, but they only played with him if he was with me, not on his own. Sean has a dog, Major, a sort of blue heeler gone wrong, with these crazy stunted legs and a body like a barrel. Not the brightest dog on the planet. He used to like coming with us to play armies, but he was hopeless at ambushes. If Sean was on your side, you could be pretty sure Major would waddle out of the hiding place and bark just as the enemy was getting close. For that reason, Sean was almost always on my side. The others never wanted Major in their team.

Sean's smart. He reads heaps of books, though he doesn't do so well in tests. His reports say stuff like *Sean should stop day-dreaming and learn to concentrate.* He used to lend me books, got me started on Ranger's Apprentice and Troubletwisters. And he writes great stories about new planets and weird adventures. The other kids at school like reading his stories but they don't like Sean all that much. He's a funny-looking kid with sticking-out teeth and glasses, and he's terrible at sport. He can't balance on a skateboard for nuts, though I gave him lessons and he kept on trying until his knees were seriously skinned. I've been worried about how Sean was getting on since the day I found myself up at those gates. So my mission is to make sure he's OK.

Until I learn Manifestation I'll be invisible in the world of the Living, so Pete says. I waft down to City Beach Primary and hover on the edge of the oval where some kids are playing footy. Brett Smith scores a goal for the blue faction and I give a silent cheer. Wish I was down in the middle of it and not up in the air, though actually this is a great view. There's Sean, sitting under a tree reading. He often gets let off sport because of his asthma. I glide in a bit closer and see that he's not actually reading the book. His eyes are on the footy match but they're sort of glazed, as if he's not really seeing it. The book is a new Garth Nix, one I haven't read. If that can't keep him interested things must be pretty bad.

I hover right beside him, partly to have a read of his book and partly to try and work out what's bugging him. Maybe I get a bit too close, because suddenly he sits up straight and I hear him say "Matt?", though his lips don't move. I shoot out of there fast before I break a rule and get myself condemned to eternal floating.

How could Sean know I was there? The Living can't see us unless we Manifest, and they can't hear us unless we make a point of clanking chains or whatever. Sean's a pretty unusual sort of guy, lots of imagination, but this was like he had ESP or something. One thing's for sure—I've got to be more careful from now on.

I'm worried about Sean. He doesn't look good at all, so I hang around until the end of school and follow him home at a safe distance. Adam and Brett go off together and David goes home with his sister. Sean walks with his head down. He doesn't stop to look at interesting stuff the way we used to. We always used to make faces at Mrs Maldon's dogs when they stuck their noses through the fence, and we used to stop and eat mulberries on the vacant block near the park. The mulberries look great today, but Sean doesn't even glance at them. He goes on up the hill until he comes to the corner where, if I was there, we'd be splitting up to go home. He says, "See ya, Matt," only, like last time, his lips don't move. He heads off home. Major waddles out to meet him and they both go inside.

It strikes me, real hard, why Pete doesn't let people come back to visit their families. It's hard enough seeing my friend in a mess because of what's happened, and a family would have to be worse. The mission starts to feel a bit hopeless. How can I help Sean if the Rules of Haunting mean I can't let him know I'm here? I'm just about to go on up to the gates and never come back when all the guys start reappearing up and down the street, dressed for a game of armies. Brett and Adam have their camouflage pants on and David's wearing a scout shirt with the badges taken off, his battledress jacket and a balaclava his grandma knitted for him— she was knitting me one as well, but I guess that'll go to one of the others now. They head off down the street, and pretty soon Sean comes out too and tags on the end of the group. Major's there as well, panting a bit as he tries to keep up.

I follow them over the highway and up into the bush, wondering how they're going to split the teams for armies now. It used to be Brett, Adam and David versus me, Sean and Major, that's if we were all there. Guess who nearly always won? Sometimes Brett would choose me for his team and then Adam or David had to go with Sean.

It looks as if they aren't splitting up today anyway. They all head on up the hill, through the scrub and over towards the quarry. We usually don't go that far. We once made a cubby up there and when our parents found out they went mental, saying it was too dangerous. It's OK really, though. You just have to keep away from the edge.

I wish I was there. Really there, I mean. The guys are going to a new place, down the side of the quarry. It looks pretty steep. Adam swears when he slips on some loose gravel. Sean's at the back, keeping up quite well but looking a bit white. Major's scrabbling after him.

Brett gets to the bottom and waits for the others. "There!" he says, pointing to the end of this hollowed-out place in the rocks. The guys come over in a bunch to look at it, and I glide in for a look too, being careful not to get too close.

There's this really deep-looking hole in between the rocks, full of water. There must be an underground spring or something, because it's usually pretty dry in this bushland, but here's this sort of dark pool, with a rock shelf on the far side and steep cliffs going up next to it, so high it's all in shadow. The other guys look impressed and worried at the same time.

"Wow," says David, his voice echoey and strange.

"How do you get around the other side?" asks Adam, having a good look at the pool, which is pretty wide.

Sean isn't saying anything. Nor is Major, who's down on his haunches having a rest, his little eyes fixed mournfully on Sean.

"Up here." Brett's already starting to climb around the sheer rock face next to the pool. Now that I get a good look, I can see there are places where you can grab onto the rock, and footholds too. The problem is, there's water seeping out of the cracks and little slimy weeds growing there, and it looks slippery.

Brett's going well, finding spots for his feet, gripping on tight with his fingers. Nobody else moves, though, until he's right around the rock wall and safely on the shelf at the other side.

"Come on!" he yells, and his voice seems to be coming from everywhere.

Adam goes next. He manages all right, though he uses some of his worst swear words when he slips halfway around and gets his new runners wet. Then it's David's turn. I don't think he really wants to do it, but it's turned into a kind of test, so he does. His face is shiny with sweat and he stops a couple of times on the way over, but he grins when he gets to the other side and Brett says "Great!"

Sean and Major haven't moved. Sean's looking over at the other guys. I don't like the look on his face—sort of set and unhappy and a bit desperate, as if he feels he has to prove something to himself.

"Come on, Sean!" yells Brett, not really unfriendly.

Now Sean's looking at the rock wall with its coating of slime.

"You chicken or something?" calls Adam.

"Shut up, Adam," David says. "He doesn't have to do it."

Adam looks a bit embarrassed, but it's too late anyway. Sean's starting around the rock wall, his feet in thongs, his shoulders tight with strain as he clings on.

I come very close to breaking the Rules of Haunting then. I could talk him around as easy as anything. I could help him hold on. He isn't so hopeless, really—he's a bit weak but he always tries things, even though he isn't much good at them. But the *no touching, no talking* rule means I can't help him.

Sean's about half way around when Major starts barking. He's got a huge bark, deep and menacing, a Rottweiler sort of bark. With the echo off the rock walls, that bark is like the sound of a sledgehammer. It pounds right into your head.

Sean hesitates. The guys on the other side have gone very still. Slowly, Sean moves his foot out to the next crevice in the rock and reaches up for a hand-hold. I don't hear it because of the barking, but I see the rock beneath his foot give way and splash into the dark water and then, almost straightaway, Sean loses his grip and falls into the pool, and the water swirls right over his head.

He's up again quickly, but he's drifted out towards the middle and he's flailing around, coughing and splashing and doing all the stuff you're not supposed to do in the water. He doesn't shout for help; he's too busy trying to breathe. I can see the guys putting two and two together and making five—Sean's asthma and his weak swimming and a few other things add up to a pretty serious situation. I can feel Brett's thoughts as he rips off his shoes and dives into the water. What he's thinking is, *Not him too.*

David crouches at the edge of the rock shelf. Adam starts to climb back around to the other side, probably thinking he might have to run for help. It doesn't take Brett long to swim out to the middle of the pool, but when he gets there Sean panics, clutching onto him and practically pulling him under.

"Let him go, Brett!" David yells. "You'll both get drowned!"

Brett hangs on, though, swallowing a lot of water as he tries to get Sean over to the shelf, but not making much progress.

I'm helpless. I can't think of a single thing to do that won't break the Rules of Haunting. But I'm not going to let two of my good friends die when I could have saved them. I'm about to take some kind of dramatic action when the barking stops. I turn and look at Major. He's fixing me with his beady and not very intelligent eyes, and suddenly I get it. The rules say no talking to the Living, fair enough. They say no getting inside people's heads. People. Not dogs.

In three seconds Major is transformed. He leaps up, eyes gleaming, and executes a perfect doggy dive into the water. He paddles effortlessly up to the struggling guys, grabs Sean by the back of his tee-shirt and starts swimming toward the bank where Adam's now standing. Sean's still thrashing around, but Major's grip keeps his head above water. Free of Sean's strangle-hold, Brett swims after them, his face white with shock.

Adam hauls Sean out, helped by Major, and does some old-style resuscitation on him. Brett collapses on the rocks and tries to get his breath back, and David climbs around from the ledge. Major sits quietly beside Sean, giving his face a lick from time to time.

Sean's OK after a while. He sicks up a few litres of pond water and coughs a bit, then they put Adam's jacket on him and start for home, talking about how they're going to explain the wet clothes to their mums. This time Major goes first, his ears pricked up like a real blue heeler's, his tail held high. Every few minutes he looks back to see if Sean's all right, then he heads on along the track.

So now I'm officially a Wraith Level One. Pete says if I keep up the good work I'll soon be promoted to Level Two. He says I performed my mission with initiative and imagination. So I'm allowed to learn poltergeist stuff and fiddle around with ectoplasm.

Sean's happier these days. The guys seem to like him a lot better now. Brett said Major was a canine hero, and everyone wants him and Sean on their team. I think what really changed their minds, though, wasn't the way Major dived in and saved Sean's life. It was Sean climbing around that rock wall even though he was scared out of his skull. I'm glad I didn't help him with that climb, because what mattered was that he did it all by himself.

He still stops and says, "See ya, Matt," when he gets to the place where we used to split up after school. But I don't think he misses me so much anymore, and though that makes me a bit sad, I know it's a good thing. As for me, I miss him, and I miss Brett and David and Adam, and I miss my BMX and my skateboard and playing armies in the bush. But I sure am looking forward to being a Headless Horseman.

☽

back and beyond

They say you can't go back. They say trying breaks your heart. Things morph and change, every moment another step on the slow path of decay. Iron rusts; copper tarnishes; glass shatters; silk tears and frays and rots. Skin wrinkles. Hearts break. The past is forever out of reach. That's what they say.

As a lover of fairy tales, I should be mindful of such warnings. Fairy tales are full of them: *Use every key except the smallest. Love me, share my bed, but don't ever ask me where I go on the night of full moon. Wander about anywhere in the castle except for the north tower.* But then, the best stories are the ones where the hero ignores good advice. They're the ones where folk release monsters and walk into traps, then by courage and cleverness make their own way out. Does the young sister decide nettles are too hard to sew, and her brothers may as well stay swans? Does Vasilissa refuse to fetch fire from Baba Yaga? Does the soldier hand over the tinder box to the witch and lose his head, end of story? Hardly. What poor tales those would be.

So I'm going back, heedless of the warnings. It feels like time. I'm going back to the Children's Library, or more precisely, to the patch of grass beyond the back door, near where they used to keep the rubbish bins. Only one child ever knew the secret of that patch of grass, and that child was me.

I'll be honest. It's possible I've conjured a false reality from dreams and wishful thinking. I've had that place hidden away inside me, locked and guarded, all these years, right next to unworthy thoughts, words I should have left unsaid, mistakes never atoned for. The Department of Unfinished Business. Was the patch of grass more than it seemed to be? I never expected to find out, and I didn't much care. It was long ago and far away. Besides, I liked the memory as it was.

Last week's news changed that. It changed everything. Seems my story from this point on will be shorter than anticipated: more flash fiction than epic trilogy. With that revelation, I've instantly become the youngest child in all those questing tales. I will not measure out my time in a slow downhill journey to the bitter end. I will be bold. I will be brave. I will use the smallest key, climb the north tower, ask the forbidden question, all three. All on the same day. Why not? Soon there'll be nothing left to lose.

Last time I visited Dunedin, a few years ago, the Children's Library building housed some kind of eatery. What will it be now, an upmarket boutique, a private gallery, a writers' collective? Offices, maybe. That could make my mission tricky. I head down Stuart Street from my B&B, thinking about that patch of grass. Paved over long ago, I expect. No matter. The toughest paving breaks down eventually. Cracks and splits like a broken heart; frets and crumbles away. Who knows what may lie beneath?

As I walk down the hill I meet my young self headed the other way, going home. She balances a stack of eight library books; the one she's reading is open on top. Her hair is in unravelling plaits and her glasses are sliding down her nose. She crosses Filleul Street with only a cursory glance for traffic. I know she does not see the cars, but riders in armour, a dragon in a lonely cave, trolls and demons and mermaids. A solemn child in a viyella frock, hand-knitted cardigan and school sandals, she walks oblivious up the hill and away from me, trailing magic.

You found it, I think. *I can find it. It is real.*

The library has changed hands again; the sign outside reads Scotia Bar and Bistro. They find me a table at the back. I feel a presence here: the Children's Librarian lingers long after her time, a woman of formidable intellect and volatile mood. There was something of the witch in her, and that left its mark on me. A good witch. These walls nurtured my writing gift. They gave me breathing space. They filled my head with dreams.

Scotia is a serendipitous find. Here I can eat a last meal that honours my Highland forebears. I order haggis, bashed neeps and tatties. I'm too keyed-up to manage both soup and mains. My stomach is in knots. I loosen them with the assistance of a Laphroaig, neat. I wonder what the patrons—only a sprinkling—think of an elderly woman dining out alone. Likely they don't even see me. Once your hair turns white, once you start to sag a bit, you become invisible except to your own kind. I have a sudden urge to turn on my fellow diners, cackling wildly and curving my fingers into talons. *You fools! Haven't you read your fairy tales? Ignore me at your peril!*

The urge passes with the arrival of my meal. As I eat, my gaze is drawn toward the back door. I can see that the kitchen is through there, and there's a sign for the loos. The place I want is out that way. Have I got the guts to go through with this, and if I have, who's going to pay for my dinner? I could leave cash under the plate. I could leave my credit card. I might become one of Dunedin's great unsolved mysteries, fodder for tabloid headlines and true crime books. *The Case of the Vanishing Author.*

I finish the haggis and eat the trendy garnish, complete with fungi. A solution for the case comes to me—magic mushrooms, a hallucinogenic trance, a night walk through the city, a fall into the depths of a construction pit to become a permanent part of a new building. Oh, yes, a new library! *Little did Susan know, as she borrowed a magical saga of druids and warriors for next month's Book Club, that the author's corpse lay entombed right under the circulation desk.* I ponder returning to the B&B to write this tale— *The Ghost in the Library*—but that would be the act of a coward.

"Dessert, Madam?"

I order the whisky trifle and a decaf long black—they'll be some consolation if my courage fails me at the last minute—then rise and head for the Ladies.

It occurs to me, as I sit on the loo studying the graffiti, that I should have brought a bigger bag. My evening purse is bulging with keys, wallet, mobile, reading glasses and pill bottle. Not that these items will be much use to me in that other place. The glasses, maybe—I could use them for lighting fires, if nothing else. I'd have been better to bring a flint, a knife, wayfarer's bread, a water-skin, warm clothing. In fairy tales, the youngest child always heads off to seek her fortune carrying, as a minimum, a crust of bread wrapped in a red-and-white spotted kerchief. I consider going back in for the whisky trifle and decide against it. But what if I want to keep a journal? The only writing materials I have are a clapped-out ballpoint and the back of a letter. That's the letter I read only once, the one that includes the words *invasive malignant carcinoma*. I unroll six metres or so of toilet paper, fold it and stuff it in my pocket. One way or another, it's sure to come in handy.

Can't put this off much longer. I creak open the door of the Ladies and go out into the yard. Warm light: the glow from the kitchen windows, through which I see the chef and her underling putting finishing touches to puddings. Cold light: the impassive blue-silver of the moon. Full moon. A time for change, no doubt of it.

I'm on the pavers, feeling my way not with my feet but with my memory. A blockish building looms on my left. Ahead are the blind back walls of shops and municipal offices. A dilapidated cottage stands against one, an unlikely survivor from times past. Over the sagging porch a wind chime tinkles gently. I can just make out the hand-lettered sign in the darkened window: Tarot Readings. Crystal Healing. Brighid's Circle, third Friday.

Where was the spot exactly? Here? Or over there? I try to orient myself by rooftops, chimneys, doorways, but too much has changed. It's been more than fifty years since I first went through. I look up at the moon, and she gazes back down, pregnant, mysterious, beautiful. Perhaps benevolent. Perhaps merely detached. I close my eyes.

I'm sitting cross-legged on the grass, my library books on one side—the Blue Fairy Book, Knight's Castle, The Silver Chair—and my school bag on the other. This is the spot, the magical spot. I'm engrossed in my reading: *Up and down the paths and avenues ran poor Beauty, calling him in vain, for no one answered, and not a trace of him could she find . . .*

"Are you all right?"

My eyes snap open onto the moonlit night, the restaurant windows, and the concerned features of a woman standing by the loo door.

"Mm, fine. Just getting some fresh air. Chilly night."

"Should be a lovely day tomorrow," she says, and goes back inside. Now I've been spotted I'd best get this done quickly, before someone notices my coffee going cold on the table and my dessert pristine on the plate. I close my eyes once more.

The books; the bag; the grass scratchy under my bare legs. *At last, quite tired, she stopped for a minute's rest, and saw that she was standing opposite the shady path she had seen in her dream.* I see the shady path. It's about ten paces away, and leads into a forest of spruce and fir, dark northern trees. Trolls hide behind stones; giants sleep in secret caves. Enter with caution. Bring your own box of tricks, or the path may wind on and on, and the forest never open to meadowland. My seven-year-old self went in armed with tales. She found a talking hedgehog and a queen with no castle and a fairy with an aptitude for bubble-blowing. She found five friends with unusual talents, and performed a quest requiring the help of mice and birds, and lived to come home again. Back to this place behind the library.

And now I will quest again, and be the hero of my own story. If there is a monster called invasive malignant carcinoma in this tale, I will slay it with my trusty . . . mobile phone? I'm shivering. Should've brought a pocket knife, a book of spells, an attack dog.

It occurs to me that I'm about to take my own monster on the quest, which is beyond foolish. I delve into the bag and bring out the letter from my oncologist. I don't need this sheet of paper. I will learn to write on parchment. I will learn to *make* parchment, and ink, and quill pens. I will find an ancient scholar to teach me.

I rip the letter into tiny pieces, reducing the big scary monster into small, manageable ones: oma, siv, ali, nan. If I meet them over there I'll tame them. Train them to scrape back my parchment, grind my pigments, sharpen my quills, serve me herbal teas. Right. Now it's really time.

I take the pill bottle out of my bag. By moonlight, without my glasses, I can't read the small print on the label. One, two, twelve, fifty? Enough for a single night's rest or a hundred years of thorn-guarded slumber? No matter.

Close the eyes again; feel the racing heart, a wild horse rushing for home; calm the breathing, slow, slower, slowest. Imagine the moon and stars above, calling me home. Sink into the story . . . *She rushed down it, and, sure enough, there was the cave, and in it lay* the Beast—asleep, as Beauty thought. Quite glad to have found him she ran up and stroked his head, but to her horror he did not move or open his eyes.

It's all right, I reassure Beauty, as I am taken up and whirled around and set down blind in another world, *your Beast still lives; in this place, love saves and redeems. In this place dreams come true. Here, valour and honour and fidelity mean something. And in this place*—I open my eyes at last—*nobody disregards an old woman, not if they have the least skerrick of common sense.*

I'm here. There is the path under the dark trees, and there the cave, and there is Beauty bending to kiss her Beast, and he opening his eyes to learn that he can be loved. It is night, and the same full moon shines down on us. I realise I have left my handbag behind. There will be no cheating at kindling fire; no phoning home. I'm on my own, and the future is mine to make.

I get up, finding to my surprise that this realm has provided me with suitable clothing for that future: I'm wearing a pair of stout wooden-heeled shoes, thick stockings, a long gown with little bone buttons, an embroidered shawl, a red kerchief with white spots. This is tucked into my belt, ready to accept what comes—a cargo of mushrooms, an abandoned puppy I might find by the wayside, a gift of magic beans, a plait of garlic. Something's sticking into me. Ah! A knife, slipped through the other side of the belt. I look up at the Shining One and give her a nod. *Thanks for the head start.*

I glance around me, assessing the terrain. In the cave, Beauty and her Beast are locked in an embrace. I note with interest that he has not morphed into a handsome prince, and that pleases me. Who wouldn't prefer the Beast, loving, honest, real in his imperfection?

A moment to reflect; a moment to consider what I've left behind. My daughter will get the letter in a day or two, the only true record of where I've gone. *Tell the girls I've gone on a quest. If I don't come back, it's because there's always a new monster to slay, a new injustice to combat, a new voyage of discovery to make. Let them remember me that way, not as an old woman who rusted and tarnished and frayed as, day by day, they witnessed her slow, helpless decline. Girls, know that each of you will be the hero of her own tale. As you are, my lovely daughter. Look for my smile in the full moon. Hear my voice on the wind. Feel my touch in the warmth of a summer day. I will be there every moment, telling a new tale of wonder.*

I wipe my eyes on a fold of the shawl. I stand up straight. I square my shoulders, and see an owl fly across the moon. The night air fills my lungs and suddenly I am wide, wide awake, more awake than I have ever been in my life. I stick two fingers in my mouth and give a piercing whistle. Silence, save for the shivering of the trees. Hmmm. Something further required here. "Hocus, Pocus, Zippity-zog," I chant, not entirely at random. And out of the dark comes a wondrous dog. He is as big as a horse, his paws are the size of footballs, his teeth gleam in the moonlight. His eyes are kindly, like those of my dear departed kelpie, Outlaw. He wags his tail with frantic enthusiasm. Perhaps he *is* Outlaw, transformed by his passage to this other place. His hair was red-brown when I knew him before. Now it's white as hoar-frost.

"Down, Outlaw," I command, and he hunkers down beside me. I climb onto his back, and we're away! We run, we run, we run like the wind! The trees stream past, a chaos of dark shapes, a river glints into view and winks out again, mountains rear up in the distance, their peaks gleaming with snow. The night unfurls around us like a shadowy cape. Run, Outlaw, run! I am Baba Yaga in her shivering house of bones! I am Morrigan swooping black-winged to gather her harvest of souls! I am Hexebart and Atropos and Granny Weatherwax! I am Draguța, I am La Loba, I am the wise old woman at the heart of every tale! I am she who shakes the earth, I am she who bursts the banks in spring flood, I am she who hears the secret thoughts of an acorn sleeping the winter long. I speak to the thunder and converse with the lightning. Out of my way, for a quest is afoot, and the path is as long as the tale I tell!

☽

the angel of death

Someone slides open the shed door and the smell hits me. It's not just the acrid stink of urine and the familiar stench of faeces, it's a deep-down, energy-sapping smell of sickness and despair. The noise is deafening. A good sign, I guess. To bark like that, you need the will to live.

There are nearly five hundred dogs in this place; that's what we've been told. None of the volunteers are saying much as the RSPCA staff hand out supplies and allocate each of us a row of cages. I get Sector F, eighteen cages in all. It's going to be a long day.

The supplies include a mask, but I don't put mine on. Puppy mill animals don't get handled much and when they do, it's often not kindly. A bitch lives pretty much her whole life in a small wire cage. She's hauled out to mate, then shoved back in to give birth. She suckles her pups for a few weeks before they're taken away to be cleaned up and sold. She's left in the cage until it's time for the next mating. This goes on until she's too old or too sick to be productive any more. She's a breeding machine. Why would she put any trust in human touch? If I was her, I'd want to see a whole face, not a mask. Either way, I'm going to get bitten more than once today, so I do pull on the heavy-duty gloves. I'm going to walk out of here smelling like an open latrine and hopping with fleas.

Sector F has small dogs, Maltese, Papillon, Chi, trendy cross-breeds. Or so I guess; these dogs haven't been bathed or groomed for months, maybe years. Some of them could be anything.

I'm quickly into the routine. First get some shredded paper in each cage to make the dogs more comfortable before I have to do any handling. One way or another they'll all be out of here by the end of today so cleaning the cages is a waste of time.

I move along the rows, opening each cage door, putting in the paper, having a quick look. Bone deformities. Mammary tumours. Untreated eye disease. A tiny Chi bares rotten teeth at me from the darkness at the back of her cage. Some of them are just one big dreadlock, caked with filth. A Cav's chewing obsessively on the wire, its mouth a mass of festering sores. The cages are stacked three tiers high, and the bottom row's the worst. Waste matter drips down through the wire mesh of the cage floors; it gathers at the low point, gluing itself to the godforsaken creatures housed there.

I'll need body bags. I go off to get them from the supply post, pausing for a few breaths of fresh air while I'm out there. One of the volunteers is being sick under a tree. A couple of others are having a smoke down by the coffee van. RSPCA staff have set up the triage area under a canvas awning, four vets, a lot of vet nurses. Volunteers are bringing out the stud dogs from the big enclosure down the end, where the males have been kept on concrete. They'll be triaged first. Lack of handling will have left them either aggressive or fearful. There'll be obsessive behaviour such as pacing, gnawing, circling. Many will be beyond rehab.

Not my concern right now. I do the rounds of Sector F again, dispensing fresh water and small amounts of high-nutrient food. The bitches devour the food in a few desperate gulps and clamour for more. The ones that haven't given birth yet are several to a cage, and some fights break out.

I hope my quota will be triaged early, straight after the males. The RSPCA people like me. They like the way I can deal with this stuff and not fall apart. As a paramedic I've seen a lot. Done a lot. You grow a hard shell. Learn how to paste on your 'calm and capable' face when you need to.

Now for the inventory. First cage, dead pup in the corner, three live ones with nasal discharge and glued-up eyes. The mother doesn't look too great either, though she's wolfed the food. I put the dead one in a bag, make a note on the inventory form—infection?—and slap a red sticker on the cage. I move on.

Two pregnant bitches together, Maltese or similar. Balls of filth, both of them. One still licking out the now-empty bowl and attempting to wag her tail; I mark her down as reasonable condition. The second has a mat of hair right over her eyes. A particular stink here tells me ear infection. I reach in, trying to clear the eyes, and get a bite on the glove; the Malty shrinks away, wetting herself. I'm not going to get a look at those eyes until I lift her out, and I'd probably need clippers anyway. Decide to leave it to the triage crew. Yellow sticker, priority two. The first bitch comes over to the wire as I'm writing, pokes her nose through, whines a bit. I have a word to her, reach in a finger to stroke her head. She backs off.

"I'm one of the good guys, darling," I tell her, but she probably can't hear me over the racket, which has gone up a notch now. Volunteers are busy in all the rows doing the same stuff I am, and the male dogs are still being led out, most of them leaping about on the end of the leads, lunging at anything and everything. Not all, though. A big biker type covered in tatts goes past with a JRT in his arms. The dog looks catatonic, eyes staring, body rigid. The guy's cradling it against his chest, talking to it. I imagine him saying, *Get through this, buddy, and you'll qualify as a patched member of the Comancheros.*

Time passes. I finish the top row, move along the second. The inventory gets longer. Cavalier bitch with severe mammary tumours. Sad eyes. Head tilt, probable ear infection. Looks pregnant again, though it's hard to tell. Red sticker.

"Back soon, sweetie." Can't promise more than that. What happens to these dogs after triage depends on a whole bunch of things. Those with no urgent health issues will be bathed and clipped, given flea and worm treatments, kennelled in the RSPCA shelter. Because this operation's so big, some of them will go straight out to the local rescue groups to be placed in foster. If every sector's like mine, a lot of the dogs will have severe health or behavioural problems or both, stuff that means they won't ever find permanent homes. My guess is half will be euthanased, if not today, then at some later point in the assessment process. A quick death in kind hands. Not a great outcome, but surely better than mouldering on in this hell-hole.

The owner was out front when I first arrived, arguing with the RSPCA boss: *livelihood, valuable purebreds, just got a bit behind with things, no right to take them* . . . She'd have had a series of written warnings, clean up your act or have your animals seized and the place closed down. There'll be a good basis for charging her. Photographic evidence, eye witness accounts. She'll get a fine; a ban on keeping more than a certain number in future. Maybe some jail time. Doesn't help these girls, though, does it?

Move on. Bitch with festering wounds, full of maggots; second bitch cowering at the back of the cage. Red sticker. Injuries probably inflicted on one dog by the other. Or self-inflicted from worrying away at a sore patch. Next cage: mange? Next cage: severe matting, damaged eye. Next: body bag. And another body bag. Nearly done.

I need to stretch my legs again before I tackle the last few cages, so I tag the body bags and take them to the collection area. I lay them on a growing heap. Run free, you poor little buggers.

It's when I'm walking back to Sector F that I sense someone just behind me. I stop. Turn. No-one there. Head on toward my cages, then stop again. I can't be hearing footsteps over the din, but I know someone's there. I'm being watched. Something touches my ankle, brushes against my calf. I look down.

There's a dog standing beside me. But every dog in this shed is either caged or leashed. This animal doesn't belong here. It's perfectly calm. A volunteer's dog? Surely nobody would be dumb enough to bring their own animal into a puppy mill.

The dog sits precisely by my left heel, staring up at me. It's a tiny, brindled thing of indefinable breed and looks as if it's expecting a command. I glance around, wondering where it's escaped from, but all I see is volunteers cage-checking. If this one's done a bolt, nobody's missed it yet.

I walk on. The dog gets up and comes with me. Seems I've cracked at last, started hallucinating. I don't look down, but I know it's keeping pace with me, walking to heel. Crazy man. Finish up and get out of here.

Bottom row. I crouch down, concentrating on the confined dogs, doing my best not to look at the one outside the cages, right next to me. Tell myself that if I can't see it, it isn't there. But I do see it, out of the corner of my eye: intent stare, brindled pelt, oversized ears. Jesus, it's an ugly little thing.

The last four cages: fifteen to eighteen. Fifteen, three pups with severe mange. Sixteen, body bag. Rigor's set in; it's hard to manoeuvre the dead Cav out, and it doesn't help that there's a live one in the cage with it, panicking. Now I'm hearing things as well as seeing them; a whimper from the little guy beside me as I finally get the body through the narrow opening, manoeuvre the door shut and wrestle the stiff corpse into the bag. A howl from the one still in the cage. I catch myself muttering a prayer to the god I stopped believing in long ago, the day I attended the fatal accident down in Donnybrook. Find myself needing to wipe my eyes. "Your fault," I say to the thing beside me. "On my own I can do this." A tongue comes out and licks my hand. "You're not making it any easier," I say.

Seventeen: another frightened Maltese, on her own. Heavily pregnant, perhaps due within a day or so. Filthy, matted, flea-ridden, but with no obvious signs of illness. Young, I suspect. Maybe her first litter. "You, we can save," I tell her. And because I don't want to look at what I know is in the next cage, I shut my eyes for a moment. Draw breath. An image pops into my mind, me on the couch at home, can of VB in one hand, remote control in the other, channel-surfing for a program that doesn't exist, the program that's another kind of life, with a family to come home to and a job that won't populate my dreams with death and despair. The image changes. It's still me on the couch, with the beer and the remote, but now I have the pregnant Maltese curled up on my knee sound asleep, her coat glossy with good health.

A voice speaks in my head, bursting the bubble instantly. *I am the angel of death.* I open my eyes, blink a couple of times, look around. The small, ugly dog looks up at me. "No, you're not," I say. I know the angel of death. Seen him over and over. On the battlefield, in smashed cars, hovering at the end of ropes hanging from lonely trees, standing in the street outside a nightclub where a young man lies in a spreading dark pool. Know him as intimately as a person can without being dead himself.

Right. Get it done. Eighteen: Chi with litter of five pups, all dead. The bitch doesn't want to give them up; bites me right through the glove. "Sorry, sweetie," I tell her, slipping the little ones into a single bag. The image comes again, uninvited. There I am on the couch, only now there are two dogs on my knee, the Maltese and the Chi. All three of us watching the football. Jesus Christ. I scowl at the ugly little dog, and it meets my gaze with perfect calm. Bloody angels.

Right on cue, here's RSPCA staffer Jenny with crates on a trolley. She manages a smile.

"Hi, Dan. Ready for triage?"

I glance down at the self-styled angel of death, then up at Jenny with her wholesome face and crazy red hair. If she could see the dog she'd make some comment, surely. "Ready," I say, getting to my feet and giving her the Sector F inventory. We load the red sticker cases first and she wheels them off, telling me to go get myself a coffee and take a break.

I should be desperate to get out of here. But I can't seem to walk away from seventeen and eighteen.

"Mutt," I say. "Cur. Mongrel."

The angel of death regards me knowingly.

"If I go out, you go out with me," I say. Because, if this really is the angel, I'll come back to find the Maltese and the Chi both gone, like that kid in the car who died when I stepped away for two minutes take a call from HQ. Like in Iraq, when I stopped to adjust my kit while Kevin went forward and trod on a mine. A moment's inattention and the wretched angel seizes his opportunity. "Heel," I say.

I put three sugars in my coffee, but it still tastes like piss. No wonder everyone's smoking. We all stink. The angel sits next to me as I gulp down the coffee, which is at least hot. It pads beside me to the portaloo and waits for me. After a while I see Jenny heading back from triage with her trolley and I go back in. The dog comes right along.

We load the yellow sticker cases. By my ankles, the dog yaps a couple of times, as if to make a suggestion.

"Shut up," I say. My rule is this: no dogs of my own. No fosters, no adoptions, no waifs and strays. Let one in and the whole thing comes falling down. First the mask, then the shell, exposing the pathetic soft creature inside. Not happening. I can do a day's volunteering at the shelter. I can do what I've done today. But when the shed door closes, I turn my back and walk away. Alone, like I've always been. "Just so you know," I murmur.

"You all right?" asks Jenny.

"Fine," I tell her. "I'm fine." She can't hear it. Can't see it. It's a figment of my imagination. Still, I stay by cages seventeen and eighteen while Jenny trolleys the yellow stickers to triage.

The Maltese is up against the front now, nibbling at my finger. Next door the Chi, her dead pups cleared from the cage, is just standing there, blank-eyed. I sit on the filthy floor beside them. The angel hunkers down next to me. I put my head on my knees; shut my eyes. Wish I knew how to pray. Wish I believed there was some point in prayers.

I am the angel of death.

"So you mentioned." I don't bother opening my eyes.

None can escape me.

"You think I don't know that?"

I bring the long sleep of no dreams. I bring an end to nightmares, Daniel.

"Thanks but no thanks. And you can keep your paws off these two. There's enough death in this place already."

I bring an end to sorrow. An end to suffering. See, they come.

I don't want to see anything but, eyes tight shut, I do anyway. All over the shed they drift from the cages, ethereal shades of dogs wafting in one direction: straight toward me. Or rather, straight toward the angel, though he's not calling them, not aloud anyway. He's waiting with head up, ears pricked, everything perfectly in line, like a poster child for the Cesar Millan obedience method.

The lost, the lonely, the neglected and forgotten. Every one that perished for want of good care. Every bitch overbred and abused; every dog kept on hard concrete and driven mad by the lack of kind touch. Every one chained up and left alone in a cold yard; every fighting dog beaten until it bit back. Every designer puppy that grew inconvenient. Every pound dog euthanased for want of a little compassion.

"Tell me something I don't know."

They are all around you, Daniel. Bidding you farewell; thanking you for your kindness. You have done your best. You cannot save them all.

I feel their tongues on my face, their bodies against mine. A small one crawls onto my lap and lays its head against my chest. I open my eyes and they're still here, transparent outlines of emaciated body and frantically wagging tail, the sudden gleam of bright eyes, silent movement all around me. And behind them, others that are not dogs but men and women, boys and girls. The kid from the car. The family from the blood-spattered house. The fire victims, the sad suicides, the cot deaths. Here's a soldier in fatigues, squatting down to offer me a phantom smoke, grinning all over his ghostly face. *Dan! Seen you looking better, buddy. How's it going?* Like old times, back in camp when we had no idea what lay ahead.

"I'm good, Kev," I lie, but my dead friend is already fading away. A ghost of a ghost. The men and women, the children and babies fade as well, leaving only the little army of dogs.

So?

"What do you mean, so?"

The ball's in your court, Dan.

What angel talks like that? What dog ever talked in words, anyway? I think maybe I've been crying; I need to get a grip before Jenny comes back.

"Listen," I say. "Maybe angels don't make bargains, but there's a first time for everything, I reckon. You take the ones that are already dead—that goes without saying—and you take the ones that won't make it through the first assessment. The rest you leave. And I take these two here." I can't believe I just broke my most sacred rule, the one that ensures my protective armour stays in place.

There's an expression on the angel's face that comes close to a self-satisfied smirk, though it's not easy for a dog to do that. *A bargain? No, Daniel. It is a gift.*

As Jenny and her trolley rattle back into view, the ghostly dogs depart with the angel leading. There's no soaring up into the heavens, no triumphant ascent to the rainbow bridge or the great dog park in the sky. They just pad away across the filthy floor, tails high, eyes bright, heading for the open doors and the sunshine beyond. Almost before I can snatch a shaky breath, they're gone.

"Dan? You sure you're OK?"

"Fine." I get to my feet, knowing my face is wet with tears, hoping, ridiculously, that Jenny hasn't noticed. "Only . . . " Jesus, this is hard. It feels like I'm cracking open.

"Only what?" She looks at me closely, eyes narrowed. "This is the home stretch, Dan. The easy part. These are the adoptable ones."

"Just . . . Can you put in a word for me? I'd like to foster a couple this time. Take them straight home today, when they've been vet-checked. Do the baths and clipping myself. Don't know if Liz will OK that."

Jenny must be surprised, shocked even. She knows me pretty well by now; knows I've done rescue after rescue and never once taken an animal home. But all she says is, "I'll have a word. Which ones?"

I indicate cages seventeen and eighteen. In my mind, the Maltese is Princess. The shell-shocked Chi, I'm still thinking about.

"Jeez, Dan. That malty looks ready to pop any minute. Sure your bachelor establishment's ready for a litter of pups?"

"Talk to Liz for me, will you?"

When we get to triage, Jenny does just that. Goes on and on about my Saturdays at the shelter and my experience as a paramedic and how valuable I've been until I'm too embarrassed to look at anyone. But proud, too. Several of the other staffers back her up. Seems they do find me pretty useful, and not only because I'm Mr Calm and Capable.

Liz, the RSPCA boss, quizzes me about how things are set up at home and whether I've ever dealt with a whelping and if I realise the Chi's going to need pretty intensive care for a while. I give the right answers, promise to pick up some supplies from the shelter to see me through the weekend, win a smile from Jenny. Liz tells me they'll pay the vet expenses while I'm fostering.

The vet, John, thinks Princess is having a biggish litter and warns me to bring her in at the first sign of any problems. He gives me antibiotics and anti-inflammatories for the Chi. Liz thanks me for my day's work. Jenny helps me carry the two crates to my car. In the triage area the work goes on, dog after dog, as the puppy mill gradually empties out. Someone's opening the body bags to take photos before they're sealed and disposed of. Building a case.

We load the crates.

"I should stay," I tell Jenny. "Plenty still to do here."

"Go home, Dan," she says. "Take your girls home."

So I do. As I negotiate the gravel road off the property, taking it slow so as not to jostle the cages, I mutter, "Devious little bugger. A gift, huh? What gift was it supposed to be, dog shit on the carpet? Or are we talking deep stuff like absolution?" I think of my friend Kev, his smiling face, his voice just the same as it always was. The suicides, the accident victims, sleeping a long sleep of no dreams.

The Chi's whimpering. I stop the car, turn to look into the crate. She's shaking and trembling, her eyes wide with terror. In her own crate, Princess has settled down on the blanket, nose resting on paws. After a bath and a clip she's going to be a beauty.

I take off my jacket and put it over the Chi's crate. Half an hour to get home; she'll be calmer covered up. PTSD. I know more than enough about that. Lot of work ahead with her.

I put the car back in gear and we move off again. I think about the Angel and that gift he mentioned. Most likely the whole thing came out of my own head, which is full of crap from the past. But it did make a kind of sense. And now here I am with these girls to look after.

As we cross the cattle grid and turn onto the main road, I decide a good name for the Chi would be Hope.

◑

by bone-light

"We need light," says Susie.

The power's gone off again; that happens a lot at Woodland Gardens. This place must have been named by a clown—instead of numbers, the floors have names, Chestnut Level, Willow Level and so on, a whole tower of trees. Woodland Gardens itself is a concrete high-rise with no redeeming features. Along with dodgy power it has blocked drains, creeping mould and lifts that make everyone use the stairs, even people who live on the top floor— Oak Level—like us. If something can break, you can be sure it'll be broken at Woodland Gardens. Down the bottom, outside, there's a sad playground with a metal swing and a climbing frame on dirty sand. In the daytime it's usually empty because mothers don't want their kids stepping on dog poo or used syringes. At night it's a meeting place for dealers.

We're sitting in our flat in the almost-dark, my stepmother, my stepsisters and me. Our torch batteries are flat, Susie's lighter is used up and we've managed to run out of both matches and candles. It's nearly dusk outside and the heater's gone off along with everything else electrical, so it'll soon be icy in here. But I know better than to suggest early bed. Susie wants our projects finished tonight, so she can get them in the mail first thing. Since it's already too dim in here for us to see our work, one of us will have to fetch light. It's not going to be Sophie or Miranda, because they're Susie's own daughters, her flesh and blood, and she never makes them go downstairs in the dark. I am my mother's daughter, and my mother is dead.

"Won't the shop be shut by now?" I say, hating the way my voice shakes. "I think they close at five on a Thurs—"

Before I can finish I'm hauled up onto my feet with Susie's fingernails pressing into the soft flesh of my arm. I sink my teeth into my lip; I won't give her the satisfaction of hearing me cry out. My heart's thumping hard.

"You think I'm stupid or something?" Her hand tightens.

"You'll have to go to the basement," Sophie says.

"Better hurry, Lissa," puts in Miranda. "It'll be dark soon."

There's a silence. I feel the weight of their gaze, the three of them, and I hear them thinking: *Go. Now. Before we make you.*

"That concierge woman's supposed to have everything," Susie says, and the hold on my arm slackens slightly. "You know, what's-her-name, the one they all talk about. Go down and ask her for candles and a lighter."

We haven't been at Woodland Gardens long. Susie got word that Dad's deployment was extended another six months, and almost straight away she sold the house that had been my home for all of my fifteen years. Home and haven. The house where my mother gave birth to me, her only child. The house where, only a year and a half ago, she gave me a gift, then died. Susie moved us so fast there was no time to ask questions. There wasn't even time to cry. It felt as if I blinked, then opened my eyes to find everything gone.

This flat is small. Two bedrooms: one for her, the other one for the three of us, with me on a trundle bed. Apart from my clothes, I got to bring one book—*Grimm's Fairy Tales*, which she had to let me keep because it was a Christmas present from Dad—and Mimi, who didn't get given to the Salvos because she was hidden in my pocket.

Susie had Wilmot put down. For that, I can never forgive her. She didn't have to choose a place with a no pets policy. She didn't have to move us at all. I thought I was going back to school at the end of the holidays and instead here we are in a completely different neighbourhood. When I asked about school—the kids at Woodland Gardens go to Westmoreland High—she said some stuff that frightened me so much I never asked again. Stuff about how screwed up in the head I was, and how much worse it would get if I was around people. Stuff about what she'd do to me if I told anyone what she'd said, ever. Miranda and Sophie never finished high school and now I have an idea why.

"Her name's Barbara," says Sophie, reminding me sharply of what's ahead.

None of us has ever been down to the basement. None of us has ever met Barbara the concierge in the flesh. But we've heard about her. Everyone at Woodland Gardens talks about her in the same way, hushed and scared like an olden-days person speaking of a witch. She's supposed to have lots of stuff down there, not only candles but old-fashioned oil lamps, fuses, all kinds of tools, probably matches and firelighters too. And weird stuff, so Kye told me. Kye is the only kid I've spoken to since we moved in here. Susie doesn't like letting us out, and we're not supposed to talk to anyone. Her reason is, the building's full of druggies and perverts. But doing the washing is one of my jobs, and that gets me as far as the communal laundry along the end of Oak Level. When I'm there I hear people talking. And I see Kye sometimes, hanging around. He told me people go into Barbara's basement and never come out again. He told me she has a human bone for a door knocker. He said his uncle told him Barbara came from some country where they do voodoo, black magic, and that weird people are always visiting her to get spells. If that was true, if magic was real, I'd ask her for a spell myself. I'd get one to bring my father home right now. He probably thought he was doing the right thing when he married Susie so soon after Mum died. He must have thought I needed a mother, since we have no other family and he's away so much. And Susie wasn't so bad back then. Dad couldn't have known she'd turn into a monster the moment he was gone.

I've thought of asking Kye if I can make a phone call from his place, to . . . I don't know who, but there are welfare people who are supposed to help the families during a deployment, and I could look up their number. Or I could call my old school, speak to Mr Turner or Mrs Moss. I've thought of giving Kye a letter to post to Dad, because I suspect Susie rips them up, or Dad would have sent some back the way he always used to. Only Susie's so good at lying, and she's his wife now. She'd tell the welfare people I'm emotional and confused, and say she's getting professional help for me. And then she'd punish me. She's good at punishments. I have lots of bruises, the kind that show on my body and the kind that are deep inside where nobody can see.

"Off you go, Lissa," she says now. "Don't take too long about it. You're way behind with the orders; at this rate you'll be up all night getting that one finished." What we make, Susie sells online. Sophie's fine shawls; Miranda's Aran sweaters; my one-of-a-kind dolls. I make a lot of dolls, so I guess they're popular. Susie won't let us use the internet, so I don't see the customer feedback. No internet means no email either. Dad could be on another planet. He's been gone eight months, and in those eight months my whole world has changed.

"What are you waiting for?" Susie snaps. "Pitch darkness? Go! Now!"

There's no refusing. And with Susie standing over me, there's no getting a coat or gloves even though it'll be freezing in the stairwell. At least I have Mimi. She's about all I do have these days.

Susie locks the flat door behind me. Locks me out. When I get back with the candles I'm supposed to knock on the door three times, count to five, then knock three times again and wait for her to let me in. The two times three knocks are so she won't open up to some kind of crazy person. Though that's what she told me I was: crazy. A crazy girl can't go to school, but it's OK for her to sit at home making dolls for her stepmother to sell. I hope my dolls go to better homes than mine, homes where people love them and look after them and whisper secrets in their woollen ears.

The hallways in Woodside Gardens are long and grey. At this time of day all the doors are shut. There's still enough light from the tall windows down the end for me to see my way to the lift, and beside it the stair door. This door's broken, falling off its hinges. I step through and start down the twelve flights.

The stairwell stinks of wee. I'm hoping not to meet the perverts and junkies Susie talks about, though the shadowy landings seem like places where bad stuff might happen. I reach Willow Level, Aspen Level, Juniper Level, and the light's almost gone. I have to slow down or I might fall. There'll be no sympathy from Susie if I break my ankle, only a reprimand for being clumsy and costing her money for a trip to the doctor. I wonder if the doctor would believe me if I told the truth about my stepmother? For a moment it seems almost worth breaking my ankle to find out. I sit down on the top step of Juniper Level to stop myself from jumping. I take Mimi from my pocket and put her on my knee. There's just enough light left to make out her little face, her dark beady eyes, her snub nose, her mouth that's not smiling and not frowning but something in between. Her black embroidery-silk hair; her moss stitch gown in my favourite purple.

"I'm scared, Mimi. Scared of Susie and scared of myself. Scared of going down to the basement."

Give me a kiss, says Mimi.

I oblige with a peck on her knitted lips.

Give me a hug.

I press her against my cheek. My mother's last gift was teaching me how to knit. How to put love and hope and courage into every doll I make, so the person who gets that doll will have a true friend in good times and in bad. Mimi was the first doll I ever made, and knitted into her body is a strand of hair my mother cut from her own head as she lay dying. "When you are sad, Lissa, when you are lonely, when you are at your wits' end, she will help you," she told me. And it was true. I don't think Mimi is truly magic—how can she be, when I made her myself with wool and needles?—but when I speak to her in the right way, I can hear her speaking back to me.

Now let me fly!

I toss Mimi up in the air. She performs a triple somersault and I catch her on the way down, setting her upright on my knee again. She's only a little doll, ten centimetres from the top of her head to the soles of her knitted shoes. In the dim light it seems to me she's looking quite pleased with herself.

Why are we going downstairs in the dark?

"To visit Barbara in the basement. To ask her for light."

Mm-hm. Mimi seems to be considering this. *We'll need that if we're to find our way back up. Did you say you were scared?*

"I'm scared of Susie because she hurts me and I never know when she's going to be angry. And I'm scared of Barbara the concierge because everyone else is."

Mimi appears to be waiting for more.

"And I'm scared of myself. A moment ago I was going to throw myself down these stairs and hurt myself on purpose, and that would make what Susie says about me true. I wasn't crazy before she came, Mimi. I'm sure I wasn't."

Was your mother ever afraid of anything? Even at the end?

I remember Mum lying on the bed, hooked up to a drip, a skeleton with a fine layer of white silk for skin. Her eyes huge; her mouth stretched in a terrifying smile. Speaking words of hope. I shake my head.

You are your mother's daughter, Mimi says. *Get up, walk down, fetch light. I will help you.*

We go on down. Poplar Level, Cypress Level, Eucalyptus Level. I can hardly see the steps now. Ash Level, Elm Level. Somewhere below me a door clangs open, and I hear someone charging up the stairs toward me. I shrink back against the wall, stuffing Mimi into my pocket for safety. My heart's in my throat. A drug deal gone wrong, someone being chased with a knife, someone desperate . . . The person reaches the landing below me and comes straight on up. *Don't see me,* I beg. *Just go on past, please, please . . .*

It's a man dressed all in black, leather pants, hoodie, chunky Doc Marten-style boots. He hurtles past me. Either he's a top athlete or he's terrified of what's coming after him. His face is as dark as his clothes; there's a hint of gleaming eyes, and he's gone. I wait, making myself remember to breathe. Wait for whatever is coming next. I count up to fifty but nobody comes. Mimi says nothing, but I imagine her thinking, *What are we waiting for?* As well she might, because since the man ran past me, it's gone so dark I can't see my hand in front of my face. I pray that Barbara the concierge is home, and that she does give me light.

The lower levels, I navigate by touch. One hand on the iron railing, the other stretched out toward the concrete wall of the stairwell, I go down foot by cautious foot, hoping there are no broken steps, no missing stretches of rail. The dark's like a presence pushing at me, weighing me down. I feel as if I'm deep underground, though I think this is only Yew Level, third from the bottom. There's no reading the signs anymore, so I start counting the steps, counting the turns in the stairs. This stairwell comes out on the ground floor; I've been down here in the day time, when Susie took a risk and sent me to the shop on my own. Back then, I thought of running away, asking the shopkeeper if I could use the phone, asking someone, anyone, for help. I didn't. Susie's got a long reach. As I go down the last flight of steps to ground level, I start wondering if she actually doesn't want me to come back tonight. She might be hoping I run into a murderer so she can get rid of me with a neat explanation for Dad. It's not as if my dolls are making Susie a fortune, or we wouldn't be living here in Woodside Gardens. I wonder what's happened to Dad's Navy pay. I wonder how it was that she could sell the house while he was gone. What if he's sick or even dead and she hasn't told me? But that couldn't happen. Could it?

The stairs come to an end. I stand still, trying to get a sense of direction. Somewhere in front of me I know there's a door that leads out to the so-called plaza, where kids ride skateboards and do graffiti during the day and adults shout and smash bottles at night. Between me and that door there's utter darkness. I can't even see a line of light around the doorway, though surely there's at least one street light working out there. I creep forward with my hands outstretched, hoping I'm not about to fall down a flight of steps I've forgotten about. My heart's jumping around like crazy.

My hands touch the concrete wall. I work my way around till I find the door and pull on the handle. It's locked.

For a bit I just stand there, thinking of the long way back in the dark, imagining myself telling Susie I failed, guessing what might happen then. Susie making me stand in a cold shower till I'm blue and shivering. Susie making me stand out on the balcony in my underwear. Susie shoving my head into the wall. Susie has a great imagination.

I sink down onto the floor and get Mimi out of my pocket. I sit her on my knee. "I don't think I can go on," I mutter.

I can't see her face in the dark, but I hear her familiar voice.

Give me a kiss.

I touch my lips to her face.

Give me a hug.

I hold her to my cheek and find that I am actually crying a bit.

Now let me fly!

I flip Mimi up into the air and manage to catch her, blind.

So, we're down here in the dark. And you're curled up in a ball crying.

"I do try to be brave." I scrub a hand across my cheek. "But sometimes it's too hard."

There is a light to be found in every darkness. You are your mother's daughter. Find it.

"But—" I fall silent, because it seems Mimi's right. The blanketing dark has lightened just enough for me to see that there *is* another set of steps, leading not up but down, and from somewhere below a faint glow is coming. I thought you could only reach the basement by the lift or a flight of outside steps. But maybe there's a third way.

With Mimi in my hand I inch across to the steps, which don't have any kind of guard rail. We go down. The dim light gets a bit brighter. There are only seven steps, and here we are at another level, with a short landing and one door at the end. The door is painted in blood-red gloss, and on a shelf beside it is the source of the glow: a lamp made from what looks like a real human skull, with a tea-light candle inside. It makes weird flickering shadows all over the stairwell walls. And there, dangling beside the door, is the knocker Tye told me about. If that's not a human shin-bone I don't know what it is. Now I'm really cold.

There's a little brass plate on the red door, and on it is some lettering, only it's not the letters I know, but a foreign alphabet of some kind. It might say anything from "Concierge" to "Visitors will be eaten alive." I gather my courage, put my hand around the leg bone and rap on the door.

I wait. It feels as if getting downstairs took a long time, far longer than it should have done, and I wonder if Barbara has gone to bed already, in which case she won't be well pleased if I go on knocking. Maybe she's out. Maybe Mimi's instincts are wrong for the first time ever.

After a while I knock again, not too hard. I call out, "Is anyone home?"

The door opens so suddenly I yelp with fright. There's a woman in the doorway, long straggledy white hair falling out of a bun, little bright eyes, skin with a million wrinkles. She's wearing a knitted garment in exactly the same purple I used for Mimi's dress, and in her arms she's holding this humongous orange cat. It is the biggest cat I've ever seen in my life and it has a mean look in its eye. I know cats, though. I see right through this one.

Barbara—who else could this be?—hasn't said a word, so I speak up before things get embarrassing.

"Sorry to disturb you. I'm—"

"Lissa from 1205. You'll be wanting light, yes?"

I gape, but only for a moment. Behind her the room looks dark and bright at the same time, full of changing light that shows me rich colours and elaborate patterns. Unlike ours, Barbara's place is full of interesting stuff.

"Come in," she says as if reading my mind, and steps back to let me go past her.

There are bones everywhere. Skulls with lights in them, their glowing eyes following me as I move cautiously across the room. Leg bones and arm bones and goodness-knows-what bones hanging from the ceiling like mobiles. Colourful pottery bowls full of tiny bones that must be from shrews or voles or something. There's a smell like incense, a lot better than the stink in the stairwell. I start to feel dizzy and have to remind myself why I'm here.

"Our power's off," I say as Barbara puts the huge cat down on an overstuffed sofa. It settles on an embroidered cushion, staring at me through narrowed eyes. "My stepmother sent me to ask you for candles and a lighter. Please."

She just stands there examining me, her arms folded. I can't think of anything else to say, so I crouch down beside the cat and put my hand carefully out where he or she can smell it and decide to be friends or not. "Beautiful one," I whisper, remembering Winslow with his silky fur and lovely blue eyes. "Aren't you a fine cat, then?"

The giant feline deigns to sniff my hand, then gives itself a cursory lick. It raises no objection when I stroke it gently.

"She bites," says Barbara.

I don't think this cat's going to bite me. She's purring now. "What's her name?" I ask.

"Rory. Aurora."

I go on petting her for a while, and Barbara goes on standing there watching me.

"Sorry," I say eventually, remembering that it's late. "I miss my own cat. Is it OK for me to have some candles, please?"

"Ah," says Barbara, and I realise the door is shut and I'm alone with her and her house is seriously weird. I get to my feet and think about the twelve flights of stairs and the dark. "I have candles," she says. "I have lighters. I have all manner of things down here, as no doubt you've heard. They tell all kinds of stories about me."

"I don't get out much," I squeak. "But I did hear you have candles, yes."

"Can you pay?"

"Oh." My heart sinks. "My stepmother didn't give me any money." Stupid! I should have thought of this.

"Nothing's free, young lady. But there are other ways of paying."

I back away toward the door. If I can get out, if she hasn't locked it, I should be able to outrun her. She's a big heavy woman and she looks sixty at least, maybe even older.

"Can you cook?" Barbara asks.

I stop backing. "Yes," I say. I've been cooking since I was a little kid. Since Dad went away I've been doing pretty much all the housework, including preparing meals for four. If that's all she wants me to do, fine. Even if it takes until midnight.

Barbara flings open an inside door to show a dark old kitchen lit by more skull lamps. The stove is one of those ancient iron ones with a wood fire in a little compartment; there's a basket of logs sitting next to it. Bunches of herbs and onions and garlic dangle from the ceiling. In the middle of the room there's a wooden table and on it are a big bowl of fruit and veg, a basket of eggs and some little sacks that look as if they might hold rice or beans. In the corner stands a big red cupboard with a design of fruit and flowers painted on it, like something out of a fairy tale. *Then she shut her little brother in the red cupboard, and when she opened the doors again he was quite, quite gone.*

"I'm going out," Barbara says. "Work to be done. You'll make my dinner, three courses, each finer than the last. Lay it out on this table before I return home, and be sure it's a meal fit for a queen. If I'm satisfied I'll give you what you came for. But take care you leave my kitchen tidy. If I find the smallest thing out of place, I'll consider eating you for my dinner instead."

Seems as if she's heard most of the things the tenants of Woodland Gardens say about her and finds them amusing, not upsetting. I'm beyond being surprised by anything at this point, so I put on an apron, wash my hands and get to work. My gran had a wood stove like this so it's not too much of a challenge. I don't let myself think about where that chimney might come out.

Making a three course dinner takes me a while. I put Mimi on the table, propped up against the fruit bowl. Rory the cat comes in at a certain point and hunkers down in a corner to supervise. As for Barbara, she's flung on a cape and gone off, slamming the front door behind her. It's pretty trusting of her, seeing as she's never met me before tonight. I wonder what work she could be doing at this hour.

I think about Susie, upstairs getting angrier and angrier in the dark. The doll I was working on will be lying on the table up there, all lonely, waiting for me to finish embroidering her face. Like all the dolls I make, she has in her a hair I plucked from my own head and knitted in with the wool. Someone's out there waiting for that doll, and unless I get this job finished and take the candles upstairs they'll have to wait a day longer, and Susie . . . I can't let myself think too hard about that; I have to concentrate. I dare to open the red cupboard and find it's a pantry full of useful ingredients. It's a long time since I've had so much good stuff to work with.

For starters I make a tomato and basil soup, with shaved parmesan and a herb scone on the side. I put together a spiced fruit compote and vanilla custard—there's no fridge in Barbara's kitchen, but the bottle of milk in the pantry is still OK, and so is the chicken waiting to be jointed and cooked. The main course will be breaded chicken pieces on herbed couscous, with vegies baked in olive oil and rosemary. In herb lore, rosemary means a strong woman, so it seems a good choice. I hope the meal's substantial enough for Barbara. She looks like she might be a big eater. I wonder who would have cooked her dinner if I hadn't been here.

It's starting to feel as if midnight might have been and gone, and my eyes are gritty with tiredness. The meal is pretty much ready, with only the couscous to steam. I make myself coffee, give Rory some chicken scraps in a bowl that looks like it might be hers, and sit down at the table for a bit. The kitchen's full of good smells; even with those skulls staring down at me, it feels safe in here. The coffee should give me enough energy to clean up, then I only need to set the table and I'm done. If Barbara likes the meal, I can grab the lighter and candles and head on upstairs, and I'll still have time to finish the doll before morning.

I find crockery, a glass, knives and forks. I check the kitchen: bench wiped clean, dishes washed, dried and put away, floor swept, fire made up, kettle steaming on the wood stove. Everything's ready. And I hear noises from outside the front door—Barbara's back.

Whoosh! Rory leaps onto the table, sending the open bag of couscous flying. Around two kilos of the stuff spill out all over the floor, the tiny granules rolling and scattering into every corner. I jump up and they crunch under my shoes. Rory has terrified herself; now she's standing on the table with one paw planted on the clean plate, fur on end, yowling. There's a rattle at the front door as Barbara sticks her key in the lock. What was that she said about eating me for dinner?

I scramble for the red cupboard where there's a dustpan and brush, and I slip over on the carpet of little grains. I land on my hip, putting new bruises on the old ones. I want to curl up on the floor and cry. Instead I look at Mimi, who's still standing beside the fruit bowl.

Give me a kiss, says Mimi.

The front door squeaks open. I struggle to my feet, reach out for the doll, kiss her embroidered mouth.

Give me a hug.

Quick, quick, I will her as I lay my cheek on hers.

Now let me dance!

I throw her high; in the few seconds we have left before fate catches up with us, she may as well enjoy herself. She twirls, tumbles, falls back into my waiting hands. Dear Mimi, my true friend in good times and bad.

Sit on the chair, close your eyes, lift your feet and keep that cat out of my way.

I manage to gather up Rory, who weighs half a ton, and sit down at the table again. I can hear Barbara walking about in the other room, muttering to herself. There's no way this can be cleaned up before she comes in, no way.

Somewhere near my feet there's a little sound like rats scuttling about. In my arms Rory tenses, making a deep-down whining noise. My body feels like it's strung on a wire, every bit of it jangly and terrified.

Hold on to that cat and keep your eyes shut.

Something small and woollen brushes against my ankle and is gone. The scuttling moves around the room, from cupboard to table, from table to bench, from bench to stove.

How much couscous does your recipe require? asks Mimi.

"A cup." This is crazy.

The scuttling moves up onto the table; becomes more of a pouring sound.

Done.

I open my eyes. The floor looks completely clean. Mimi is exactly where she was before, regarding me with her woollen gaze, and the couscous is back in the bag, most of it anyway. The enamel cup I had ready for measuring is filled precisely to the top.

The door opens and there's Barbara, tall and imposing, her dark eyes taking in the tidy kitchen, the neatly laid table, the various serving dishes waiting. I put the cat down, then move the couscous over to the bench and measure a cupful of water into a small iron pot.

"Please, do sit down," I say a bit shakily. "Are you ready for the first course now?"

She sinks weightily onto the chair. "I could eat a horse," she says, sounding as if she actually means it.

Barbara eats the tomato and basil soup, the parmesan and the herb scone without saying a word. While she's getting through that, I steam the couscous, which seems none the worse for its stint on the floor.

"Good." Barbara wipes her mouth with a large hand. "What's next?"

I serve the couscous, the chicken pieces and the baked vegetables: creamy potatoes, golden pumpkin, ruby-red beets, glistening onions. My mouth is watering, but she doesn't suggest I sit down and share her feast, and I don't either.

When she's eaten about half the main course, she sets down her knife and fork and stares at me. "I need entertainment," she says. "A story. Think you can manage that?"

I'm OK at cooking and I guess I'm OK at stories too, thanks to *Grimm's Fairy Tales*. I start to tell her a story about a girl who goes into the woods to find an old witch who lives in a hut on hen's legs, only Barbara keeps interrupting and asking questions, and it turns into a story about a girl whose stepmother takes her away from everything familiar, until the only friend she has in the world is the little doll her mother taught her how to make. A girl who only gets let out when her stepmother wants something; a girl who's lost touch with the good things of her past, and only sees the cruelty and loneliness of her future.

"Is this the doll?" Barbara asks, looking at Mimi, who stares back boldly from her spot by the fruit bowl.

I tell her. I explain about the other dolls I make and how Susie sells them as fast as I can get them finished. I don't tell her about the strands of hair; that feels too secret, even though Barbara's listening with interest and her expression's quite kindly. She's finished the main course, a meal big enough to go around all four of us at 1205 with leftovers to spare.

"Ready for dessert?" I ask politely, wondering what the time is and whether Susie will have given up on me and gone to bed by now. Maybe I can sneak in without waking her up.

"Mmm." Barbara stretches, moves her chair back a bit from the table. "Who taught you to cook, Lissa?"

"My mother."

"She did a good job. You could be a chef someday."

I say nothing. You don't get to be much at all if you haven't finished high school. I bring out the fruit compote and the custard, and I make a pot of tea.

"Sit down," Barbara says at last. "Fetch yourself a cup, a bowl and a spoon."

We eat the dessert course together. It tastes wonderful; each mouthful reminds me of summer and sunshine and being safe. It reminds me of Mum and Dad and the way things used to be.

"Well, then," says Barbara when the compote and custard are all gone and we're sitting over our cups of tea. "You've told me your story, and a fine one it was, full of joy and sorrow, good times and bad. Now it's my turn. I'm sure you have plenty of questions for the old woman in the basement with her voodoo spells and her cantankerous familiar. Go ahead, ask them."

My mind fills with questions. I'd love to know about her past, and what brought her to live at Woodland Gardens, where she doesn't belong at all. I'd like to know what the brass plate on the door says, and what language it's in. I'd love her to tell me what work she does out there at midnight. And I want to know about spells: whether there's one that will rescue me from Susie.

Suddenly it seems dangerous to ask much at all. It feels like prying into something best left alone.

"I only have one question," I say.

Her eyebrows go up.

"Is magic real?" I ask, hoping she won't laugh her head off.

She doesn't say anything, just looks at me, and I remember the thing with the couscous. I think of the hair I put into my dolls, as if that might somehow make them as real to their owners as Mimi is to me. Of course magic is real. But then I remember Susie and my bruises and how I've never been brave enough to ask Kye if I can use his phone, and I think no, it can't be.

Barbara goes on looking at me and sipping her tea, and I think she isn't going to answer at all until she gets up, goes to the red cupboard, opens a little drawer at the bottom and brings out something that looks a bit like a melted candle. When she shows it to me I see it's like a doll, with arms and legs and a head, but blobby and crude as if someone got tired of making it halfway through.

"What if I told you this was a voodoo doll?" she asks, and a shiver runs through me. It doesn't take much to imagine this little thing with pins stuck all over it, or being held over a lighter flame until it drips away to nothing. "What if I taught you how to work a curse?"

Now the room is bristling with magic, the *Grimm's Fairy Tales* kind where girls try to hide terrible secrets and wicked stepmothers dance in red-hot iron shoes. I think about how different my life could be if Susie didn't exist. Then I take a deep breath, reach out and pick up Mimi. "No," I say. "Not even if it gets me out of trouble. Not even if it fixes up the future the way I want. It'll cost too much. That kind of thing always does."

Barbara smiles. She reaches over toward the stove, opens the iron door with her bare hand and throws the wax thing inside, where it sizzles, making a vile smell. She clangs the door shut. "You'll be wanting that light, then." She stands, takes one of the skull lamps from the shelf and hands it to me. There's a wire running through a couple of holes on the top, so I can carry the skull. The tea-light candle inside has been burning a while; this lamp may be out before I even get to Oak Level. Perhaps the power will be back on by then. Perhaps Susie won't hurt me. After the voodoo thing, I can't seem to make myself ask for more.

"I'll see you out," Barbara says, leading me through the room with the embroidered cushions to the red front door. When she opens it, Rory streaks out, quicker than her bulk suggests is possible, and darts up the steps to the ground floor.

"Thank you," I say. "It's been interesting talking to you."

Now she does laugh, but in a good way. "And you," she says. "Hasten upstairs, Lissa. Dawn is breaking, and a new day comes."

A new day? Already? I see that she's right, because up the top of the seven steps the door to the plaza is open, and as Rory sprints out, the darkness starts to lift. Out there, it's nearly dawn, and upstairs in 1205 Susie's going to wake up and find I've been away all night. Can I really have been talking for as long as that? Did I somehow fall asleep and not even notice? Either way, this is a disaster.

"Farewell, Lissa," says Barbara softly, and the door closes behind me.

Grimly, I start the long climb. Pine, Cedar, Yew. Beside each painted name there's a little silhouette of the tree; nice idea, wrong place. Beyond the stairwell windows the sky turns violet, pink, gold. Elm, Ash, Eucalyptus. Let her be still asleep. Let me get inside and be sewing before she wakes up. But that isn't going to happen, because I have to do the twice three knocks on the door. She's going to kill me. Cypress. Poplar. My legs are on fire; I have to stop and catch my breath. I sit down on the steps with Mimi on my knee, and look out the window as somewhere beyond the concrete towers the sun edges over the horizon.

Down below, the stairwell door opens. The guy who walks through is not much older than me. His hair's the colour fairy tales call golden, and he's wearing snowy white overalls with a logo on the pocket, a smiling sun with Day and Son, Fresh Food Deliveries underneath. The guy's carrying a little crate, and in it are loaves of bread and bottles—old-fashioned glass bottles—of milk. Like the one in Barbara's pantry. "After you," he says politely.

We go on up, me first, the milk guy—Day Junior—second. I wait for him to ask me what I was doing sitting on the stairs at what must be about five in the morning, or to comment on the skull lamp, but all he says is, "Going to be a lovely day."

"Mm," I say, my mind full of Susie. Why am I so stupid? Why didn't I ask Barbara if she'd let me use her phone to call the welfare people, instead of cooking her a giant dinner and asking her about magic? No wonder I'm in so much trouble.

Day Junior and I climb through Juniper, Aspen and Willow. Outside, the sun comes up and proves him right; weather-wise, at least, it's shaping up to be a beautiful day. Seems as if he plans to start his deliveries at the top. When we get to Oak Floor, he balances his crate on one arm and uses the other to hold the broken door back so it can't fall on me as I go through.

"Thanks," I say, and head off toward 1205, not looking back to see who on Oak Floor can possibly afford a fresh food delivery.

The hallway is full of light; outside, the sun's climbing. I reach our door, knock three times, wait, knock three times again. The door flies open. She's been waiting. Her face is all squeezed up with rage. Her arms stretch out to drag me inside.

"Here," I say, holding out the skull with its pitiful, flickering candle inside. Too little, too late. Susie takes it, and the look on her face makes my flesh crawl. My fingers move to touch the comforting shape of Mimi in my pocket. She's not there. Somewhere on the long climb up, I've dropped her.

No time to think. I turn my back on Susie and bolt for the stairwell. Day Junior hasn't got past the first doorway, and when he sees me rushing down the steps he comes after me.

"Hey! Slow down or you'll hurt yourself. What's wrong?"

I gasp out an explanation, and instead of laughing at me he helps me search. As we go down, Willow, Aspen, Juniper, checking every step, I do wonder why Susie hasn't come after me, but nothing's as important as finding Mimi. Without her, a bit of me's missing, and I don't have a lot to spare.

It's Day Junior who locates Mimi, wedged between concrete step and iron railing on Poplar Level. He extracts her carefully, dusts her off, hands her back to me. "Safe and sound," he says. "Must have jumped out of your pocket."

I'm just starting to say thanks when there's a massive *Boom!* from somewhere up above. The two of us shrink back against the wall, Day Junior acting like a fairy tale hero as he spreads out his arms and shields me. The noise is over quickly, but now there's a strange light from up there, not the rising sun or a little skull lamp but a big, hot, hungry light. And people shouting. *Fire!*

Day Junior takes my hand. "Downstairs, quick!"

I hesitate for about two seconds, then people start streaming down the stairs from the floors above us, and the only thing we can do is go down with them. There's an alarm woop-wooping, and smoke starting to fill the top of the stairwell. People are in their nighties and pyjamas, with kids wrapped in blankets and old folk clinging onto the dodgy hand-rail, but nobody's panicking, and we all make it down to the ground floor and out onto the plaza where the Day and Son delivery van's parked, gleaming white in the sunlight.

The fire fighters arrive and we get moved away from the building. The fire's on Oak Level. I can see smoke billowing out of the windows. I look around for Barbara, but I can't spot her or Rory in the crowd. Still, the fire's a long way up; in the basement they should be safe. Firies head up the stairs; down here on the plaza there's a truck with a massive extension ladder and hoses being screwed onto water mains and lots of activity. Someone asks Day Junior to move the van. He asks me if I'm OK and I say yes, so he hops in and drives it away.

I haven't seen Susie. I haven't seen Sophie or Miranda. But Kye's here with his mum and his little brother, and they live on Oak Level. I can't make myself go over and talk to them. My head's gone muzzy and my legs feel weak. I collapse onto a bench with Mimi on my knee, staring up at the thickening smoke and thinking about that lump of wax Barbara threw into the stove. How it sizzled and burned. How it filled my nostrils with a smell like death. I want to say a prayer, but I can't think what should be in it, so I put my head down on the bench and press Mimi against my cheek and close my eyes. Magic *is* real, just like in *Grimm's Fairy Tales*.

The day after the fire, I'm leaving Westmoreland Hospital, where they've kept me in overnight for observation. A social worker from Defence Welfare is letting me stay at her place until Dad gets home on compassionate leave. Her name's Siobhan, she lives near my old house and she's told me she has three cats called Winken, Blinken and Nod. Siobhan seems to know a lot about what's been happening to me, even though I've hardly said anything. She tells me a Mrs Barbara Jaeger rang the office and told her where I was and that I needed help. And Mrs Moss from school rang too, a while ago, asking why I hadn't come back this term and if I was OK. I ask Siobhan if Mrs Jaeger is the concierge at Woodside Gardens and she says yes, and that Barbara said to pass on her best wishes for the future.

Before I go home with Siobhan, I visit my stepsister Sophie, who's in a different ward getting treated for smoke inhalation. Miranda's in surgery this morning—her hands got burned—so I can't see her. Sophie looks terrible, hospital sheet-white with big bruises under her eyes, but she scrapes together a smile.

"Lissa. You're OK," she whispers.

"I'm OK. And you will be, too." I know the next thing I should say is that I'm sorry about Susie, but the words won't come out. I'm sorry it happened the way it did. But I can't be sorry she's gone.

"Look in the drawer," Sophie says on a rasping breath. "Got something for you."

I open the drawer in the bedside table, and there's the little doll I was making before Susie sent me down to get light. She's unharmed, just waiting there quietly for me to fetch her so I can finish embroidering her face. She's lying on the lacy shawl Sophie was knitting, and under that I see Miranda's Aran sweater with the fancy cables. I want to laugh and cry at the same time.

"Our Dad's coming," Sophie says. "They let me call him. He cried when he heard my voice. All this time, he didn't know where we were."

I start to understand why my stepsisters were sometimes unkind to me. I guess they were every bit as lost and afraid as I was. I feel strange, sort of sad, sort of relieved, but mostly just very tired.

"Miranda stopped to grab our work as we were running out." Sophie's looking at the doll, which is on my knee now. "That's how her hands got burned. I'm sorry we couldn't save your book, Lissa. I know you loved it."

A book is only a book. It's the stories in it that matter. "Thank you," I say, putting my hand on hers.

"Mum," Sophie whispers. "She threw that skull thing across the room, and suddenly there was fire everywhere. I don't know how it could . . . I don't understand . . . " Her voice fades to nothing.

"They think it may have been an electrical fault," puts in Siobhan from the doorway.

There's a silence, then I say to Sophie, "Let me know how you're getting on, OK?" When it's finished, this doll will be for her, and I'll make another for Miranda. Companions for a new life.

Siobhan comes in to put a little card on the bedside table, with contact phone numbers and addresses so Sophie and Miranda can find me if they want to.

"I have to go now," I say. I look at Sophie, and she stares up at me with her shadowy eyes, and the thing unspoken between us looms as huge and dark as the monster in every child's worst nightmare. "It'll be all right," I say, which is the best I can do at the moment.

Before she closes her eyes, Sophie whispers something. Maybe, *sorry.*

On the way to Siobhan's house, we drive past Woodland Gardens, where the clean-up is still happening. I don't look up at Oak Floor. An old woman in a purple dress is walking across the plaza, with an enormous orange cat dawdling along behind her. I fish Mimi out of my pocket, hoping Siobhan's too busy driving to notice. I have a big question for my doll, a question about right and wrong and magic and responsibility. It's a question that's too big to be put in words.

Give me a kiss! demands Mimi.

I touch my lips to her woollen mouth.

Give me a hug!

I hold her against my heart, hoping the faceless doll in my other pocket won't get jealous. Her time will come.

Now let me dance!

One flip is all she gets, and not a very high one. I stand her on my knee, gaze into her knitted eyes and ask my question.

"All right?" asks Siobhan, giving me a sideways glance but keeping her hands firmly on the wheel.

"Fine," I tell her. "Could you drive around the block before we go home, please?"

Being a social worker, Siobhan is probably used to people acting weird. At the next corner she turns left and we begin a circuit of Woodland Gardens.

Start working on it now, Mimi says, *and by the time you're an old woman with white hair, you might know the answer to that question.*

As we come around the plaza again, Barbara's still there, waiting while Rory does her business in a patch of dirt. I don't open the window and shout. I don't ask Siobhan to stop. I just look across at the two of them and mouth the words, "Thank you." Barbara turns and looks straight back at me. She lifts her hand in a sort of wave. Her mouth is not smiling and not frowning, but something in between. We drive on past, leaving Woodland Gardens behind us.

O

author's notes

"Prickle Moon" was written for this collection. Growing up in Dunedin, New Zealand, I was familiar with hedgehogs—their ancestors came over with early settlers from Britain. They lived in bushland and in people's gardens, and we used to put out bowls of milk for them in the evenings. Sadly, they often became road kill, since venturing out at night in a city environment was fraught with peril for a creature of such gradual habits. The entire story of "Prickle Moon" came to me in a dream during a visit to Dunedin in early 2012—a rare gift from the gnarly old goddess of the wood. There are some familiar names in the story. Willie Scott is named after my father, William (Bill) Scott. I apologise to my dear friend Helen for making the misguided laird of Gimmerburn a member of Clan Buchanan.

"Otherling" was first published in 2000 in a chapbook entitled *Voyager 5: Collector's Edition*. This marked Voyager UK's fifth anniversary. At the time I was reading the Icelandic Sagas as part of the research for my Viking novel, *Wolfskin*, and "Otherling" has a strongly Nordic flavour. "Otherling" made encore appearances in *Realms of Fantasy*, *ASIM*, and the Tachyon Publications anthology *Epic*, edited by John Joseph Adams (November 2012.) There are lots of twins in my novels; I find their special bond intriguing and inspiring. In "Otherling" I go down a dark path, looking at the way a subsistence society, reliant on the wisdom of the gods for survival, might view the birth of such a pair. It's a story about personal sacrifice and impossible choices.

"Let Down Your Hair" was first published in *The Big Issue* Summer Fiction edition, Christmas 2005. My Rapunzel story is about the enduring strength of true love and the power of storytelling to teach, heal and find ways through locked doors.

"Poppy Seeds" was written for this collection. I love the rhythmic flow of traditional storytelling with its tropes and repetitions, and I tried to capture some of those elements in this quasi-folk tale. One character was inspired by a wonderful picture book called *Stick Man* by Julia Donaldson and Axel Scheffler.

"In Coed Celyddon" was written for the anthology *The Road to Camelot*, edited by Sophie Masson and first published in 2002 by Random House Australia. *The Road to Camelot* contained stories by fourteen of Australia's best-known fantasy writers, each featuring a character from the Arthurian legend at a turning point in his or her young adult years. The boy of this story became a courageous warlord who united the sixth century tribes of Britain to keep out the invading Saxons. Coed Celyddon (the 'Scottish Wood') was the scene of one such battle. The original Arthur—from the Welsh Chronicles—did have two loyal friends, Cei and Bedwyr, and a dog called Cabal. My story could be history, but it also contains the seed of the legend.

"Juggling Silver" appeared in the anthology *Tales for Canterbury*, published by Random Static in 2011. The anthology was produced to raise funds for victims of the devastating Christchurch earthquake, and was divided into three sections: Survival, Hope and Future. "Juggling Silver" was the last story in the Hope group.

"'Twixt Firelight and Water" was written for the anthology *Legends of Australian Fantasy*, published in 2010 by Voyager Australia, and edited by Jack Dann and Jonathan Strahan. The story is related to my Sevenwaters series, set in a magical version of early medieval Ireland, and fills in the tale of enigmatic druid Ciarán and his raven, Fiacha. When I wrote the story I had just emerged from a tough year of cancer treatment, and the triumphal happy ending reflects the positive thinking that helped keep me strong during that challenging time.

As well as fantasy stories, this collection includes four of my ventures into romance/women's fiction. In 2000 my novel

Daughter of the Forest was a finalist in the Romantic Book of the Year awards, and I was invited to contribute a short story to *Woman's Day* magazine. "Gift of Hope", which appeared in the December 4 edition, was the result.

"Letters from Robert" was published in *Woman's Day* in October 2005. Midford is a blend of the suburbs of Guildford and Midland, east of Perth. Guildford, settled in 1826, was as far up the Swan River as barges could safely carry goods; there they were unloaded and transferred to bullock carts for the long slow journey inland. Guildford is full of wonderful old colonial houses, where I'm certain ladies like Clarinda took tea and exchanged the latest gossip.

"Jack's Day" was published in *Woman's Day* in March 2011. The setting is Prevelly Park, near Margaret River. The SAS (the Special Air Service regiment of the Australian Army) played a covert role in the Vietnam war. The characters in this story about a military family are entirely fictional, though as I am a contemporary of the Vietnam veterans and the mother of a soldier, the themes are fairly close to home.

In 2006 I attended a publishing panel in which someone said the next big thing in romantic fiction was baby boomer adventure travel. I was unconvinced, but when an opportunity came up to contribute another story to *Woman's Day*, I thought I'd have a go at writing a credible romance with characters of around my own age. "Far Horizons" appeared in the magazine in January 2007. I realised, on putting this group of romantic stories together for the collection, that I must have a thing for men with blue eyes.

"Tough Love 3001" was written for *Elemental: The Tsunami Relief Anthology*, edited by Steven Savile and Alethea Kontis (Tor, 2006.) All profits from *Elemental* went to the Save the Children Fund to help survivors of the Boxing Day 2005 tsunami in Southeast Asia. "Tough Love 3001" arose from my experience of running a critique group with an extraordinary mix of participants. It was only one step from there to aliens.

Back in the 1980s, my household included a twelve-year-old boy who liked playing armies in the bush with his mates. The characters in "Wraith Level One" are very loosely based on those kids. The original version of this story was full of eighties slang, which disappeared when I reworked it for this collection. In many ways, though, it still reflects that era: a time when kids went off on their own and did dangerous stuff after school, without mobile phones. This is the story's first publication.

"Back and Beyond" was published in 2010 in the anthology *A Foreign Country: New Zealand Speculative Fiction* (Random Static, Wellington). I think of "Back and Beyond" as magical autobiography. The story is full of things that are important to me: family, books and libraries, fairy tales, ancestors, love of place, hope, courage and a belief in natural magic. And, of course, dogs. The story contains my child self and my adult self, and is set in a real place—the old Children's Library building in Filleul Street, Dunedin, which now houses the very fine Scotia Bar and Bistro. Although I had breast cancer in 2009, my prognosis was more positive than that of my fictional counterpart and I plan to be in this world a while longer. Is "Back and Beyond" a story about suicide? It depends on whether you believe in the magic of books.

"The Angel of Death" was written for this collection. My four dogs are all rescues. In this story about the clearing of a puppy mill (an intensive dog breeding facility) I have combined elements from rescues I know about in Australia and abroad, so although it's the RSPCA that carries out the rescue in "The Angel of Death", the protocols described in the story are not necessarily those they follow. Sadly, places like this exist in most developed countries, and my depiction does not exaggerate the conditions rescuers are often confronted with. If this story makes even one reader think twice about buying a puppy from a pet shop or online, it will have achieved its purpose. Those cute fluff-balls advertised on Gumtree may well come from a place like the one in this story, and their parents may live out the whole of their wretched lives without meeting a single angel.

The Russian story Vasilissa the Fair, with its nearly all-female cast, is one of my favourite fairy tales. I'm especially fond of the crone Baba Yaga, who, like the fire she guards, can be both destructive and life-giving, and who must be approached in the right way if one wants a favour. "By Bone-Light" is my first re-imagining of the story, but it probably won't be my last. It was written for this collection.

GUILDFORD, JANUARY 2013

◑

acknowledgements

"Prickle Moon" © Juliet Marillier 2013. Appears here for the first time.

"Otherling" © Juliet Marillier 2000. First published in *Voyager 5: Collector's Edition*.

"Let Down Your Hair" © Juliet Marillier 2005. First published in *The Big Issue*, December 2005.

"Poppy Seeds" © Juliet Marillier 2013. Appears here for the first time.

"In Coed Celyddon" © Juliet Marillier 2002. First published in *The Road to Camelot*, edited by Sophie Masson.

"Juggling Silver" © Juliet Marillier 2011. First published in *Tales for Cantebury*, edited by Cassie Hart and Anna Caro.

"'Twixt Firelight and Water (A Tale of Sevenwaters)" © Juliet Marillier 2009. First published in *Legends of Australian Fantasy*, edited by Jack Dann and Jonathan Strahan.

"Gift of Hope" © Juliet Marillier 2000. First published in *Woman's Day*, December 2000.

"Letters from Robert" © Juliet Marillier 2005. First published in *Woman's Day*, October 2005.

"Jack's Day" © Juliet Marillier 2011. First published in *Woman's Day*, March 2011.

"Far Horizons" © Juliet Marillier 2007. First published in *Woman's Day*, January 2007.

"Tough Love 3001" © Juliet Marillier 2006. First published in *Elemental: The Tsunami Relief Anthology*, edited by Steven Savile and Alethea Kontis.

"Wraith, Level One" © Juliet Marillier 2013. Appears here for the first time.

"Back and Beyond" © Juliet Marillier 2010. First published in *A Foreign Country: New Zealand Speculative Fiction*, edited by Anna Caro and Juliet Buchanan.

"The Angel of Death" © Juliet Marillier 2013. Appears here for the first time.

"By Bone-Light" © Juliet Marillier 2013. Appears here for the first time.

AVAILABLE FROM TICONDEROGA PUBLICATIONS

978-0-9586856-6-5	Troy by Simon Brown (tpb)
978-0-9586856-7-2	The Workers' Paradise eds Farr & Evans (tpb)
978-0-9586856-8-9	Fantastic Wonder Stories ed Russell B. Farr (tpb)
978-0-9803531-0-5	Love in Vain by Lewis Shiner (tpb)
978-0-9803531-2-9	Belong ed Russell B. Farr (tpb)
978-0-9803531-3-6	Ghost Seas by Steven Utley (hc)
978-0-9803531-4-3	Ghost Seas by Steven Utley (tpb)
978-0-9803531-6-7	Magic Dirt: the best of Sean Williams (tpb)
978-0-9803531-7-4	The Lady of Situations by Stephen Dedman (hc)
978-0-9803531-8-1	The Lady of Situations by Stephen Dedman (tpb)
978-0-9806288-2-1	Basic Black by Terry Dowling (tpb)
978-0-9806288-3-8	Make Believe by Terry Dowling (tpb)
978-0-9806288-4-5	Scary Kisses ed Liz Grzyb (tpb)
978-0-9806288-6-9	Dead Sea Fruit by Kaaron Warren (tpb)
978-0-9806288-8-3	The Girl With No Hands by Angela Slatter (tpb)
978-0-9807813-1-1	Dead Red Heart ed Russell B. Farr (tpb)
978-0-9807813-2-8	More Scary Kisses ed Liz Grzyb (tpb)
978-0-9807813-4-2	Heliotrope by Justina Robson (tpb)
978-0-9807813-7-3	Matilda Told Such Dreadful Lies by Lucy Sussex (tpb)
978-1-921857-01-0	Bluegrass Symphony by Lisa L. Hannett (tpb)
978-1-921857-05-8	The Hall of Lost Footsteps by Sara Douglass (hc)
978-1-921857-06-5	The Hall of Lost Footsteps by Sara Douglass (tpb)
978-1-921857-03-4	Damnation and Dames ed Liz Grzyb & Amanda Pillar (tpb)
978-1-921857-08-9	Bread and Circuses by Felicity Dowker (tpb)
978-1-921857-17-1	The 400-Million-Year Itch by Steven Utley (tpb)
978-1-921857-24-9	Wild Chrome by Greg Mellor (tpb)
978-1-921857-27-0	Bloodstones ed Amanda Pillar (tpb)
978-1-921857-30-0	Midnight and Moonshine by Lisa L. Hannett & Angela Slatter (tpb)
978-1-921857-10-2	Mage Heart by Jane Routley (hc)
978-1-921857-65-2	Mage Heart by Jane Routley (tpb)
978-1-921857-11-9	Fire Angels by Jane Routley (hc)
978-1-921857-66-9	Fire Angels by Jane Routley (tpb)
978-1-921857-12-6	Aramaya by Jane Routley (hc)
978-1-921857-67-6	Aramaya by Jane Routley (tpb)
978-1-921857-86-7	Magic Dirt: the best of Sean Williams (hc)

THANK YOU

The publisher would sincerely like to thank:

Elizabeth Grzyb, Juliet Marillier, Sophie Masson, Pia Ravenari, Jonathan Strahan, Peter McNamara, Ellen Datlow, Grant Stone, Jeremy G. Byrne, Sean Williams, Garth Nix, David Cake, Simon Oxwell, Grant Watson, Sue Manning, Steven Utley, Bill Congreve, Jack Dann, Janeen Webb, Jenny Blackford, Simon Brown, Stephen Dedman, Sara Douglass, Felicity Dowker, Terry Dowling, Jason Fischer, Angela Slatter, Lisa L. Hannett, Kathleen Jennings, Kim Wilkins, Cat Sparks, Pete Kempshall, Ian McHugh, Angela Rega, Lucy Sussex, Kaaron Warren, the Mt Lawley Mafia, the Nedlands Yakuza, Amanda Pillar, Shane Jiraiya Cummings, Angela Challis, Talie Helene, Donna Maree Hanson, Kate Williams, Andrew Williams, Al Chan, Kathryn Linge, Alisa and Tehani, Mel & Phil, Brian Clarke, Jennifer Sudbury, Paul Przytula, Kelly Parker, Hayley Lane, Georgina Walpole, everyone we've missed . . .

. . . and you.

In memory of
EVE JOHNSON (1945–2011)
SARA DOUGLASS (1957—2011)
STEVEN UTLEY (1948—2013)